the
Eagle
Tree

NED HAYES

the Eagle Tree

Little
a

Published by Little A, New York

www.apub.com

Amazon, the Amazon logo, and Little A are trademarks of Amazon.com, Inc., or its affiliates.

ISBN-10: 1503936643
ISBN-13: 9781503936645

Cover design by Tim Green, Faceout Studio

Printed in the United States of America

With gratitude to Jill, Kate, and Nick

1

I saw the Eagle Tree for the first time on the third Monday of the month of March, which could be considered auspicious if I believed in magic or superstition or religion, because my middle name is March, and this is the name that I like people to use to describe me, and I do not respond if you call me by other names. My mother continues to call me Peter, despite the fact that I have told her that I am March.

So seeing the Eagle Tree for the first time on the third Monday of the month of March might have been auspicious if I believed in things that are not true. But I do not. I do not believe a lot of the words people say, because people say things that are not true. People even have names for different things that are not true. I do not believe in anything that I cannot see with my own eyes or hear with my own ears. And I name all of these true things with their true names.

I believe in trees. I can touch them. And they have true names. They do not change in terms of what they are to me.

On the day I first saw the Eagle Tree, I was fourteen years, four months, and three days old. On average, I climb 5.6 trees every day. Some days I climb thirty trees. Some days I only make it to four, which is just one beyond my base. My base is three trees. I always climb at least three trees every single day, rain or shine, sick or well.

In the past, when we lived in the house with yellow paint and three steps in front of the door, I climbed three trees every day, the ones across the road from my house. I would climb those three trees every morning, before my mother woke up. I do not think she knew I did that, but maybe she did, because at breakfast she was always telling me to wash my hands before I ate. Even now, when I follow the rule to wash my hands, sometimes there are bits of bark on my skin, or needles and leaves under my fingernails, and perhaps she saw this kind of residue. I do not notice this typically, unless she draws it to my attention.

When I wash my hands, I have to look at my skin. I see that my fingers are callused from gripping tree limbs, and my nails are short and grubby with bark. They are like the claws of a bird that lives only in trees.

On the third Monday of the month of March, I was climbing the Western Red Cedar—*Thuja plicata*—next door to our new house with the blue mailbox. I did not go to school that day. And my mother did not go to work, because she picked me up in the morning from the place I was over the weekend. It was the first day I was back in our new house.

In fact, I was in the backyard of the house next door for the very first time. We had just met the man next door, Mr. Clayton, and I had just seen his name on the black mailbox next to our blue mailbox, which made it easier for me to remember his name.

Then, after meeting Mr. Clayton, nineteen minutes and forty-two seconds later, I was able to climb the tree that grows in his yard. That day was the very first time I had ever been in that Western Red Cedar. It was my second tree of the day.

Because I did not yet know the pattern to climb the Red Cedar, I had to spend much time charting my route and counting my steps. That is why I did not notice the Eagle Tree until I reached nearly fifty feet up into the limbs of the Red Cedar. I was counting my steps and memorizing the route for future use.

When I close my eyes now, I can see precisely how it happened; each step is a picture in my mind.

As I clear the canopy of the smaller trees that grow near the houses in this neighborhood, I pull myself into my twenty-seventh move, lifting my right leg to rest on a small branch. I test the small branch. It is not stable, and I decide not to go any higher. The bandages on my arm are bothering me again, and I consider taking them off, but I remember the rule my mother told me about the bandages.

Nevertheless, when I think of taking off the bandages, I stop moving. I stand on the branch, and I look out from the Red Cedar. Then I realize what I see.

From this angle, I can see the valley of trees on the other side of the river of roofs in front of me.

The wind picks up, shaking the smaller limbs and dropping dust and shards of Red Cedar bark on me, but I grip tight, still staring.

I can see something on the other side of the valley—actually, above and beyond the valley—and although it is as huge as a water tower, I know at first sight that it is organic.

It is a tree. It is a tree larger than I have ever seen in my life. The great trunk rises above the forest canopy, a round cylinder nearly bare until the top, where projecting limbs jut out in stunning perfection at the highest altitude. Even from this distance of a mile or more, I can see protrusions on the limbs that look like growths or nests. But nests are unlikely; most birds like to nest within the canopy. This tree is a thing of perfection, distinct and alone.

At the time, I did not know that it was called the Eagle Tree. I just thought of it as a very large tree.

When I saw the extraordinary tree, I immediately tried to measure it. I could see it was at least fifty feet above the forest canopy. I could feel the desire rising in me, like a sudden surge of sap coming up from my roots, echoing out of my mouth.

My mother stood underneath the relatively small Red Cedar I was in, and she called up to me, but I could not hear her voice because of the wind and because of the sound coming out of my own mouth. The sound burst out of me in ululating rhythm, and I almost sensed that the big tree was singing back to me, swaying in the wind.

I knew then what I had to do.

On that first morning I saw the Eagle Tree, I remained in the Red Cedar for exactly 121 minutes. While I stared at the distant tower with its craggy pinnacle and outgrowth of branches near the summit, I was trying to gauge precisely how far away it was from me. And from my current height, I could see part of the road pattern, so I was trying to figure out which roads might be able to take me to the tree, and I was still trying to figure out how tall exactly the tree might be from its base to its apex.

One hundred and twenty-one minutes was unusual for me, for in recent years I have not remained in a tree longer than twenty-seven minutes at a time. I have been told that many people my age can climb a tree quickly. It takes me longer because I have to plan my climbing slowly in my mind. That is how my mind works, in plans and steps. Nevertheless, I am not allowed to be in trees longer than twenty-seven minutes. That is the rule: I cannot stay in trees for long periods of time anymore.

When I was younger, I used to take a very long time to climb a tree and then I would stay there for many hours, but after some incidents that involved fire trucks and long ladders and yelling men with loud megaphones that hurt my ears, new rules were put in place so that I could no longer make this a habit. There are also now rules that prohibit me from transferring to trees with adjoining branches. Tree transfers tend to end with me deep in the forest canopy and out of sight of my mother. Sometimes I also fall during tree transfers, and that one time I had to wear casts on my wrists for 25.5 days, which bothered my mother for some reason. The casts were also irritating to my skin.

So at this time in my life, I tend not to remain in a tree very long. Instead, I have multiplied the number of trees that I climb, making do with quantity of trees rather than time in a single tree. This has changed my sense of trees; it has made it necessary for me to learn the dimensions and shapes of many trees instead of just one, which I have come to appreciate as a geometric benefit of multiple trees.

Nowadays, I come down to the ground shortly after climbing each tree—all the way down, so that my feet touch the earth for at least three minutes, per my mother's instructions. Also, typically after climbing three trees, I make an attempt to tell my mother or my uncle where I am and what trees I will climb next, before I do so. This agreement and change in my behavior was achieved only after my mother informed me of the Arizona contingency plan.

Staying in the Red Cedar for exactly 121 minutes was therefore atypical for me. I was making loud sounds, and I think Mr. Clayton eventually went inside. But I think my mother remained at the base of the Red Cedar. Her voice was hoarse and her hands were shaking when I came down, which led me to believe that perhaps she had been making sounds to me.

When I came down, my uncle was in our house. Uncle Mike is my mother's brother. He was wearing his green Seattle Sounders cap. I like it when he wears his hat, because I can look at the hat instead of his face, but I looked toward him so we would be connected in the way he wants to be connected. Still, I looked at his hat.

My mother talked to me some more. She and Uncle Mike told me that I must not climb any more trees for the remainder of the day, which was unfortunate and, I thought, not necessary. I knew which tree I had to climb next, and it was not easily accessible to me at that time.

It was 11:06 a.m. when I came down from the Red Cedar. My mother insisted that I stay with her the remainder of the morning on that third Monday of March. She also insisted that I hear her and acknowledge the words and intent of what she was saying, which is a challenging request for me. But with effort, I was able to do so. I am not required to look at her eyes while she speaks, which is fortunate, because I kept turning my head to look toward the forest that contained the Eagle Tree.

First, my mother began by explaining that she had called Uncle Mike on the phone and asked him to come to our house. She had called him because she was frightened and did not know what to do. I did not ask her, "What is the problem?" Each time I have asked her that question in situations similar to this, she has raised her voice very loudly, and when she raises her voice loudly, I lose track of what she is trying to communicate to me.

"Peter, listen to me," she said repeatedly, and so I did not turn away from her. She and Uncle Mike sat down on the sofa in the living room, and after some time, I also sat down—in a chair. I chose my chair carefully. It was not exactly facing them; it was turned slightly so that I was not forced to see their faces constantly moving and changing as they spoke to me.

"Peter," she said. "I know that time is important for you. So tell me, how long were you up in that tree?"

"One hundred and twenty-one minutes," I said.

"All right." My mother made a sound. A sigh. "This is the second time this month that you've been out of sight like that. And after this past weekend and what happened with the—"

"I don't want to talk about it," I said. I looked at Uncle Mike's hat.

"Nevertheless, it happened. After our whole conversation with Mr. Clayton about the rules for climbing his tree." My mother sighed again. "I think we need to consider the move to Arizona."

"What?" I said loudly, and my hands started going. I was not sure I had heard her correctly. Why was she talking about moving to Arizona again?

I dislike Arizona. There are no trees there, nothing to climb.

"He wouldn't have this issue if you hadn't taught him to climb so high in the trees," said my mother to Uncle Mike.

He sighed underneath his hat. Then Uncle Mike turned his head toward my mother. "Well, most kids can climb trees. I know kids on the spectrum usually can't, but I just wanted him to fit in. I thought knowing how to climb trees would help him, because kids on the spectrum should be able to climb too. I just thought it would be a little thing, just one tree, or maybe two—"

"What did you say?" I said to my mother. I can be much louder than Uncle Mike.

"Honey—March, I am just discussing the situation with Mike," said my mother. "I feel that you need to pay attention to the clear rules we've set around dangerous—"

"It is not dangerous," I said. "I climb every morning. Some evenings. I create a climbing pattern for each tree. And I know precisely what pattern to follow on each tree. It is not dangerous. I know the rules. It is not dangerous."

"You might know the rules. But you didn't follow them. You were out of sight for so long, and all I could hear was your loud howling. I thought maybe something had happened to you up there. Do you hear me? Do you understand what I'm saying?"

"Arizona," I said. "Arizona."

My mother rubbed her hand over her face, as if her skin were tired. "Peter—March—there is only so much I can take. This weekend pushed me over the edge. I'm sorry, but I can only take so much."

Then her voice crumpled, the sound breaking apart. "I—I—I'm not saying we have to move to Arizona right now. It's just that with you going off on your own like this . . . I need to have some peace of mind. I need some help."

My hands were flapping furiously now, striking against my chest and against the cushions, and then against the lamp next to the chair. Uncle Mike caught the lamp before it fell; he lunged forward, and then he was standing beside me, holding the lamp. He adjusted his hat with his other hand.

"Look, buddy," he said. "Your mother isn't trying to upset you. You've just got to understand that you can't go out of sight like that without at least trying to tell her what you're doing. Why were you up in that tree so long?"

I can hear the sound rising from my mouth; the hum of it reminds me of the upper canopy, of the insects that buzz unceasingly across the top of the forest line. Beyond that, I see the darkness of the valley on the other side of Boulevard Road, and then beyond that, the peak of the great trunk, rising above everything I know. So high that it would be part of a second canopy if there were an old-growth canopy here. So high that the ecosystem of the forest below would hardly affect it. Perhaps it has no limbs on the lower extremities because it has no need for the rest of the forest at all. It is a solitary giant, circumspect in its height, removed from everything below.

I am so glad we moved to this new house with the blue mailbox, because this new house has allowed me to see the tree.

I blinked. I glanced up, and my mother was now also standing next to the chair, her hand clenched tight in Uncle Mike's hand, looking at me hard and talking fast and loud.

"I just don't know what to do when he gets like this. I need to connect with him. I don't know if I can just let him go, if I can allow him to just disconnect like . . ."

Her eyes were leaking, and I looked away quickly.

"I saw a tree," I said.

And then I could see that my words were too loud, because they both flinched when I said those words. So I said my words again, but softer this time. "I saw a tree. Across the valley. I want to climb it. I was looking at the tree. That is all I was doing."

"There," my mother said after a moment. "Was that so hard? Just to tell us what you were doing, what kept you up in the tree next door. I wish . . . I wish it was easier for you."

"Arizona," I said once more. My dad's mother—my grandmother—lives in Arizona. And the cousins. Every year, we go to Arizona to visit my grandmother and cousins. My father moved there two weeks ago.

"He's visiting Grandma," I said. "Then he will come back. Then we will be together in our old house again."

"I don't know about that," my mother said. "The situation is complicated. In fact, I don't know if he will come back from Arizona."

In some parts of Arizona, I have read, there are many trees. But not in my grandmother's part of Arizona. There are no climbing trees near Scottsdale. I once climbed a bush there, but it was not the same.

My mother talked about moving to Arizona quite a bit before my father left. But even if we don't move there, he will come back to Olympia to climb trees with me. That is what he said he would do. I do not care to move to Arizona. I will not let us move to Arizona.

When I thought about Arizona, I could see only empty orange desert in front of me. I do not like the orangeness; it erases every tree, every branch, every leaf.

The thought of that emptiness surrounded me and overwhelmed me. Sound came out of me to fill the emptiness.

"Things have to change sometimes," my mother said. "We can't go on like this forever."

But the sounds coming out of my mouth were so loud now that I could hardly hear her words. Now my hands were flailing through the air like a windmill, and I could feel spittle on my chin. The feel of it was cold against my skin.

"Hey, March," said Uncle Mike. "You saw a tree." His words cut through the fog that was rising inexorably around me. "Would you like to drive out and see where it is? Find that tree?"

I stopped breathing.

"You can't climb it with him," said my mother. "You can't let him climb another tree today. Not after this weekend. You understand me?"

"No, no, I get it," said my uncle. "We'll just go look. Right, buddy? We'll just go look."

There were spots in front of my eyes. Red ones and black ones. I started breathing again.

"I don't know," said my mother. "Is it wise to allow him to—?"

"Come on," said Uncle Mike. "Let's go take a look at that tree."

I was now breathing many deep breaths, filling my lungs and pushing the air back out. I was no longer moaning. My hands were still moving in little circles, but I could not prevent that. My legs were already moving toward the door, toward his truck, so that we could go find the tree so I could climb it. Right away.

2

On the Friday before I discovered the Eagle Tree, we moved into the new house. The new house is smaller than the old house. That is because only my mother and I live here. My father does not live with us anymore, so we now live in a smaller house.

Our house has a living room almost precisely twelve feet square, with a sofa and a chair in it and a bookshelf with books. There is also a kitchen downstairs. The kitchen has a small table with chairs, and a counter, and a sink with warm water and very cold water, but no steaming-hot water. The kitchen also has two doors that are made up of glass windows—one of those windows is now covered with cardboard and tape. The windows, except the one that is covered, look out at the backyard.

You can leave the kitchen to go back into the living room, or you can go to the bathroom on the other side of the stairway. Or you can use the stairway that has fourteen steps if you wish to go upstairs. The fourteen steps lead upstairs to the two bedrooms.

The bedrooms are the same size: I measured them. My mother has the bedroom in the northwest corner, and I have the bedroom that is closer to the southeast. The windows in her room look out at the trees in the backyard. I think the reason I do not have a window with trees is that in our old house, I broke my arm climbing out of the window to go to the trees to climb them. So now I have a window with no trees.

The new house's kitchen has large windows and doors that my mother says are French. The doors open onto the backyard, where there is a Maple. It is only forty feet high. Maple trees are difficult to identify precisely, since there are many varieties. But based on the leaves, the location, the height, and the coloration, I believe that it is most likely that this Maple is a Bigleaf Maple, *Acer macrophyllum*.

There are other plants in the backyard as well. Ferns and lilies. Wisteria and rosebushes. And a smaller tree that I believe is a young Sweet Cherry. *Prunus avium*. I cannot determine the exact variety yet.

I did not sleep in this house the first three nights we lived here. I was in the hospital, where they kept putting bandages on my arm and I kept taking them off. But then on the fourth day we lived here, I was able to come back to our new house.

In the car coming from the hospital back to our new house, my mother talked to me. I was trying to listen to both the car engine's hum and her voice, so it was hard to concentrate. But then she brought up Arizona. This is what she said:

"Look, we had to move to this little house after your father left, and I don't like it any more than you do. If you really want us to be together, you and I could move to Arizona with him. It would—"

"No," I said.

"Arizona is a lovely state, March," my mother said. "And we could live with your father again. You need to understand—"

"It is too hot there," I said. But really I do not care about the heat. I care about the trees. If trees could grow in that heat, I would not mind moving to Arizona. But if I talk about trees again, I do not think my mother and I will keep talking.

She will just make a decision without me. That idea is very scary to me.

My mother sighed. "It's not too hot in the part of Arizona I'm talking about moving to. Your father says that he's open to reconciliation if we move . . ."

It occurred to me that perhaps my mother should know about other options. I am familiar with many parts of the country that have better trees to climb than Arizona. The car's engine made it hard to think, and I closed my eyes to concentrate.

"Kentucky," I said. "Tennessee. Those are options I would like to talk about."

My mother paused. She took a breath, and I thought she was looking at me, but I did not look into her eyes. Finally, she spoke again. "Why, might I ask, *Kentucky*, of all places?"

"The Appalachian Mountains. They have one of the biggest hardwood forests in the world. Today, they do, at least. This will change in the future."

"Trees," she said. She turned the wheel of the car, and I swayed to the side. I opened my eyes again. "More trees than here even, I'm betting," she said.

"Yes," I said. "But not for long. The Appalachians could turn into desert or savanna before too long, and I would like to climb those trees before they go away and it all turns into Arizona."

"The trees will go away?" said my mother. "I'm afraid I don't follow you, March."

"If the global temperature rises by only four degrees Celsius over the next fifty years—and it's probably going to do that—then all of the Appalachian forests will die. Already, the Elms and the Chestnuts are gone, and the Hemlocks and the Flowering Dogwoods. And I didn't get a chance to climb them yet. Before we know it, the forest will just go away and die off."

The car turned back the other direction, and I swayed back toward my mother. I know what it is like to be a tree, pushed back and forth in the wind.

"Oh, March," said my mother. "I'm sure there will be more trees to climb. It's pretty much impossible for a whole forest to die like that. You'll have years and years to climb trees. I want to talk about reality here, okay?"

"It is not impossible," I said, and my voice became very loud, because when we talk about reality, it is important to be factual, and when I speak loudly, I am very factual. I spoke loudly over the hum of the car's engine.

"When the global temperature rises another degree or two, all of the Red Spruces and the Fraser Firs will be gone. Then the Sugar Maples and the Mountain Ashes will die. These kinds of trees cannot live in that temperature zone. Ninety percent of Fraser Firs are already dead there."

"Well, I'm sure you can find a Fraser Fir to climb somewhere else, March."

"No, I can't. Fraser Firs are unique to the Great Smoky Mountains. I have never climbed one, and they are dying from acid rain and the balsam woolly adelgid."

"What is that?"

"A moth."

There was a long pause. The sound of the car's engine had become a much louder hum.

"I do not want to live in Arizona," I told her.

"Pat Tillman lived in Arizona," said my mother. "Did you realize that?"

When she said that, I knew she wanted me to think good things about Arizona because of that fact.

A man named Pat Tillman invented a game I like to play. He called the game Tarzan. I have never asked why he gave it that name or where it comes from, but I like the word. It buzzes on my tongue.

Pat Tillman's Tarzan game requires very fast tree transfers on a steep hillside. If you are good at the game, you are transferring between trees that have no limbs touching, so you are jumping from one tree to another. The first time I tried it, I fell immediately to the ground. I was not very coordinated then. I think I broke my toe when I fell, but I did not tell anyone about that first fall, because I did not want my mother to tell me I could not play Tarzan.

I kept playing Tarzan after that, and eventually I got good enough at Tarzan that I could do it on very steep hillsides and in sparse tree sites, not just in dense tree growth. For me, it takes a lot of planning. I have to look up at all the tree holds before I make a single move. But when I have planned a climb or a tree transfer, I can execute it with some precision. If I don't fall first.

Pat Tillman also used to play a game that is on television that is called football. However, I do not like balls, and I am not particularly interested in feet, so I have never seen this other game he played. Pat Tillman did not invent that game, but after he played that game, he volunteered to fight in a war.

"Pat Tillman lived in Arizona," repeated my mother in the car.

"Yes, but he does not live there anymore," I replied. If Pat Tillman were living there, I would go even to Arizona to do Tarzan jumps with him. But he doesn't live there anymore, so we can't.

"He is dead," I said. "He died in the war."

Then the car stopped by the blue mailbox, and I recognized that we had arrived at our new house. So I got out of the car. My mother had to remind me to close the car door afterward. I had forgotten to close the door because there were other things to look at in our new neighborhood.

There are many trees in our new neighborhood, and I had not yet climbed any of them. The first night I was in the house, I attempted to climb the Bigleaf Maple in our backyard, but I was unsuccessful. The day I got back from the hospital, as soon as we got inside the house, I asked my mother if I could climb a tree. And she said, "Jesus Christ, March, can't we just eat first? Let's eat breakfast. At the very least, some food."

I climbed the Bigleaf Maple in fourteen steps and twenty-two minutes. The Cherry tree was even faster for me. When I came down from the Cherry, I saw the Western Red Cedar, *Thuja plicata*, next door. My mother said she would talk to the neighbors for me, to find out if I could climb the Red Cedar.

The man who opened the door had skin the color of a mature Douglas Fir and curly gray hair like steel wool on the top of his head. My mother introduced me to the man and said his name was Mr. Clayton. After my mother and Mr. Clayton talked for some time, he took us to his backyard, and we looked at the Red Cedar. The great roots of the tree arched upward into a rounded bolus covered with thick, red, peeling bark that curved into a narrower trunk with uncut limbs lifting toward the sky. The Red Cedar was perfect for climbing. Already I was calculating the steps I would take to move from the ground into the lowest branches of the tree.

Mr. Clayton also looked at the tree. He moved his head up and down and squinted at the reddish limbs. The shadow of the lacy twigs and leaves fell across his face, and so as he moved his head, he looked mottled brown and black for a moment, as if branches had grown across his brown skin.

Mr. Clayton turned toward my mother. "What exactly does he aim to *do* up in that tree?" he said.

"Just climb it," said my mother. "That's all. Then he'll come straight down."

She looked at me. I looked away immediately, but then I realized that she was looking at me to confirm my plans. I knew this because she has told me that when she looks in my direction, she expects that I will know that she is checking in with me. Sometimes I remember this—usually when we are out in public. Most of the time, especially at home, I do not remember this fact.

This was one of the times I remembered.

"I will climb the tree," I said. "Then I will come straight down." I had confirmed what she said. I thought this was the right thing to say.

Mr. Clayton rubbed his chin and slid his gaze toward me, and I prepared to glance away from him, but part of me wondered what it would be like to be able to freeze his face. I liked his face, but I could not look at his face directly. So I thought I would like to freeze him and look at him very closely, without the possibility of him ever moving. And then it occurred to me that it would be interesting to freeze everyone around me and look at them closely, to examine them like I examine tree bark when I climb. And they'd be just as still as a tree, and then I could understand them better.

But then I realized that my mother had said my name several times in a row, and she had gripped my arm, and this broke my concentration on the idea of freezing people and looking into their faces without being uncomfortable.

Her grip on my arm made me very uncomfortable, and I stopped breathing. Because she was still gripping my arm, I tried to think back a moment to what she had said before she touched me.

"You can promise Mr. Clayton here that you'll just climb his tree and you won't hurt the tree in any way," my mother said. But I did not think she was actually talking to me, because her mouth was facing Mr. Clayton and she was looking at him.

"We have an agreement," she said to Mr. Clayton. "He spends not more than twenty-five minutes in a tree before he comes down. Isn't that right, Peter?"

I looked down at my mother's hand. My mother was not exact, but I did not correct her statement. She was still holding on to me. It was hard to not breathe. If I kept not breathing, eventually I would pass out. I had done that before. I did not want to pass out here. I wanted to climb the tree.

"Yes?" she said.

"Yes," I said. And she let go of me. Then I breathed again.

So I made that promise to follow the rule to my mother and to Mr. Clayton. But then when I got up to fifty feet high in the Red Cedar, I saw the Eagle Tree across the valley, and I forgot the rule.

And that was when I stayed in the tree for 121 minutes. I wish now that I had not done that. It meant we might have to move to Arizona. But before we moved to Arizona, first I would climb the Eagle Tree.

3

Uncle Mike offered to take me to see the tree. But my mother told me I must get a jacket.

While I was searching through my new closet for my jacket, Uncle Mike talked to my mother, and he also went next door to talk to Mr. Clayton. I found out about this conversation when I came downstairs and we got in Uncle Mike's truck. Uncle Mike told me that he had talked to Mr. Clayton about my sighting of the very large tree. Mr. Clayton had explained to him that many people call it the Eagle Tree, because a pair of bald eagles nested in the broken top crag of that tree for many years.

Now I knew that the informal name of the tree was the Eagle Tree. I said the name to myself several times after Uncle Mike told me. I knew the informal name now, but I did not know what species or variety the tree would turn out to be.

Uncle Mike drives a large truck the color of White Elm bark, which means it is a light-gray color. I know Elm bark, even though most of the American Elms, *Ulmus americana*, have been killed by disease now.

The gray truck has four windows, one of which will not roll up the final one-eighth of an inch to make a seal with the window frame.

That means that the right rear passenger window makes a thin, high whistling sound when the truck is moving. Often I have to cover my ears, because the sound is a saw going through my head. However, if Uncle Mike remembers that the window will make the sound, then he opens another window, which makes the sound go away from that right rear window. Sometimes when I cover my ears, he changes the other window so it works. Sometimes he does not see me cover my ears, and he does not change the window, and then I can hear the sound in my head through the whole ride.

He has asked me to talk to him about the sound, so that he remembers to change the window. But I did not talk to him about the sound on the drive to the Eagle Tree. By the time the sound started, it was too late to talk to him; I had to cover my ears. And I cannot talk to him when my ears are covered. It is one of the rules. I cannot talk to people when my ears are covered, because it is rude. And I could not remove my hands from my ears to talk to Uncle Mike, because then the sound would get deeper inside me. However, despite the sound in his truck, I appreciated that Uncle Mike was taking me to see the tree.

The forest had a sign that said "LBA Woods." Once we passed the sign, the trees leaned over the road, and soon the light was dim, as the trees grew very densely together. When we arrived, I was so excited that my hands would not stop moving. Uncle Mike had to open the truck door for me.

The line of the horizon was covered in green, and light filtered through the trees, rays of sunlight splitting around the vast trunks, the branches above us fluttering in a faint wind. The green needles were silver underneath. It was almost too much for me to take in. I flinched as a leaf from an Alder was caught by the wind and fluttered down through the forest. A distant bird shrieked.

"These woods are presettlement," Uncle Mike said. He pointed at a large fallen tree that was lying across the terrain ahead; it was as big as a hill in itself, and small trees sprouted from the top of the great mound. It was a nurse log, but larger than any I had seen in the woods behind our house or in the woods in Watershed Park, where I usually climb.

"That's an old-growth tree," Uncle Mike said, "and more significantly, there are— Watch out, March!"

I let out a grunt. I had stumbled into a deep pit that was half-covered by blackberry vines, and I was forced to turn my attention from the vast canopy overhead to the ground in front of me. But I did not slow down in my headlong rush through the bushes and the stinging nettles. I was interested in what he was saying, but Uncle Mike does not need me to say words for him to continue speaking—my mother often needs this, for some reason. Instead, he simply keeps telling me information that is useful.

"You've already found a place where a tree fell," he said as he pulled me out of the crater. "See, a truly ancient forest is full of root craters. The ground gets really uneven, because when the trees fall, they create these big pits, and the smaller trees try to fill them up. You with me, March? God almighty, look at your arms."

I looked down at my arms. Below the bandages, on my forearms, the vines had scratched me, so that there were lines of blood along both of my arms. It was an interesting pattern. I was considering whether to add to the pattern with more scratches when Uncle Mike took a cloth out of his pocket and wiped the blood away.

I still looked down at my arms. I could see where the pattern was before. I could imprint it there, if I focused.

"Gosh, I can see what they mean," said Uncle Mike. "The people protesting to save these woods are right—these trees are almost untouched." His voice was different somehow. It was exactly the sound in his voice that I heard at the funeral of my great-uncle.

Uncle Mike's words resounded in his chest as he spoke, as if he were a hollow tree. "It's an undisturbed old-growth forest. You can tell because there are gaps in the forest canopy, between the trees. The trees in a regrowth forest are mostly the same height, so the canopy above is pretty consistent in height—you see what I mean?"

Shadows moved across my face as the leaves far above shifted in an unseen breeze. They wafted back and forth, like Mr. Clayton's face shifting in the light, from one dark color to another.

I was standing still, looking up at the shifting leaves, when the family of deer appeared. They stepped quietly out of a grove of Cascara Buckthorns, *Rhamnus purshiana*, all of which were growing so close together that it was hard to believe even a single deer could make its way through the branches, much less a family of them.

A large mother deer stood taller than me. And beside her were two fawns, whose limbs seemed thin as blades of grass. Their spotted skins flickered in the uneven forest light, blending into the mottled colors of the fallen leaves and vines and branches that compose the forest floor.

"Well, buddy, I'm sure glad you stopped moving your hands and making those sounds," whispered Uncle Mike. "Otherwise, the deer would never have come out."

I looked down at my hands and arms. I could still imagine the patterns that the thorny vines of the wild blackberry made on my skin. They were shadows too, permanent shadows on my skin. But I no longer had the urge to add to the pattern. And Uncle Mike was right— my hands had stopped moving before the deer appeared. I had been looking at the Buckthorn grove, and I hadn't made a sound for most of that time.

I knew it was important to be silent in the forest if you want to be part of the woods, but I did not realize how quiet and still I had become.

The deer disappeared seconds later, blending back into the grove from which they came, as if they were part of the trees and had stepped into our reality for only a moment.

After the deer, we moved through the forest for another thirty-four minutes, stumbling over vines and evergreen huckleberry, and losing our way several times in the darkness of the woods. Finally, Uncle Mike found a clear space in the forest, a miniature meadow. There, in the center of the meadow, was the tree I had been hungering for.

The Eagle Tree.

The tree was a vast cylinder of wood. It filled the sky. The limbs stretched out above me, a great canopy sheltering the rest of the trees, as if they were its children. I stood back and felt the breath coming sharp and quick in and out of my mouth. I reached up with my hands, feeling the air in the meadow around the tree and stumbling through evergreen huckleberry bushes and sword ferns as I got closer and closer to the densely scaled ridges of the tree's bark.

When I reached the tree, Uncle Mike reminded me that my mother did not want me to climb, because this tree was too high. I do not know what she based this assessment on, as the brush at the forest floor and the variability in the canopy that surrounded the Eagle Tree made it difficult to get a precise height from our house. But I estimated using basic geometric principles. The Eagle Tree was probably taller than two hundred feet. Perhaps as high as three hundred.

My mother had said I must not climb the Eagle Tree. However, she had not said anything regarding climbing other trees in the old-growth belt that surrounded the tree. The overhanging branches and the large root system of the Eagle Tree prevented companion trees from growing right next to it. Maybe the tree liked this; maybe it liked to have its roots alone on the forest floor. I did not know if this was intentional on the part of the Eagle Tree, but by clearing part of the forest it could grow without impediment.

When I am stressed, my arms sometimes move on their own in big flapping motions, as if I might take off, and my hands spin like a hummingbird's wings. I would like to think that the Eagle Tree cleared the canopy around it the way the flapping of my arms sometimes keeps away other people that I do not want to interact with.

However, despite this cleared area around the base of the tree, many other trees reached their branches into the zone of the Eagle Tree. They stretched toward it.

So I stepped back and decided to climb a Western Larch, *Larix occidentalis*, which was growing on the edge of the clearing around the Eagle Tree. This tree's upper limbs touched the Eagle Tree.

It is very unusual to see a Larch on this side of the Cascade mountains. The Larch is a member of the family Pinaceae. There are over ten species of Larch around the world that are deciduous needle trees. But we have only one in the Pacific Northwest, and that is the Western Larch. It is unusual, because it is a conifer that drops its needles, and also I had never before seen one here in Olympia.

I would climb this Larch as a consolation prize for waiting to climbing the Eagle Tree. I would climb the Eagle Tree's immensity another day, when I had worked up the courage.

The Larch was the closest tall tree to the Eagle Tree, but it was only about one hundred feet high. Uncle Mike said some words to me when I started climbing, but by the time I remembered to listen to him, I was already twenty-five feet up, and I just kept going.

The out-of-region Larch I am climbing is leaning inward, as if the Eagle Tree contains a magnet to pull all other smaller trees toward it. I am pulled in its direction too.

As I hitch myself high in the Larch, I get a better look at one of the Eagle Tree's long branches, and I realize that the Eagle Tree might be a species of Pine. If it is the type of Pine I am thinking of, it would be very unusual to see it this close to the coast. What is it about this hilltop that grows out-of-region trees?

I wait in the Larch for a long time, watching the Eagle Tree. I do not move. I hardly breathe. The sun drifts lower in the sky. The shadows change. And just as I am thinking I will climb down out of the Larch, I see something move in the upper part of the Eagle Tree, on a single large branch that reaches out from the crown at the top.

It is a bird. But it is not a bald eagle. The eagles are long gone from their nest at the top.

I recall the pictures of birds that I looked at last winter in the book called *Birds of the Pacific Northwest Coast*. The pictures I saw then are stored in my memory with photographic precision. Uncle Mike does not believe that I can remember which page number a picture is on in a book I looked at last year. But I can. And that is what I do now.

On page 43 is a picture of the auk family, and the beak of the bird in the Eagle Tree is curved like it is the relative of an auk. Lower down on the page, underneath the paragraph about the extinct great auk, is a bird that looks like this bird. In the picture, it has curved stripes of black and white. The book calls it marbling.

But this bird in the tree is fluffier than the bird I saw in the book. There are differences. The wings are shaped a little differently. The eyes are not precisely the same.

This bird looks at me with black eyes. They glimmer, small obsidian rocks in the gloom. I stop breathing entirely. I do not blink. I hold my breath until I see red spots in the corners of my eyes, and my hands grow numb. But then the bird turns its head away and pecks at something on the tree branch. I breathe again.

The differences between the bird in the book and the bird on the tree limb I attribute to age and sex and observance. The bird on the tree may be younger; the bird may be a different gender. I am perhaps seeing the bird from a different angle. I know that there is a greater than 80 percent likelihood that my identification of the bird is accurate.

It is a marbled murrelet. A juvenile murrelet. And it has disappeared from view.

After I climbed down from the Western Larch, I went to the car, where Uncle Mike was smoking his pipe and reading the paper. "About time you came down. It's getting pretty dark. I was about to come in there and get you out of the tree myself."

There was a pause, and I realized he wanted me to say something.

"Okay," I said. "I am here now."

"Good," he said. "Look at me." I glanced at him, and he began to smile, and I looked away quickly, before his face changed. "You okay?" he said.

"Okay," I repeated. "I am here now."

"Yup, I heard that." He gave a long sigh. "Let's go then." He turned the car on, and the engine made a high hum, a sound I matched with my next breath. I could keep this sound going a long time—the whole way home, if I was lucky. It is good to be in tune with the engine.

"Anything distract you in the forest?" he said. "Your mom might worry that we're so late. Thought I told you to be down earlier."

"Murrelet," I said to him.

"Is that right?" he said. He sighed again, but he did not say anything else for a long moment. I did not know if he heard me correctly. Because the marbled murrelet is a very rare bird to have seen—that is, if I identified it correctly.

Then he spoke again. "Tell me about this mur-let. Is it a tree?"

"No, of course it is not a tree," I said. I could see the pages of *Birds of the Pacific Northwest Coast* in my mind, and I chose some sentences to describe the murrelet accurately and precisely. I thought Uncle Mike probably did not want to know all of the information I could see on the page, so I tried to condense what I knew about the murrelet.

"The marbled murrelet is a seabird. It lives in the ocean. The marbled murrelet lays a single egg inland on an old-growth tree branch."

"Ah," said Uncle Mike. After a minute, he asked a question. "Okay, why do they build their nests here?"

"The murrelet doesn't have a nest. They just lay an egg on a branch." I do not tell Uncle Mike that I have never heard of one laying an egg on a Ponderosa Pine, but there is a lot unknown about the murrelet. Then I remember another recent discovery. "They found a murrelet chick in an Alder and on a cliff. So who knows where they lay eggs? They are a mystery to scientists."

"A mystery, huh?" Uncle Mike laughed. "The egg is abandoned on a solitary tree somewhere? Yeah, I'd say they're mysterious!"

"The egg does hatch," I said. "The chick comes out. The parents fly back and feed it with fresh fish from the ocean."

"Wait a second—ocean birds here? We're over ten miles inland, March. We're not right on Puget Sound. Why would an ocean bird lay an egg here?"

"That is what the book said. Murrelets lay an egg in an old-growth forest. They can go as far as fifty miles inland. The chick lives alone on the branch and eventually spreads its wings and flies back to the ocean."

"With its parents?"

"No, alone. The parents leave it alone for a long time. No one knows how the chick knows how to go to the ocean. Or which direction the ocean is in. It is a rare bird. It is a mystery. No one knows much about them. No one gets close to them. No one sees them."

"No one gets close to them. No one sees them," Uncle Mike repeated. "So how do you know that you got close to one? That you saw one?"

"I identified it by comparison to the picture I saw on October 14 in *Birds of the Pacific Northwest Coast*."

"So you don't know for sure. Could have been anything."

"No," I said. "I do not know for sure. But I do not think it could have been anything. It was likely a marbled murrelet."

"Well then," said Uncle Mike. He did not say anything else all the way home. I did not say anything else either. I was in tune with the engine.

I was looking forward to coming back to climb the Eagle Tree. Maybe the next day.

4

The next day was Tuesday. I have school on Tuesday. My school is Olympia Regional Learning Academy, or ORLA. It is a public school, but it does not have the different classes and teachers that my mother and Uncle Mike told me about when they described to me their time in middle school and high school. The students in my class do not move to other classes with other teachers. We have only one teacher.

His name is Mr. Gatek, and he has hair that makes him look like a man named Albert Einstein. I have a poster of Albert Einstein on my wall. Only Einstein's hair was white, and Mr. Gatek's hair is a light brown, similar to the brown of a hazelnut from the *Corylus cornuta*. I do not have a poster of Mr. Gatek on my wall.

There are also other desks and other students in the classroom. In the past year, there have been sixteen students who have desks. For forty-seven days, there were seventeen students, but then one student left, so now we have only sixteen again. I am one of the sixteen. I number the desks in my mind, and that is how I keep track of the number of desks.

My mother and I stayed in Olympia after my father moved to Arizona because my mother said it was best. But I also read an e-mail that she sent to my father that explained that the Olympia Regional Learning Academy provides a "consistent and supportive environment" for me and for who I am, and that she would not be moving to Arizona to be with my father.

In Arizona, they don't provide this in the public schools, because the Republican governor there is killing education. That is what my mother wrote in the e-mail to my father. I do not think my father ever wrote back to her.

I do not know what a Republican is, or how you can kill education. Education is not a living thing; it is an action that you perform to someone else to give them knowledge. And most of what I learn at ORLA is not knowledge. I have learned all about trees on my own, for example, and most of the time at school Mr. Gatek and other people seem to be telling me to stop learning so much about trees and stop talking so much about trees, and instead to do things that have no relationship in my mind to knowledge. They have me do art, even though I am not good at art. And they teach me the history of human beings, for which I cannot see an applicable purpose.

Also, we read books that have very few facts in them, but instead have stories about things that could not happen. People try to explain the stories to me, but most of what they say sounds like how Pastor Ilsa explains the Bible to me, when she says it is "true" even though it is not factual. This is confusing.

Mr. Gatek also teaches me things that are only tangentially related to knowledge. He wants me to learn people's names and learn special ways of talking, like not raising my voice and modulating my tone as I talk, and even how to make my face move so it appears I am smiling even when I do not feel like smiling.

At school, they also want me to be able to stand in lines in the cafeteria instead of just going straight to get food, and they want me to clean up the place where I sit after I eat and also clean my desk, and sometimes I even have to use a broom or a vacuum cleaner in the classroom. This is very irritating, because both the broom and the vacuum cleaner must be held at unnatural angles for my hands, and I dislike the sound of the vacuum cleaner intensely, and sometimes I must cover my ears.

In the background of the vacuum sucking, there is a high whine, which sounds to me like how I imagine a tsetse fly sounds. Tsetse flies live in midcontinental Africa, and they transmit trypanosomes, which cause sleeping sickness in human beings. Sometimes when I am vacuuming and I hear the buzzing in the background, I imagine that a tsetse fly has landed on me and bitten me and that I am falling asleep. I stand still until someone comes to wake me. Once this made Mr. Gatek very angry. He was very loud that day. I was asleep with the vacuum in my hands for only eighteen minutes and forty seconds.

But most of the time Mr. Gatek is not loud at all, even when I say my certain words over and over again. He usually has a quiet voice, and I like the way he says words and sounds.

When I was five and six and seven years old, before Mr. Gatek, there was a certain book in our classroom at Lincoln Options Elementary School. It was my first introduction to real information about trees. It was *A Child's Guide to Trees*, and it was my favorite book. I would use my finger to trace the pictures of the trees in the book, and I would memorize the images and match the images to the trees I saw outside.

When it was reading time, and I wanted the tree book, I would point at the bookshelf and say words to Mrs. Hawkins. I would say, "Donut, coconut, coffee and cream." Or sometimes I would say, "Cadillac Seville," which was another phrase that I used at the time. On other days I would say, "Water, water, water." This is a phrase that continues to intrigue me. And every single time, Mrs. Hawkins would know that I wanted the tree book, and she would bring me the book when she passed out books to everyone to read.

Once we had a substitute teacher, though, and someone else asked for the tree book, and I said, "Orange Julius," and the substitute teacher gave me a book about oranges and orange things, and I threw the orange book across the room, and it hit another child in the head, and then I had to go home for the rest of the day.

The sounds of certain words used to fascinate me. And the change in tone as people say them. My mother and I went to a coffee shop once, and there was a waitress who helped us, and she called back to the kitchen, "Donut, coconut, coffee and cream." She said this phrase in a peculiarly musical way, and I repeated this phrase very loudly every day, over and over, for many days. I am too old now to use the same phrase every day, but sometimes I find other phrases pleasing.

Other people in my class at ORLA say things now too. One boy said, "I have a note, I have a note" over and over again. He said it every time he had to go to the bathroom, or when it was time for recess or the end of school: "I have a note, I have a note."

This was before I turned eight years old, when I used to repeat phrases all the time, before I realized that you could use language for communication.

But when I moved from Lincoln Options to the Olympia Regional Learning Academy, Mr. Gatek did not allow me to have my favorite book until I said either the name of the book or the word *book*.

It took almost a week before Mr. Gatek understood which books I wanted to read, and then he was able to teach me the titles of those books and demonstrate to me how I should ask for those books. It was difficult for me to understand this, and I was very frustrated with the stupidity of Mr. Gatek for a long time. I said many different phrases and pointed and flapped my hands, but nothing worked until I used the words that he taught me for those books. And that was when I realized that I could communicate with other human beings to get things that I desired.

I was eight years old and eight months and two days when I realized this important fact, and then after that realization, I read everything I could find, and I used words to say what I wanted.

Trees do not require you to make certain sounds to be understood. They are simply present and ready for you to climb at any time. Trees are easier.

On Tuesday morning, I sat down at my desk, but the classroom was mostly empty. Mr. Gatek was at his desk already—he was holding papers and looking at them—but no other students were there yet. I started to talk to Mr. Gatek about the big tree I saw when I climbed the Red Cedar next door, and how I want to climb that tree. Then I talked about what we saw in the forest. Then, only partway through, Mr. Gatek said, "March, I'm going to have to ask you not to tell me about this tree right now. I have to grade homework. But I would be happy to hear more about this at lunchtime, all right?"

So I stopped talking.

Then other students came into the classroom, and it became noisy. I put my hands over my ears, and I thought about the big tree in the old-growth patch of forest.

The other students do not know as much about trees as I do. In fact, they do not know about *anything* more than me. I am better at science and math and writing than anyone else in my class of students.

However, there is an exception to this rule. I am not better at history or art. I have tried to draw a tree, but there is a girl in my class who can draw a much better tree. My tree was eight lines. It was a stick tree. Her tree was very accurate; mine was not. I believe the tree she drew was a Maple. An *Acer leipoense*, most likely. The picture she drew is on the wall beside my desk.

I do not know the girl's name who drew the tree. We have been in class together for five years.

5

After school on Tuesday, my mother took me to see a woman who has a sign on her door that says "Rhonda Ramsey, MA, Child Development Therapist." The same words are on a card on her desk. I find it easier to remember people's names when they have a nametag like this, so I remember her name: Rhonda.

I had to start seeing Rhonda because, they told me, sometimes my body is hurt and I am not aware of that. Since I was most recently in the hospital, over the weekend, I had been assigned to see her every week. This is now a rule—every Tuesday I must see Rhonda.

The office where Rhonda works has a small bowl with water burbling out of a little pot in the middle. It appears to be constantly moving, like the small waterfall I found in the creek behind our old house after it rained heavily last winter, but I believe the water in the bowl is the same water, recycled. I do not see the point of the small bowl with the moving water. But next to the bowl of water is a very small Japanese Maple, and the smallness of the tree and the partial exposure of the root structure is fascinating. I want to touch the miniature tree.

"March," Rhonda said, "do you understand that there will be a hearing about your mother's ability to care for you?"

"Why would my mother not have the ability to care for me?" I said.

"You've had some problems with hurting yourself. This hearing will decide if you have the capacity for self-injury. It's important for you to know that—"

"No," I said. "Stop talking about that."

I did not understand what she was talking about. I did not want to know. Rhonda sighed.

"Why do you think you are here, March? Why do you think you were instructed to come see me in this office?"

I thought about the answer to her question. I thought that what caused my mother to be concerned was that my inner arms and thighs often have abrasions on them.

Sometimes these cuts and bruises occur when I am gripping a naked tree trunk that has only a few limbs. I wrap my body around it, as a sloth would, and pull myself upward on the trunk. I do not notice at the time they happen, and in fact, I do not typically notice any injury at all. I only realize that they have occurred later on, when my mother or Uncle Mike draws my attention to them.

"I was injured," I told Rhonda. What happens to me in the trees seems to be a concern to my mother, because sometimes things happen when I am up in a tree and she does not know about it until many hours later.

"How recently were you injured?"

I looked down at the patterns on my arms when Rhonda asked this question. There was also the bandage on my upper left arm. I didn't want to talk about that part. But I could talk to her about the other patterns on my arms.

"The only time I had to go to the hospital because of a tree-trunk injury was when I pulled myself upward on a fifty-foot Douglas Fir that did not have any projecting limbs for thirty-five of those feet, and then when I slid back down the trunk, my skin tore on the bark and there was too much blood, and my mother took me to the emergency room, where they cleaned out the wounds and wrapped my arms in bandages that made it difficult to climb trees for one week, but I did not have any stitches that time at the hospital—I do not typically go to the hospital, and the hospital is not my favorite place," I said. Then I took a breath.

"All right," said Rhonda. "Thank you for that information. But let's get clear about why you are here. There will be a commitment hearing."

"I do not know what that is," I said.

"Okay, let me explain. You were in the hospital recently, correct?"

I thought she already knew the answer to this question, so I did not know why she was asking me. Perhaps she had forgotten what happened. I had not forgotten.

"Yes," I said. "For a different injury."

This was the first time I had an appointment with Rhonda. She talked to me about the rules of her office. Most of her rules are about time. Time can be difficult for me. It is a continuous thing, and it has no boundaries. Sometimes it moves very fast and sometimes very slow. Whenever I make a plan to climb for a certain amount of time, like climbing a tree, my plan is not what happens. It is not possible to plan or move precisely in time, and that makes me scared.

But Rhonda seemed to understand this already. I was curious about how she knew, but I did not ask, because she described my experience of time as a stream that moves fast and slow, and her description was accurate. She told me that the rules of her office involved time. No one could leave the office before the end of our time together, not me or her. Unless for the bathroom, of course. And another rule was that both of us would get time to talk. She has a timer that is bright red and looks like a red tomato with white markings, bright square ants marching around the rim. When it is time for me to talk, the timer will start. When a sound goes off—she showed me the source of the sound, which is a loud bell that hurts my ears—then I must stop talking, and Rhonda can talk. Or, if she chooses to do so, she can set the timer for me to talk again. She said this was a way of controlling and measuring time, and that it had helped other people like me to control time.

I wished I had a machine like this at home, so that I could control how long I could be in a tree. But I did not tell her that.

Instead, she said she would ask me a question, and she would set the timer for me to talk to her about the answers to the question. Her first question was very simple, but I did not have very much time, I thought, so I talked very fast. She asked about trees, and she asked me what my favorite tree was. This was an easy question.

"The Ponderosa Pine is amazing, because it can grow in places with as little as twelve inches of annual rainwater. What's really interesting is that when the land is dry, some of the trees do not grow much above the surface—only a few inches—but underground, they are growing very deep taproots, to seek out water. That's what I would do, if I were a Ponderosa Pine—seek out the water underground, where it hasn't all dried up."

"Is that what you would like, March, to be a tree?"

I thought about her question, but I did not answer her. Sometimes I think I would like to be a tree. Sometimes I think I am a tree, just located temporarily in a moving body, like one of the Ents from *The Lord of the Rings*, a book that my mother read to me before I could read for myself.

But Tolkien is confusing. I prefer books that give me factual information about trees. The most recent book that I read is the *Encyclopedia of Forest Sciences*, in four volumes. From that set of books, I have clarified my knowledge of trees in the Pacific Northwest. I now know more about the following tree species: Ponderosa Pine, Engelmann Spruce, Western Juniper, Incense Cedar, and Golden Chinkapin. I have never seen a Golden Chinkapin. They grow in Oregon.

Tolkien did not write a factual book. He wrote a book of imagination, and it was hard for me to understand, so I remember very little of it. Except the Ents. I remember the Ents. They are imaginary creatures that are made like trees, but talk and act like human beings. They move slowly, as a tree would, except when in a storm, and then they move swiftly. I like the Ents.

"I like factual books," I told Rhonda. "I do not like Tolkien, although I was an Ent once."

One year, at school, we had a party called Halloween. People dressed up in different costumes, of characters they would like to become in their dreams.

I was an Ent. I stood in the center of the room in my costume, and I did not move during the entire party. I did moan in the wind once when a teacher tried to move me, but other than that I made no sound.

"I think I was an accurate Ent," I told Rhonda. Then I realized that the timer was still going for me, and so I kept talking about the Ponderosa Pine, my favorite tree.

"The Ponderosa Pine is famous for its extensive root system, which can eat up all the water underneath a stand of trees. The Ponderosa Pine is usually found on hillsides up above fifteen hundred feet, especially in Washington State. I have never been able to climb one, and now that the ponderosa pine beetle is eating all the Ponderosas in the world, I might never be able to do so."

"How does this make you feel, March?" said Rhonda. Her voice had something in common with the flowing water. It seemed to be at the same speed.

I ignored the water, though, and I ignored what she said, because I didn't have time for it. There was more information regarding the Ponderosa Pine that was important to communicate.

"Ponderosa Pines have orange-colored bark, and on the trees that have been on these hillsides for hundreds of years, the bark forms into large orange plates."

"All right," said Rhonda. "That's good to know." Then the timer went off, and the ringing sound fuzzed my head for a moment. Rhonda made a noise, as if she wanted to talk, but I had one more thing to say.

"But wait," I said. And I held up my hand, like Uncle Mike does sometimes when he wants me to remember something really important. "It is easy to mistake a Ponderosa Pine for another tree. If you really want to confirm it is a Ponderosa Pine, just lean into the deep furrows between the plated bark. The old-growth Ponderosa Pines can—sometimes—smell of vanilla. It is very similar to the smell you are wearing now in this office."

Now the timer was reset, and Rhonda said it was her turn to talk. During her turn, she told me that she would work with me to do check-ins on my body, so that I could realize when my skin was torn, or when I was in pain, or when I was hungry. So that I would not be dependent on other people to draw my attention to what I need. We practiced some check-ins on my arms and legs until the bell went off again, and then the timer made a beeping noise again, and it was my turn to talk again.

"Your mother said you were in a tree yesterday for a very long time," said Rhonda. "Can you tell me about that?"

"Yes. It was a Red Cedar," I said. "The Western Red Cedar, *Thuja plicata*, is a member of the Cypress family—Cupressaceae—so it tends to end up in the same range as the Western White Pine, the Western Hemlock, and the Grand Fir." I took a deep breath, and I found more to tell her about the Western Red Cedar.

"What's interesting is that in terms of optimal growth zones, it's almost exactly the opposite of the Ponderosa Pine. No arid spots. It likes to live right next to a stream or a marshy part of the forest. The Western Red Cedar likes wet places. The Western Red Cedar loves the Pacific Northwest, because it is a tree of moist maritime climates. It thrives where we have cool summers and wet but mild winters near the ocean. See, that's just like Olympia!

"The Red Cedar has a trunk shaped like elongated triangles. Its base is wide and is anchored by a widely spread-out root system—kind of like the Japanese Maple there." I pointed at her little tree, so she would know what tree I was talking about. "See, its roots do not go deep, but horizontally all over the forest floor. And then as the tree goes up, it narrows to a thin peak."

"All right," said Rhonda. "But—"

The timer had not gone off, so I kept talking. I moved my eyes back and forth between the water in the bowl and the Japanese Maple. "Of course, if you want to reliably identify a tree, you need to know the foliage and the bark, and the Western Red Cedar bark and cones are distinct. The foliage is not coniferous—there are no sharp needles on the Red Cedar. Instead, the tree has flat intricate fronds that branch out like lace. It droops down, hanging fingers from each branch. In certain lights, it looks like a tree made of ferns. The cones are very small, and they rest on the lacy foliage like little flowers."

"That sounds pretty," said Rhonda.

"But also, you can tell a Red Cedar from the smell of its crushed needles. I wish I could drink it." I did not tell Rhonda that I did try to eat it once. I put Red Cedar needles in my mouth and chewed on them. But the taste was not at all like the smell, and I did not enjoy it. My mouth felt as if I had tried to drink gasoline. Gasoline is also not good to drink: I tried that too once, but it was even less pleasant than chewing on Red Cedar.

"You know a lot about Cedar trees," said Rhonda.

"Western Red Cedar is the one I am talking about. There are different varieties of trees called Cedar in the world. The one I am talking about has a layer of reddish fiber in the bark that peels off in long narrow strips like cloth. In fact, I have read that Northwest Coast Indians used to use the bark for all sorts of clothing and fishing nets and sails." I looked at her miniature Japanese Maple the entire time I talked. I would keep talking until the timer went off.

"Also, I have found that many living Red Cedars have hollows in the lower parts of the trunk. You could live inside a Red Cedar. Maybe I will do that someday, when my mother's rules for trees change."

"Is that what you'd like to do, March? Live in a tree?"

"I *climb* trees," I reminded her. "And the Western Red Cedar is great to climb, because all the lower limbs are retained by the tree, and climbing up the conical base is very helpful. In fact, the base of the old-growth Red Cedar can be ten or twelve feet wide, and they can grow up to two hundred feet tall. Unfortunately, their thin tops can snap off, so they get spiky tops that have dead, bleached limbs on the very top. The largest Western Red Cedars are probably one thousand years old. In Olympic National Park, there are trees that are over twenty feet in diameter at the base."

I paused, and then I could see the tops of the trees in my mind. "But the tops have snapped off, about a hundred and thirty feet above the ground."

The timer still hadn't gone off, and I began to tell Rhonda about other species of trees that I would like to see and climb in the Pacific Northwest, but then we were out of time, and she told me I must stop talking.

"Well, thank you for telling me about trees," Rhonda said. "I am sorry we are done for the day. It was very nice to meet you, Peter March Wong."

"Just March," I said.

"March," Rhonda said. "We are a half hour over on time, so I will have to meet with you again next week to explain the things we will work on together."

Work on together. That sounded interesting to me. Would we build models of trees? Would we build something else? Perhaps she could work on a system with me to capture tree processes on film. Perhaps we could build a fully functional tree that was speeded up, so it would be easier to see the processes happening inside. These would be good things to work on together. I was glad I was seeing Rhonda. She seemed interested in trees.

6

I had now determined which trees I would climb before breakfast before my mother woke up, in the new house with the blue mailbox. Every morning, I would climb the Bigleaf Maple and the Cherry in our backyard. Then I would climb the Western Red Cedar next door.

I do not stay up in the Red Cedar very long; I go just high enough to be able to spot the Eagle Tree. Then I descend from the tree and go inside, and by that time my mother is usually awake and we have breakfast together.

When we eat breakfast, I create a mental list of every tree I saw that morning, and I match that list against the list I made the day before, to determine if I have seen any new trees. I am still learning all the trees in this neighborhood. In our old neighborhood, I knew all the trees within a 1.2-mile radius of our house. And by the time I was thirteen years old, I had climbed them all. But our old house was in a neighborhood near downtown where there were not as many trees, and the trees were nearly all domesticated, and many were European or East Coast imports and not native Pacific Northwest species.

Our new house with the blue mailbox is on the east side of Olympia. In this part of town there are many areas that still have forest, or undeveloped land with trees growing. It is like a candy box of trees to look at, and I feel a hum inside me as I look at them as I anticipate climbing each one of them.

The trees that I have not climbed give me a hollow feeling in my throat. It is a tangy, metallic taste, a hunger inside.

For there are many, many trees everywhere I look. And I have never climbed these trees.

But the day after I first visited the Eagle Tree, my mother said I had to wait for the weekend, and that she had a surprise for me. She was giving me this surprise because I did a good job with the therapist, Rhonda, and with school this week. And she said I deserved it after being gone from my new house all last weekend. I hoped that the surprise would be going to see the Eagle Tree again.

When the weekend came, though, the surprise was not the Eagle Tree. Instead, it was a trip with Uncle Mike to a hiking place where he thought we might be able to find a Ponderosa Pine. It is my favorite species of tree, but a tree that I've never been able to climb.

Uncle Mike and I got in his truck on Saturday morning. He told me we were going very high, up by Mount Rainier, which is a large mountain that sometimes you can see from where we live in Olympia, sixty-five miles away. We drove for a long time, but during most of that time I had my eyes and ears covered. Until Uncle Mike realized about the truck window by my head and opened his own window, and the faint whining sound faded away. Then I could open my eyes and look outside.

All around us, as we drove, were expanses of forest. Trees went whipping past so fast that I could not make out their species or variety. The forest swept past us.

Now that we were driving through a forest, I could tell that we were in the midst of many trees, and this fact was calm and smooth inside me. It was like the water running endlessly in Rhonda's office, but stronger than that. It was a deep current beneath the surface of a stream.

When we reached the stopping point, we were up very high, and I could see over the top of the vast forest we drove through to get to this spot. It was an immense ocean of green. I looked around, scanned from side to side, to take in the trees I could identify. There were outreaching branches sprouting with leaves and blossoms, cones and conifer needles.

Trees filled my vision.

"Those ones over there are Birch. Am I right?" said Uncle Mike. He pointed at three small trees immediately ahead.

I looked at the triplet of trees closely. They had grayish-whitish bark and green leaves and the last remnant of one leftover blossom. They were obviously deciduous, which means trees whose leaves die every year, and then the tree pushes fresh growth out every spring.

"People think that those are Paper Birches, but they are not," I said. "They are Red Alders."

Uncle Mike went to the trees and touched them. "White bark, not red."

"Sure," I said. "They have whitish-colored bark, but it does not peel off like Paper Birch bark. They are called Red Alders. Any Alder is *Alnus*, of course. This one is *Alnus rubra*."

I was not interested in the Red Alders; they were not particularly interesting to climb. But I was interested in the small Douglas Fir next to them.

I go to the tree, and I find a hold on its side, on an old broken stump of a branch, and I swing myself up into the lower limbs, all of which are true. The trees reach up above me toward the sky, stretching out their great limbs in an intricate pattern that reminds me of the pattern of light I can make when I flap my fingers in front of my face. It is comforting to filter the light that way, and I feel the tree doing it for me now, the pattern shifting back and forth as I climb.

Later in the morning, we walked farther up the mountainside to see if we could find a Ponderosa Pine. We were coming out of the tree line when Uncle Mike paused and looked around at the open hillside, where a shadowed heap of snow lingered from winter.

"I want to talk to you about something," said Uncle Mike. "I met someone. And there's a little bit of a complication that you should know about."

I was looking at the hillside. There was the twisted shape of a tree that was curled close to the ground, and then farther away, there was a tall singleton I thought might be a Grand Fir or an Engelmann Spruce. I started walking.

"Where are you going?" said Uncle Mike. "There's no more trees to climb."

"Two trees," I said. I pointed at the small twisted one and the tall distant spire.

"That's just brush there," said Uncle Mike. "And that other tree over on the hill—that's too far away. I want to talk to you, March. I want you to know—"

"That one is not brush," I said. "Whitebark Pine."

I didn't take the time to explain to Uncle Mike that what looked like a brushy outgrowth near at hand were Whitebark Pines that had grown together as a krummholz thicket. *Krummholz* means "crooked wood" in German, and that's what it looks like, a shrub of old, twisted wood. The one I saw now could be four hundred years old—at least, a man named John Muir once found one that old. And I knew it was Whitebark because of the stiff yellow-green needles and the tiny cones.

I didn't tell Uncle Mike all this about the Whitebark because I had already moved past the krummholz. It was not a good climbing tree, so close to the ground. And I was aiming at the Fir or Pine up ahead.

"Look, okay, I can see that one tree," said Uncle Mike. "But I need to tell you. About this woman I met. See, I think you should know that—"

"I will climb it quickly," I said. "Then I will come back." I was still walking.

"I'm betting it's only a Grand Fir. And it's time for a break."

But I did not listen. I pushed my feet to move faster, even though I could feel the muscles in my legs burning and I could hear, behind me, Uncle Mike yelling about not going so fast over rough terrain.

Finally, I reached the solitary tree, and I stared up into the crown. I could now definitely confirm it was not a Grand Fir. Grand Firs have crowns made up of densely packed, flat, horizontal branches that sweep down and then level out toward their tips. And also I could see cones on the ground, and I have rarely seen Grand Fir cones on the ground. Usually, just the seeds fall from the cones.

Uncle Mike sighed and stumbled after me. "Slow down, March! I'm not young anymore, you know. Let's just rest for a bit before you climb that Fir."

"Not a Grand Fir," I said. "Not at all." Grand Firs—*Abies grandis*—are a member of the Pine family, Pinaceae, and they live mostly on the east side of the Cascade mountains, where my mother and Uncle Mike grew up. Which is why Uncle Mike thinks he recognizes it. But it would have been unlikely for a Grand Fir to be here in this terrain and in this climate. I am often surprised how lazy people are in their thinking.

Most people haven't seen Grand Fir cones, but I have—because I've climbed to the very top of a Grand Fir before. The cones are little barrel-shaped things—two to three inches long—and they sit on the uppermost branches. They look a little like the cones of the Pacific Silver Fir and Subalpine Fir, and they stay green or greenish purple until they fall.

I wished Uncle Mike were right, because Grand Firs are solid and reliable climbing trees.

But this one was not a Grand Fir. I was working to identify this tree. Inside my head, I could see cards of tree information as I analyzed what I could see and feel. There was no dome top, to start with; this tree had a tall, narrow crown. Tassel-like branchlets hung down. Close at hand—close enough to climb without technical assistance. So I hitched my leg into the tree and found a foothold about four feet off the ground. The next hold was two feet above that, and then three feet five inches above that one.

When I climb, I feel I am a piece of machinery, gears moving in synchronicity.

By the time Uncle Mike came to the base of the tree, I was approximately twenty-seven feet off the ground.

The bark is thin with a dark-purple tinge. Scales flake off in my hands as I climb. The branches I grip hold needles, so I roll the stout, prickly needles between my fingers. Resin oil covers my skin with my first six moves.

The needles are connected to the twigs by small wood pegs that stay there after I detach a few needles. They are warts on the twigs. And the needles when I crush them have a strong piney odor.

It is possible that this tree is a type of Spruce. I have read about Engelmann Spruces, but unlike Sitka Spruces, they are intolerant of oceanic climates, and they do not grow far west of the Cascade mountain range. But there are exceptions—and this may be one. An exception would grow in a rain shadow, like the dry hollow we are in right now.

The tree I am climbing is not a recent arrival. It is seven feet thick, and probably 179 feet tall. If it is an Engelmann, it is nearly as large as the biggest one known. That one is in Idaho.

"Hey, what's going on up there?" calls Uncle Mike. "Didn't I tell you to wait for me?"

I think I should confirm the tree's identity. A breeze strikes it, and I hold on tight. At the end of the branch tips, there are plump pollen cones.

The branches sway, but I do not fall, and at the end of the branches, the cones burst open in a yellow cloud of pollen that drifts on the wind. At this elevation, it would be more likely to be a hybrid between a White Spruce—*Picea glauca*—and an Engelmann. But around me, I can see the wrinkled Engelmann Spruce cones, and I can see the pollen cones on the ends of the branches.

The shape of the needles locks the identification for me. The needles are precisely four-sided, as if formed in a machine, and when I roll them in my fingers, I can feel the edges turn against my skin. This is a pure breed, not a hybrid.

"Engelmann Spruce," I call down to Uncle Mike. "One hundred percent Engelmann. Confirmed."

"Well." Uncle Mike sighs. "Aren't we all glad to hear that?"

"Yes," I say. "Yes, we are."

"How much longer do you think you'll be up there?" says Uncle Mike.

His question makes me think about time. If this Engelmann Spruce is nearly 180 feet, then it is taller than the Subalpine Fir and the Whitebark Pine we saw. And a true Engelmann would take up to three hundred years to grow to this size. The only way one gets started is in a windstorm, a spruce beetle outbreak, or a fire . . . and then the cycle starts all over again.

This tree has been struck by lightning—there is a scar spiraling down the trunk, about a hundred feet up. Uncle Mike is saying something, but I am not listening to him.

I am climbing higher. So far the branches all seem true. Now I am at sixty-five feet and at move number thirty-seven.

Then there is a sudden bright sound—a rending crack as a branch breaks, shattering under my feet.

And I fall.

I had not examined the deeper layers of the bark of the Engelmann Spruce, and I had not looked closely at its needles to see if the branch was dead. That was my first mistake.

I plan my climbs so carefully in my mind because I am not naturally very coordinated, and it takes a great deal of concentration for me to climb a tree. On this occasion, I saw only hold number thirty-seven in the ascent, then I simply moved to that branch when I got to that spot in the tree. If I do not have a plan, I cannot move. I am not good at improvising, which is something that Pat Tillman was very good at doing.

When I fell, every future move exploded apart in my mind, a deck of cards thrown in the air.

The branches are a storm around me, and I fall into a deep well of green. The needles and limbs rush past. While I am falling, I can see the limbs that I have previously touched to ascend to this height. It is a whirl of green and brown branches. But since I do not have a plan, even though I can see the branches I used in my past moves, they are not connected in a list. That makes it very difficult for me to think to my next move.

I am facing up toward the top of the tree, and it keeps moving back and forth, but the branches I am passing are below me, and I do not have eyes in the back of my head, like my old teacher Mrs. Hawkins used to say she had in her head. So I cannot see the branches below me before I hit them.

Then I hit the largest branch yet. It strikes my shoulders, and then another branch hits my back. And it occurs to me in that moment that if I were playing Pat Tillman's game, then I would use the momentum of landing on that branch to propel myself to the branch to the left, which looks very solid.

But then I have fallen off that branch. It is too late. However, when I hit the next branch with my legs, I remember what I was just thinking, and I use the impact to propel myself to the left, and I find a new hold—one I had not planned on—on the next branch, and I am still falling, but not as fast now. And I use that branch to slow down. Then I grab a handful of small limbs, and my hands sting with the needles in their grip. But I am able to bring myself to a halt. And I stand and look out from a spot far below the now-broken branch from which I fell. I am only eight feet away from the ground.

I am breathing very fast and very loud. The top of my shoulder is scratched, and my cheek too. But mostly I can feel my breath rushing in and out of my lungs, a fountain of sudden air.

The bandage has come loose on my arm. But the rule is that I must leave the bandage on my arm, so I push it carefully back in place before there is any blood.

I am standing solid on a very large branch now, holding on to the very small branches above me. I look at the needles to check if the large branch is alive. It is green and true and solid. The sunlight around me comes through a cloud for a moment, and everything seems to move. But it does not make my heart race like it did when I was falling. The light around me shifts and fades and brightens again.

Now it seems to me that I am sailing through time like the captain of a ship—standing tall, moving through centuries and millennia, at the vast and ponderous speed of a tree.

"You okay up there?" comes Uncle Mike's voice from below. It is as if he is underwater, deep below, like in a submarine, and I am floating on the surface of the water.

I think I have learned something about falling. It is not necessary to have a plan; sometimes you can simply act. This is an idea I can hold on to.

After I climbed down from the Engelmann Spruce, we drove home. On the way home, Uncle Mike and I agreed that we would not tell my mother about my fall.

7

On Sunday, we went to church. Pastor Ilsa's church is where my mother and I go to church. Ilsa's church is called the United Churches of Olympia. It is called United Churches because two churches grafted themselves together many years ago. Like two trees of different origins now sharing the same sap and melding their bark together into one seamless whole. At least, this is how my mother explained the church to me. I like the explanation.

The United Churches—both of the parts of it—is a Christian church. People here believe in God and believe in Jesus Christ. We go to this church even though I am not a Christian and I do not believe in God.

In the United Churches, someone reads from the Bible at the beginning of the service. This is the part that usually confuses me. I do not understand the Bible, but Ilsa says she does, and I believe in Ilsa, so I guess it's not all silly stuff like babies born in mangers, and donkeys who can talk. But I do not understand how it works, and words that do not work I generally do not like. I like things I can take apart and understand, or things I can read about and understand.

Ilsa says she likes to talk about God because she cannot entirely understand God. But that is not how I feel at all. I need to understand things all the way down to the root.

Part of why I like trees is that I can understand how they work, but I cannot duplicate how they work. They are bigger and stronger than me in every way. Maybe this is how Ilsa feels about God and the Bible. She talks about God being stronger and bigger than her in every way, but she says that God shares similar feelings about poor people and the environment and trees. Sometimes when I talk to Ilsa, I wish I believed in God. I think that if God existed, I would like Ilsa's God, because Ilsa's God would be like a tree.

I like the idea of God being like a tree. God would be alive and always growing and nearly everlasting. Ilsa and I have had many conversations about trees, because she studied botany in college before she became a pastor, and the fact that I like talking to Ilsa is part of the reason that we are still going to this church. That is what my mother says.

Ilsa sometimes talks about the ideas of a theologian she knows named Sallie McFague. Ilsa told me that Sallie McFague proposed a thought experiment. I do not know precisely what a thought experiment is, but it sounds interesting. The Sallie McFague thought experiment is an idea about the body of God. She said, "What if we thought of the world as the body of God?"

It is the only quote from a theologian that I think I understand.

The morning after I climbed the Engelmann Spruce, Ilsa was giving a sermon in the pulpit at the church. But she was not talking about trees. She was talking about God. I was not particularly interested in most of the words Ilsa was saying. I do not understand most talk about God.

However, I heard Ilsa say the word *miracle* several times, and that word stayed in my head, like a small stone dropping through deep water, flashing in the light from above.

Trees are a miracle in themselves; they do not require God to be miraculous. If trees are part of the body of God, like Sallie McFague said, then maybe I could believe in God. And since trees are already miraculous, and we cut them down and destroy them, I do not think it would change anything if people knew they were cutting down God or hurting God.

But I don't think the idea of God is necessary to sustain or create trees. And there are many things that make trees miraculous by themselves.

One example is the nitrogen cycle. I found information about it written down in a book by a man called David Suzuki, and this is a book that Ilsa gave to me, which is why I think of it when I see Ilsa talking in her special church robe. The nitrogen cycle is a kind of miracle.

The nitrogen cycle requires bears. Brown bears catch salmon in streams and rivers. Then the brown bears carry the salmon farther inland, and they bury these nitrogen-rich fish in the ground for later retrieval. But bears have short memories, and often they forget the fish where they left them, far inland from the streams. And the fish bodies decompose, leaving a reservoir of nitrogen in the ground. This creates a rich and fertile environment for large trees to grow, and in fact without the nitrogen deposited by the bears, very large old-growth trees would probably never have been able to continue their growth cycle. Five hundred years ago, if someone had removed all bears, none of the old-growth trees we have now would have grown. Instead, we would have small, stunted trees that died early in their life cycles.

In a very true sense, bears created the old-growth forests. But now the nitrogen cycle is broken. We do not have bears in Olympia anymore, that I know of. There are no bears to plant salmon in the forest.

After I read David Suzuki's book, I took salmon from my dinner plate and I buried it in the woods, hoping to assist the growth of a large tree. But then my mother found out about what I did with my dinner, and she was not pleased. We do not have salmon often enough for me to do this regularly, and when my mother is displeased, my tree climbing is often restricted. So I do not do this anymore when she is home.

I have considered other alternatives—like catching salmon myself, or buying it at the store and depositing it in the woods—to keep the nitrogen cycle going. But my mother explained that this cycle was created by thousands of bears over hundreds of years, when salmon was much more plentiful and no one had to buy it at the store. Also, if there were thousands of bears and I am the only one now burying salmon in the woods, then this is unlikely to restart a cycle that was ongoing for many, many years.

So I do not have a ready solution to the nitrogen-cycle breakage issue.

After church is done every Sunday, my mother drinks coffee and talks to other people in the back of the church. I eat cookies, and I read books. Sometimes, people come to me and talk to me. Some of these people make me uncomfortable, and then I wave my arms and make sounds, and then we leave early. But other people do not make me uncomfortable. Pierre is one of these people.

Pierre is married to Ilsa. He is a professor of botany and science at The Evergreen State College. Ilsa and Pierre met when she was a student of botany in college, and then they both enrolled in a graduate program for botany, but partway through, Ilsa almost died in an accident, and after she survived the accident, she said a miracle had happened. Then she felt like life had changed for her, and she left the botany school and instead went to a school for theology, and in the end she became a minister.

Pierre is a professional botanist, and he talks about trees with me. He is knowledgeable about how trees work. He has never asked me to call him Dr. Smekins or Professor Smekins, but that's what everyone else calls him.

Pierre is the only one who understands all my questions. And he likes my questions; he has never been annoyed by me.

As soon as I saw him the Sunday after I climbed the Engelmann Spruce, I went up to him and started talking. "I was thinking about the nitrogen cycle this morning," I said. "David Suzuki and the nitrogen cycle."

"Well, it's good to see you too, March," said Pierre. "Good morning to you!" When he spoke, some crumbs flew out of his mouth and landed on my shirt, since he was eating a cookie when I started talking to him. Despite the crumbs on my shirt, I kept talking to him.

"I tried to duplicate the nitrogen cycle by burying salmon in the woods," I said. "To grow trees, you know?"

"Ah," said Pierre. "I can't imagine that worked very well. Did it?"

"No, it did not." I made a frown with my face. I remembered being disappointed by not having good results with my experiment, and I wanted Pierre to see that on my face. "I do not think I can fix the break of the cycle on my own."

Pierre is good for me to talk to. Sometimes he has been very helpful, as when he explained to me that when someone holds out a hand, they expect that hand to be squeezed and gently moved up and down for between one and three seconds before it is released. It is a greeting ritual, Pierre told me, but I don't need to do it with him. This is fortunate, because I do not like to do it. I do not like to touch skin.

"You're familiar with Reimchen's work on the nitrogen cycle?" said Pierre. He finished his cookie and wiped his fingers on a napkin.

"No," I said.

"To prove that plants and trees were using the decaying salmon as a fertilizer, Dr. Reimchen traced a nitrogen isotope, N15, which is found only in the deep waters of the Pacific Ocean." While he talks, Pierre tends to twist his fingers in his white beard, and I like to see his fingers move back and forth in his beard. It reminds me of moss in a tree.

"The N15 isotope appears in the growth rings of trees in the coastal rain forest in the Pacific Northwest," I said.

"Yes. Yes, it does, bright boy," said Pierre. "And of course, the question for the scientists was, how did the nitrogen isotope get there? Reimchen figured out that spawning salmon swim up into mountain streams, and then end up under the trees, caught and buried by bears."

"That's what I was thinking about," I explained. "The bears helping old-growth trees grow."

"Yes, but it gets even better than that!" Pierre snapped his fingers and picked up another cookie. He took a sip of coffee. I was impatient. I could not think of what could be better than bears helping trees.

"See," said Pierre. "The cycle doesn't stop there. It seems that by fertilizing forests, salmon are actually protecting their own habitat. Trees on the banks of salmon-filled rivers grow faster than those along salmon-free rivers. The nitrogen helps create trees that keep salmon streams shaded at the right temperature for the fish. Isn't that fascinating? It's a virtuous circle. Know what I mean?"

After we talked about the nitrogen cycle, Pierre asked me about how my week had been and what I had done. I told him I climbed an Engelmann Spruce, up by Mount Rainier. I described the cones and needles I saw, and how I confirmed it was an Engelmann Spruce.

"I remember climbing an Engelmann once," said Pierre. Pierre then told me about when he climbed an Engelmann.

"I remember the tree above me," he said, "like a vast, frozen, vertical dragon, twisting itself up into the air, lunging for the clouds, talons wrapped tight around the rocks at its feet, dug into the soil, supporting the great upward thrust of its racked spiny arms covered in a bristled embrace."

He stopped talking and turned toward me slightly, and I averted my eyes from his beard. I do not like the feeling of being looked at, and Pierre remembered that a moment later and turned back away. He is not someone who insists on looking at me while he is talking, which is another reason I enjoy being with him.

"You know what I mean?" he said.

It took me a few minutes to understand what he meant, but in the end, I thought I liked it. Pierre meant that the tree was like the mythical creature called the dragon.

I think he makes up fantastical stories about trees to help more people be comfortable around trees, the way that Pierre and I are. But I am not sure. Maybe he likes talking in stories.

As I thought over his words, I remembered the tree on Saturday. I could see it in my mind again. Above me, the great skeletal expanse of limbs, all held up by their own years-long stretching extrusion, and along the length of each great limb, another set of blossoming branches, each one emerging in endless sequence, like a Mandelbrot set.

"How old do you think your Engelmann is?" said Pierre.

I do not know how old it really is; Pierre knew this. But he wanted me to guess. So I thought about the question.

At the center of any tree is the great pillar of the central trunk, which expands year by year—so subtly that no one can see it happen— by accreting a thin new layer of living material and then another. It's like building a cathedral by applying paint every week and waiting for it to dry before applying the next thin layer of material. The incredible thing about trees is that the method works. Cut apart a tree and you'll see each angelic layer applied, in times of drought and times of moisture alike. The tree simply keeps growing, higher and higher, expanding its territory, pushing out new growth.

I thought about how thick the Engelmann's trunk was under my hands, and I imagined the layers of xylem accumulating, moment by moment.

"I think it was at least three hundred years old," I said finally. "I think that tree had at least three hundred rings."

Pierre made a sighing sound. He took a bite of cookie. "It really is astonishing, isn't it?"

He was waiting for me to say something. "What?" I said.

"The unheard signals of trees. Each tree hears signals from an unseen internal time system, and from the weather, and perhaps even from the stars, and when it receives the signal, every winter, it cuts off access to the storehouse of supplies, and each of its forward scouts dies off. That's when the layers of the tree go down. Then the tree renews its conquest of the air every spring. You know what I mean?"

That is what Pierre says at the end of everything he says to me. Usually I do know what he means, and I can answer affirmatively. But this time, I did not know about some of the things he had talked about. I do not care about storehouses or scouts and conquests. I do not know anything about them.

"I fell," I said. "When I was in the Engelmann. Sixty-five feet up. Uncle Mike said I almost broke my back. But I caught a branch on the way down."

"Well, that's not good." Pierre made a chuckling sound. "But it turned out okay, I suppose. Glad you're still with us."

"You fell?" said a voice. "No one told me about your fall." It was my mother's voice.

Pierre gave another chuckle, but his fingers stopped moving in his beard. He knows that sometimes I tell him things that I do not tell everyone, and I think he knew that this was one of those things. My mother spoke again, but my hands were fluttering in front of my face now, as I re-created the patterns of leaves and light on my eyes.

Eventually, my mother was close enough to me and was talking clearly enough to me that I was forced to pay attention.

"It was an accident," I said. "And I won't have any more of those accidents."

"You can't be sure of that," said my mother.

Pierre gave another chuckle. "Your mother is right," he said. "Hard to be sure. Especially in big trees. Perhaps some climbing gear like the Forest Service provides to—"

My mother spoke sharply, her voice snapping and cracking like the sound of a limb breaking. "No. No Forest Service climbing gear. That would just encourage him to climb even higher. You should know better than to suggest that, Dr. Smekins."

"Right. Right then," said Pierre. His fingers smoothed out his beard with small nervous jerking movements. "Sorry."

"But in very large trees, I would need gear like that," I said. "When I climb the Eagle Tree, then I will need to use professional gear, and—"

"You can't climb the Eagle Tree," said my mother. "Not until you are eighteen years old, at the very least, March."

Pierre held up a finger. "A question," he said.

"Yes?" said my mother. Her voice was still sharp and cracking.

"This, uh, so-called Eagle Tree he's talking about—you wouldn't be talking about the very large, nearly five-hundred-year-old tree that grows at the top of the LBA Woods, would you? That land has been public property for years," he said, "but I think there's a proposal to sell it to a private company. I read that the city council is trying to decide."

"I don't know," said my mother. "Does it matter?" She had turned herself toward Pierre, and I found myself breathing a little less fast, with a little less hum underneath my mind.

"Well," said Pierre. He took a deep breath. His fingers were quiet in his beard, as if this part were very important. "That very large and very old tree is indeed an extraordinary specimen. I'd like to believe it is an extreme out-of-region Ponderosa Pine. But I'm not sure, since I've never examined it closely. If it is a Ponderosa, it would appear to have been here since the terrain was raw prairie. Since it survived the transition, there are theories that it may be a specialized variation, an anomaly in the genetic line of the Ponderosa. If, in fact, it is a Ponderosa, it would be the largest one ever found on this side of the Cascade mountains."

In my own ears, I can hear myself talking suddenly, very high and very fast. "A Ponderosa Pine? Really? Is that what it is—a Ponderosa Pine? Did you know they—?"

But my mother talked over the sound of my voice, which is something that never, almost never, happens. "March," she said. "I don't care what kind of tree it is. You can't climb it."

Pierre was still talking, pleading with her. "But a Ponderosa—here in Olympia! The tree is probably two hundred feet high now, even with a broken snag at the top, where the eagles landed up until last year. That's why they call it the Eagle Tree. It's amazing—know what I mean?"

My mother talked over him, just as she talked over me.

"Peter March Wong, you will not climb the Eagle Tree. Not now, not ever. *Two hundred feet high?* It's too dangerous. You will promise not to climb that tree. When you're eighteen years old, I won't be able to prevent you any longer. But you will not climb it now. Promise."

"I can't promise that," I said to her.

I saw Pierre's fingers going faster in his beard, and I wondered if his fingers moved in his beard in a way similar to the way my hands move in front of my face when I am feeling something strongly. His fingers curled back and forth, back and forth, weaving the strands like moss. He had stepped back; he was no longer in the way of my mother's declarations.

"All right," my mother said. "How's this then?" She sighed. "You will promise that you will not climb the Eagle Tree before you are eighteen years old unless you have spoken to me and I have responded to you affirmatively."

"Affirmative. All right."

This meant that there was a possibility that I could climb it someday. I could use logic to convince her why I needed to climb the tree before I was eighteen years old. That is three years, seven months, three weeks, and one day away from this present moment. And perhaps I just needed to find the correct logic, the right reasons. Then I could climb the Eagle Tree.

8

O n Sunday after church, I talked to Uncle Mike. He said he would take me back to see the base of the Eagle Tree on the next day, to confirm if it is a Ponderosa Pine. He also told me that my mother had talked to him about ensuring that I did not try to climb the tree. That was all right with me—I would see the tree again, and that was exciting in itself.

All day on Monday at school, I could not stop my hands from flapping. And little high shrieks came out of me, like birds buried deep in a dark forest of possibility, finding their way by echolocation. Mr. Gatek told me it was very disruptive to the class, and I had to sit by myself.

But I could not help what my body was doing. After all, I had never seen a confirmed Ponderosa Pine. I had no idea a Ponderosa could even grow here in Olympia. I let out another shriek. This sound grew to a high whine—a spaceship taking off in my mouth, the sound whistling out beyond hearing.

Ponderosa Pine can't be confused with other trees, because it is the only one that has long needles in bundles of threes. And each cone has a prickle on the back of each scale. I planned to use these characteristics to identify the Eagle Tree for sure the next time I saw it.

After all, as Pierre said, it would be very unusual to have a Ponderosa Pine growing here.

Uncle Mike picked me up at home after I rode the bus from school on Monday. His truck was still the color of Elm bark. But he had shut the window, so I did not have to cover my ears while I rode. Instead, I could merely hum along, in tune with the engine. When the car stopped in the parking lot under the trees, I saw the forest all around us, and I had never been so happy.

As we went deeper into the woods, I could feel the temperature drop incrementally and the air fill with the condensed moisture from the trees. The ground was soft and warm with light and growth, and yards deep with fermenting bark and moss and decaying vegetation. I closed my eyes, and the sun hit my face, and I felt I could almost hear the ceaseless excavations of the mites and worms and beetles that are the flowing bloodstream underneath the dead-pine-needle-and-earth skin of this vast organism.

I reached down to feel the soil, and I touched the outreaching roots of the trees that bore horizontally and vertically hundreds of feet through the forest. I stroked the earth with my palm, and I could almost feel that nearly invisible network of capillary roots that sucks moisture and nutrients out of every inch of the soil I was standing on. I breathed in and out. I was part of the forest. I was alive.

I was concentrating on the forest floor so hard that I did not hear at first when Uncle Mike called out to me.

There was a white chalk line ahead, running straight through the forest, and it was perpendicular in front of me, so I could not approach the Eagle Tree without crossing that line. I was about to make a right angle across that curious white line, to see if it made a circle around the tree, but just before I approached it, Uncle Mike reached me, and I realized he had been saying my name.

"Come here, March," said Uncle Mike. "I think all that land ahead has been sold—it's now private property. We're not allowed to go near the Eagle Tree anymore."

I was listening to Uncle Mike, but my legs would not stop moving toward the Eagle Tree.

"Is it a rule?" I said.

"Yes, March." Uncle Mike sighed. "Yes, there's a new sign here, so it is a rule. You cannot cross the white chalk line. If you see this sign, you cannot move forward past the line. Here, take a look. Read the sign."

I looked. On a metal post was a large yellow square with writing on it. A sign where there was no sign before. The writing was red, and it said in very large letters:

POSTED
Private Property
No Trespassing
Violators Will Be Prosecuted

When we returned home, I walked around the couch in a circle. I was staring at my shoes while I walked, but I could not see my shoes. I was still looking at the floor of the forest, and I was seeing again the pattern of the leaves moving across the light in the sky, and across my skin. My mother was talking, but most of what she was saying I did not hear.

My shoe came untied, and I tripped over the laces. So I stopped walking for a moment. *Someone should tie my shoe so I can keep walking,* I thought. But I had stopped, and I could now hear what my mother was saying.

"March, you've got to understand that sometimes people own land, and they can do what they want to do with that land." My mother poured a glass of water for Uncle Mike. He had taken his Sounders hat off his head, and he was twisting the hat in his hands. "They own everything on that property, even the trees," she said.

"You cannot own all of a tree," I said.

My mother threw her hands up in the air, and for a moment she looked like a tree herself. But just for a moment. She stood up and said something to Uncle Mike. "I don't know what to do," she said. "I mean, how do you work with that logic?"

I did not understand her question, and I did not think she was talking to me. But I repeated what I had said, in case there was any doubt. "You cannot own all of a tree."

My mother sighed, and then she walked from the living room into the kitchen. I opened my mouth to say again what I said, louder this time, so that she could hear me in the kitchen.

But Uncle Mike started talking before I could speak again. He talked softly while he petted my arm. His voice was soothing, like the deep, smooth flow of a stream. The current of his voice was strong and even; it flowed with the motion of his hand. I felt like a cat being petted.

"Can you explain what you mean by saying 'all of a tree,' March?"

"A tree," I said, "can be composed of a root system that, including the capillary branches, can stretch out more than a mile from the originating point of the main trunk, and perhaps even miles beyond, and a tree also creates its own microclimate around it, composed of the carbon dioxide funnel it sucks in and the off-gassing of atmospheric elements that the tree excretes, like oxygen, that animals breathe, including human beings, so the actual property line that holds the tree's trunk cannot hold all of the tree—the root system and the microclimate cannot be wholly owned by the property owner—and furthermore—"

Then I stopped talking and took a deep breath, because that was a lot to say without breathing, and my vision was beginning to narrow as it does when I have not breathed in enough air and I am about to pass out from lack of oxygen. I wonder if trees experience a similar sensation when carbon dioxide is removed from the environment. I wonder if trees that are located next to a freeway, and are enveloped by clouds of gasoline fumes from the cars on the freeway, find themselves choking and gasping for clean air. Trees can, in fact, react to painful stimuli. Electrocardiograms demonstrate that a tree's autonomic response to pain is similar to a human being's response. However, I do not think anyone has performed this kind of electrocardiogram analysis on a tree that cannot breathe.

In any case, I took a deep breath, and then I could talk again. "Furthermore," I continued, "certain species of trees, such as Aspens, actually exist as hundreds of miles of joined trees. So the human property lines are an arbitrary boundary on the living mass that thrives beneath the surface of the land. If the human property line does not encompass the entirety of the living mass of the interconnected grove, then the human being is not 'owning' the entirety of the tree."

"All right, all right," said Uncle Mike. He slapped his hat back on his head, and I could look at him again, because I could look at his hat. "I understand what you mean."

I took another deep breath. But this time I did not open my mouth to talk again. I was enjoying the petting and talking that Uncle Mike was doing.

"Here's the thing, though, March. Although you may have a valid point regarding the actual physical ownership of the property and the trees that are located on that property—"

I started to talk, but Uncle Mike interrupted me. "*Mostly* located on that property, I should have said. You have a valid point there. But the problem is that the law is clear about physical ownership over that area, and you can't simply go to that property, or climb any of the man's trees, without getting his explicit permission. It's not allowed, by law."

"Then the law should be changed. I climb trees at the school and the park all the time."

"We've been over this before, March. That's public property. Anyone is allowed to climb the trees. But as you found out when the firemen took you out of the tree at Burfoot Park, not all trees *should* be climbed, and they have ordinances against climbing trees, even in public parks."

"And I climb trees in this neighborhood all the time," I said, "except for Miss Stevens's trees."

"Right," said Uncle Mike. "Think of the owner's trees—even the Eagle Tree—as similar to Miss Stevens's trees. They are off-limits to you for now. Maybe we could talk to them and—"

"Is he mean like Miss Stevens then? Is that why I cannot climb those trees? Because the owner of the tree could be a mean bitch like Miss Stevens?"

Uncle Mike sighed a long sigh, and for a moment he stopped petting me. "I wish you wouldn't use those words," he said. "I wish your mother hadn't said that word. She was angry. It's not a good way to describe another human being. Do you understand what I'm saying?"

"Yes," I said, but really I did not understand. I just said that so he would keep petting me.

After a moment, Uncle Mike continued, but his voice sounded different now, less smooth and more jagged, like rocks sticking up above a dry streambed, the water disturbed and chaotic. He was not petting me.

"Honestly, March, I don't know if this guy is mean or nice. It's just that the rules are there for a reason, all right? And you can't just make up your own rules on someone else's property. Do you understand?"

"Why are the rules this way?" I said. I started walking around the couch, and pretty soon I could see the forest floor and the patterns again. "Why? Why?"

"I don't know, March," said Uncle Mike. "I don't know." Now the streambed that made up the sound of his voice was entirely dry of water, just hoarse sand and dry rocks left behind.

"Dinner is ready," said my mother from the kitchen. "Are you staying, Mike?"

Uncle Mike stood up. "No, I'm sorry," he said. "I've got to go. I have a date tonight."

9

We are part of a system that includes trees. Without trees, we will eventually all die. Yet there are many examples of how we are killing the trees around us, and hurting them, as well as hurting ourselves. The Ponderosa Pine, my favorite tree, is one of the trees most endangered by global warming and climate change. Pine beetles used to die during the winter, and they would eat only a few trees before they died. But now, because of global warming, they can live all year long, and they devour many trees. They have killed—and are killing—all of the vast Ponderosa Pine forests. This means that the vast forest can no longer absorb carbon, but instead ejects carbon into the atmosphere. Because of the death of most of the Ponderosa Pine trees from the pine beetle, the entirety of British Columbia is now a carbon source, not a carbon sink. This is a problem for lots of reasons. One of them is that we human beings breathe oxygen, not carbon dioxide.

I do not like this idea that we have begun to kill off—at great velocity and accelerating speed—all of the things that sustain us. I didn't like it at all when I first thought of it, but most people around me do not seem that disturbed by it, even though the knowledge of this is obvious and readily available to anyone who looks up trees on the Internet.

I guess most people are not as bothered by the death of a species as I am. Even if that is the human species.

At least, no one seems bothered, because no one has taken action to amend it. So they must not care. That is the only explanation I can think of for the lack of reaction to this fact.

I talked very loudly about all of this at recess at school one day the week of my second visit to the Eagle Tree. I talked especially to a boy with hair like yellow corn silk from my class. He likes insects. He brings insects to school, and he reads books about insects. But he is not as interested in trees. I told him that his hair looked like *Stigmata maydis*, the true name for corn silk.

"Can I touch it?" I asked him. My mother told me to ask before I touch someone's hair.

"What? Why?" he said.

"It looks like corn silk," I said. "*Stigmata maydis.*"

"Why do you keep saying that?" he said.

I did not touch his hair. But now I had a new name for him. I called him Stig. I talked to Stig more about trees and human effects on trees.

Eventually, he pushed me. Apparently, he was not interested in what I was saying. But I was still talking to him. So he pushed me again. And the second time Stig pushed me, I fell down.

"Go away, Aspy," he said. "We don't want you here."

Another boy said this to us both once, and Stig said it to me now.

When Stig with the corn-silk hair pushed me down to the ground, I bumped my knee very hard and it throbbed very painfully, and so I stopped talking and I just stayed there on the ground thinking about the Eagle Tree and Ponderosa Pines.

I lay there until Mr. Gatek came to get me after recess was over. I did not tell him about Stig with the corn-silk hair. Because then everything was all right, once Mr. Gatek came to get me. Except for the fact that I still hadn't climbed the Eagle Tree.

After I was pushed at school recess when I was trying to talk to Stig with the corn-silk hair, I came home, and my mother found out I was pushed, and she had me call my father. She said this couldn't keep happening to me at school, and she thought if I talked to my father, he would understand.

So I tried to explain this all to my father on the phone, but I think he got confused. I ended up describing the changes in the pine beetle's life cycle in a lot of detail, and I think he thought that I liked the pine beetles and thought they were interesting. In fact, he bought me a little book of insects and sent it to me after that conversation. I do like insects, but I am not as intrigued by them as I am by trees. I thought my father should have given that book to Stig with the corn-silk hair, because he likes insects more than me. But I have the book, not Stig.

The conversation with my father lasted two hours and fourteen minutes of one day, and he had to get off the phone partway through what I was saying, and I had never gotten to the real part of the story that I think is the most interesting and disturbing, which is that the pine beetles are destroying the trees, and that we need the trees to live, and that I am worried about the trees. Instead, I spent most of the time I had on the phone with my father talking about the beetles, and that was only the introduction to the real story, and so I didn't get a chance to tell him what really matters. And that made me sad.

I did not even know if my father knew that the oxygen he breathes comes from Ponderosa Pine forests, and that many of those forests are now gone. It would make me even more sad if he died from not being able to breathe oxygen and he never knew why. I would feel better if he knew why. So that made me anxious as well.

When my mother asked me why I was sad the day after I received the insect book in the mail from my father, I tried to explain some of this to her too. But mostly I ended up talking about oxygen, and then I got upset and waved my arms around and made noises that made her hold her ears, and I think she was sorry afterward that she asked me.

That week was not a good week.

I just wanted to climb the Eagle Tree, and no one would take me there. To make myself feel better, I decided I would climb the Bigleaf Maple in our new backyard again. It was very damp and misty—which some people from outside the Pacific Northwest consider to be rain, but I do not. This is typical weather for the Pacific Northwest and Olympia. It is often wet in Olympia, but we have an average of only 49.95 inches a year of actual precipitation. That's less than in Denver. In Olympia, the air is damp, and water collects and drips from everywhere. We do not get big downpours, but we get damp and spongy.

I don't care. It helps the trees grow, and I climb the trees.

That afternoon, in the mist, I changed the way I typically climb the Bigleaf Maple. The usual limb I use to ascend at the eleventh move up the tree was wet with water, and when I first gripped it I could feel the slickness against my palm, and before I got up on it, I realized that I could not stand securely on that limb. Then I remembered my fall from the Engelmann Spruce, and I felt for a moment like the limbs of the tree were whirling around me again, and I almost closed my eyes and fell backward. But I didn't. Instead, I stood very still in the tree for a long time to figure out a different way to climb the tree, and finally I created a new route up the Bigleaf Maple. This new route is composed of thirty-seven moves instead of fourteen. But it works in the rain.

After I completed the climb in the damp mist, my hands were covered with a muddy residue of bark and rainwater, and I was exhausted. But I was very happy. While I was in the Bigleaf Maple, I realized there was a way for me to go to the Eagle Tree without anyone taking me there. I could go on my own, and I could do it tomorrow. So I was making my happy moan when I came in for dinner that night. After that, I went to bed.

I had a plan. I had a plan to secretly go to see the Eagle Tree, on my own.

10

Every day, after school, I take a bus home. The first two times that Uncle Mike took me to go see the Eagle Tree, we drove on a street called Boulevard Road. Now that I had been in the house with the blue mailbox for nearly two weeks, I recognized that each day after school, at approximately 3:45 p.m., the bus turned onto Boulevard, and we passed through the same roundabout that Uncle Mike turned on to get to the LBA Woods, where the Eagle Tree is.

I had never gotten off the bus at a stop that was not at my house. It is a special bus for my class only, and we are supposed to get off only at the stop for our own house. On this day, when my bus went past the street that we turned on to go to the Eagle Tree, I could feel a humming in my chest, like my heart would burst through it. And then the bus made its regular stop.

Then I stood up, and I followed the kid who gets off at that street.

The bus driver knows where my stop is, and he said to me, "Hey, that's not your stop," and I thought I would have to sit back down again. But then I remembered what the boy in our class used to say all the time: *I have a note, I have a note, I have a note.*

So that's what I said to the bus driver. "I have a note."

And then I kept walking. Off the bus. Down the road. Into the woods.

After I left the bus stop, I saw the Eagle Tree rising above the forest canopy, a vast pillar towering fifty feet above the surrounding forest. If there were other trees at that height, they would create a second canopy, with a second layer of forest life at that level.

I walked down the road from the bus stop. As I walked, I tried to follow a crack in the pavement. I imagined that the crack was created by one of the roots of the Eagle Tree, reaching out all the way from its great height and moving for years underneath the soil, pushing slowly through the accumulated pipes and foundations and asphalt until it finally cracked through the pavement and led to this small hump, creating a map to the Eagle Tree just for me to follow.

But as I got closer to the end of the street and the end of the houses and approached the forest, the crack ran out. I stopped momentarily there, because I did not know what to follow anymore. And now I could not see the Eagle Tree at all. The trees on the lower slopes of the hillside shielded the Eagle Tree from me. I moved from side to side on the road until I could see it again. Then I moved forward once more.

I was on the same road that Uncle Mike and I drove on when we came to see the Eagle Tree the first time. After we got to the fence, he would not allow us to go any farther, and then we got back in the car and drove to the other side of the hill, to look at the Eagle Tree from there. But I was not on that side now. I was here on the first side, and I knew that soon I would encounter the sign again. But this time, I did not want to read the sign that Uncle Mike read last time—the big yellow one. And perhaps the sign might not be there at all.

I began to name the trees.

I saw the deep bark ridges of mature Douglas Firs. I whispered to each one its true name: "*Pseudotsuga menziesii.*" Then the patterns changed on my face, and I looked up to see deciduous leaves fluttering in a distant wind; they were from various broadleaf tree species, but most of them were Red Alders. "*Alnus rubra,*" I said to them. And there were also some Bigleaf Maples. A Bigleaf Maple leaf caught the wind and whirled down toward me, landing near my feet. I picked up the leaf and spoke to it. "*Acer macrophyllum,*" I said quietly to it. I tucked the leaf in my pocket. Then as I kept walking, I found that I was in the middle of a group of Western Red Cedars, and as I touched them, I said their name too: "*Thuja plicata.*" I said its true name to each one of them as I stroked their red-flavored bark.

I did this for a long time, but then I noticed a shape of a person moving parallel to me on the other side of the grove. I moved a little bit slower, hoping that the person would move past me. I like to be alone with the trees.

But the shape of the woods seemed to slow that person down as well. So I ignored that person, and I kept naming trees. Ahead of me, I saw a Western Hemlock. I called out to it its true name too—"*Tsuga heterophylla.*" Then I jumped up on top of an ancient giant nurse log, and I could look across a small meadow at a field of young trees. This was a clear-cut, and the trees were growing back, but the cut-over had probably been there since the time I was born. I looked across the growing trees, and I could see the tips of some of them droop. The drooping ones were Western Hemlocks.

I looked down. The small tan Western Hemlock cones papered the forest floor. The cones are delicate and only an inch long. This part of the forest is changing rapidly from Western Red Cedar and Douglas Fir to Western Hemlock entirely; it is now becoming a patch of Western Hemlock forest. I had been in a Western Hemlock grove before. Western Hemlock forests harbor a lot of undergrowth—Vine Maple, evergreen huckleberry, rhododendron, salal, sword fern, Red Alder, salmonberry, bracken fern.

The Western Hemlock's foliage is also distinctive—its needles are small, flat, blunt, and of unequal lengths, but always short. In fact, the species name itself—*heterophylla*—means "variable leaves"—and the needles have white bands on the underside and are dark green on the top, with variable patterning. I walked forward under the foliage, and I could see the tree's delicate, spray-like appearance. It is not like any other needle-leaved conifer.

Then the sight of the other person in the woods came clear to me for a minute and interrupted my thoughts. This time I tried to speed up, but the person sped up too. For the next twenty minutes, the person continued to move at the same pace that I moved, as if the person were my shadow.

Finally, I moved in a big circle around a huge stump of a tree that must at one time have been even taller, and bigger around, than the Eagle Tree. Now it was only a stump. But when I came around the big stump, I almost ran into the person. It was a woman. She was a little bit bigger than me, with angular features like a bird.

She moved like a bird too, but not like a forest bird, which is a quick-moving tiny thing that has to be wary of predators and only touches down in the forest floor momentarily. No. This woman moved slow but sure, her movements certain. She was like a blue heron, sitting in the shallows, watching all around her, and reaching out methodically to take what she wanted.

"I want to talk to you," she said. She held out her hand, but my mother was not here, and I do not like the rule about touching other people's hands. And the woman did not seem to mind; when I did not hold her hand for three to five seconds, she put her hand back by her side very smoothly, as if it were not a problem to hold out her hand and then remove it. This made me happy.

"You've gone around naming all the trees, haven't you?" she said.

"I only give the trees their true names," I said.

"Well, my true name is Maria Elliot. What is yours?"

"It is March," I said. "March Wong."

"Well, it's very good to meet you, March Wong," she said. "How did you learn to give trees their true names?"

"From books," I said. "What other names would I give to a tree?"

"Well," she said. And for some reason I do not mind looking at her face. I think this is because her face is so calm and still it is like water, or like a statue. She was still talking to me, and I was listening again. "See, you give the trees their English names, and I have heard you use the Latin names as well. But surely you know that Native Americans had other names."

She pointed at a nearby Western Hemlock. "This one here," she said, "this one was called S√qʷxʷbíxʷ by the people you call the Nisqually for a thousand years before Europeans came here."

"Sko-pets?" I said.

But I pronounced it wrong, and she corrected me. "Sko-puts," she said. I tried it again until I got it closer to what she'd said.

"That's one name. We have several names for different *tsuk-hwul*." I did not understand what she meant, but she was touching a tree. "And this one here," she said, "the large one with the scaly bark?" It was a Douglas Fir. "This one has cones, *sk'aelk*."

"Ska-elk," I tried. This was very interesting to me. I did not know these older names. Giving true names is important.

"But all these trees have English names now," I said. "That is what people call them. No one uses the Native American names."

"I do," she said.

"Why?" I said.

"Well, I'm Native. All of this—all of Olympia, this is all Nisqually land. Salish languages, like Lillooet, have many names for trees of various types and species. These woods have always been here. The true names have always been here."

"I know those names now," I said.

"You tried," she said gently. "You don't know them the way I know them. But I think we do have something in common. I'm a naturalist, like you, someone who studies trees." And then she smiled at me, and I looked away. I do not like to see people's teeth.

"I am employed by the Environmental Defense Council here in Olympia. I focus on trees in our ecosystem."

"I know a lot about trees," I said.

"Right. I know that," she said. Her voice had something bright in it, a birdcall. "I've been listening to you for the last hour. It's actually very enjoyable. Would you like to continue?"

So then I started naming trees again. I used the Latin names, not the Nisqually names, but she did not seem to mind. Together we walked through the forest for twenty-six more minutes.

Finally, she stopped walking. "It was very good to meet you," she said. "Remember, my name is Maria. Here's my card. Call me if you have questions about what is happening to the woods here, and what our organization is doing to help."

She put a flat white card in my shirt pocket without touching my skin, which is something I appreciated. I was comfortable with how she put the card in my pocket.

"You've seen the sign up ahead, right?" said Maria.

I closed my eyes, and I tried to close my ears. But I have never suc-ceeded in closing my ears the same way I can close my eyes.

In any case, she did not say anything else about the sign that I could not see. Instead, when she saw my shut eyes, she said, "Yep, I feel the same way. They've put up a fence now. You'll see it. Anyhow, you enjoy the forest while it's here, okay?"

I opened my eyes again, and I nodded my head. Up and down. For yes. Yes.

"Later," she said. "Good to meet you."

After she left, I named the trees some more. And then I saw a flash of yellow in the distance, and I remembered not to look at the sign in the woods.

11

Uncle Mike said that such a sign tells you that you cannot go past the sign, and that it is illegal to do so, and that if you read the sign, you should know this. That is why we were unable to go to the Eagle Tree the first time. That is why Uncle Mike made us turn around and go back home. He saw the sign.

The first time we came, we were close enough to the Eagle Tree to see the size of it, and it was even bigger than I expected. But the second time we came, we were not able to approach close enough to touch the Eagle Tree or to measure it. That was because of the sign that Uncle Mike read.

But if you do not *see* a sign, then you do not know what it says, and then you can go past the sign. Therefore, I planned to not see the sign. I would shut my eyes and move through the forest with my eyes firmly shut, and in this way, I would ensure that I did not see the sign, and I would be allowed in the forest, and I could go all the way to the Eagle Tree.

So now I was looking for the faintest hint of that bright yellow that was the color of the sign. As soon as I saw it, I would shut my eyes and move forward. I would count my steps and estimate how far my feet had taken me until I knew for certain that I was past the sign.

I moved one direction and another, peering through the forest growth. Finally, I saw the snag tip of the Eagle Tree, jutting up above the forest canopy. I could feel my heart pumping faster at the sight. The Eagle Tree was like a lighthouse to me, a beacon of hope, a sign of great life that towers over everything. It drew me in, saying, *Climb me, climb me.* Trees like this keep me oriented in a storm of things I do not understand.

I kept the Eagle Tree in sight as I continued to negotiate my way through the forest, naming trees as I went, muttering their proper names under my breath.

Maria Elliot was left behind. The road was left behind. The houses were left behind.

This time I was on my own, and I decided to push through the forest on my own, instead of taking any human path. This allowed me to do some climbing of small trees and stumps and deadfalls as I approached the Eagle Tree. I was tuning up, I thought, for my big accomplishment—for climbing the Eagle Tree.

I saw a flash of yellow in the distance, and I thought it was the sign. I snapped my eyes shut. I held up my hands in front of me, and I moved forward again, using the photograph of the forest that I'd captured inside my head as a reference for when I should lift my feet to step over fallen logs and small bushes, and when I should duck my head under overhanging branches.

For a long time, this worked.

My eyes were shut, but I could still see the image in my head.

I have been told I have a photographic memory, but mostly my photographic memory is useful inside of forests and around trees. I can see a tree's branches and know exactly where I will put my feet on each limb and where I will place my hands in order to climb the tree.

I did that now, with my eyes shut. I was now in the dark.

I did this for a long time, and then I reached the end of my photograph. I knew if I opened my eyes, I would be close to the sign, so I dared not open my eyes. I did not want to see the sign.

So I stumbled forward. Branches hit my face, and once I staggered over a nurse log and hurt my leg. Then I was limping forward.

And then my hands ran into something I did not expect. My hands touched cold metal, loops of metal. I moved my fingers back and forth, and the metal was in every direction ahead of me. I did not feel a sign, though. I had not run into the sign.

I slid my feet to one side. I took several steps in that direction. Then I moved forward again. But the loops of metal were still there, a surface that I could not penetrate. I moved in the other direction. There, too, I could not move forward.

But the surface was not entirely flat—it was not the sign. I was not in danger of seeing the sign.

I opened my eyes.

The loops of metal were part of a fence. The fence was very tall, and there were spikes of wire at the very top, in circles that could poke your skin if you climbed up there. I could see through the fence; it was made of links of metal tied together at each corner, diamonds of empty air held by small metal frames.

There was a man on the other side of the fence. He was approximately twenty-one feet away from me, closer to the Eagle Tree. He was smoking a cigarette, and he was standing beside a truck. There had been a road chewed into the forest on that side, and at the end of the road, that is where the truck and the man were standing.

He was looking at me. I curled my fingers into the metal loops of the fence. I wanted to pull down this fence. I wanted to tear it down with my fingers. I wanted to get to the Eagle Tree and climb it. Why couldn't I do that?

The forest had been broken in half by a fence pushed through it. The fence was a straight line. Trees are never in straight lines; that is one reason I like them. But the fence was very straight, and it cut directly across the forest. The base holes for the main fence posts were dug deep. The people who dug those holes had uprooted sapling trees, leaving them unprotected and thirsty in the open air. The fence itself was aluminum and shiny. There were bright-red signs that said "No Trespassing" on every other piece of fence. Others said "Violators Will Be Prosecuted" and "Security on Patrol—Do Not Trespass—Private Property."

Uncle Mike had taken me a different way the first time. He took me along the path that led past the LBA Woods, and that path had human footprints all over it. At the end of that path was the yellow sign, the sign I did not want to see again.

Inside the fence was a big truck and other equipment. It was as if an alien mother ship had landed here and planted this fence. At one point the fence would have been stopped by a large stump that was now a nurse log with saplings growing in it. But instead of the fence-builders going around the stump or removing the stump entirely, they cut a slice right out of the middle, so that the giant nurse log was split on either side of the fence.

It is a strange thing to see a fence pass completely through the middle of a huge dead tree. The stump of that tree is as big around as the Eagle Tree is. It is a shame that it is dead now, because it would have been over two hundred feet tall when it was alive and thriving. I can imagine its head tossing in a faintly felt wind in the upper canopy.

Now there is a fence thrust through its dead footing, and its root system is impaled by a fence post. I guess some people would say that I should not care about it, because this is a dead tree, not a living one.

But everything in the forest contributes to the whole. The dead trees are just as much a part of the ecosystem as the living ones; they contribute nutrients and seedbeds for the next generation of life. The whole system is part of one whole.

Therefore, it was a very strange thing to see this fence planted across the middle of the forest, as if to say "on this side is one ecosystem" and "on this side is a different ecosystem." Human beings are fond of doing this, but in the great timescale and reality of the natural world, a fence is an entirely artificial and temporary boundary, like a line drawn in the wet sand at the verge of the ocean, telling the waves they can come no farther. The waves don't care—nature does not acknowledge human lines or meanings. The waves will sweep over that line and dissolve it, given a short amount of time. The forest will sweep over this fence and dissolve it, given sufficient time.

I looked down at the line of white chalk on the forest floor that was a guideline for the installation of this fence. Already, a procession of ants was creating another line—a line of black insects—across that white chalk. And branches and leaves had started to cover and blur that white chalk. Each morning's dew and each day's misty weather had washed a little bit away from the chalk line, even though it was only a day or two old. The fence itself was as insubstantial as that chalk line in my mind. The forest would devour it; the trees would eat it up.

However, regardless of how much I would like to be part of the forest, I am not as strong as the trees, and the fence was tall. It must have been nearly eight feet tall. I could have climbed the fence, except for the coils of barbed wire at the top. Although I did not care about the scratches I might incur upon climbing it, it was possible I would get stuck up there. And that was not something I wanted to do. So I was looking up at the top of the fence, and wondering what to do, when I thought of Pat Tillman.

My mother told me that Pat Tillman, in the war, was shot by bullets that were fired by soldiers who wore the same uniform he wore, and that afterward he died, in that same war, in a place called Afghanistan, far away from Olympia.

I have read about Afghanistan, and although Apple and Eastern Aspen trees used to grow there, because of the war there are not very many trees left in that country. So I do not think Pat Tillman had a chance to play Tarzan in Afghanistan before he died there. I hope he did, though. Tarzan is a great game, and I am glad he invented it.

I decided I would play Pat Tillman's game now. I backed away from the fence, but I was careful to stay close enough to the fence that I would not encounter the sign.

I needed to find trees that were tall enough and close enough together that I could use their branches to transfer. It is a simple game in a close-knit grove. It is much harder when the trees are of disparate species with limbs that do not grow in the same dimensions at similar heights. If you jump from the eight-foot-long, four-inch-wide limb of a Douglas Fir, for example, onto a one-inch limb of a Bigleaf Maple, it is possible you would snap the limb, and that would cause the tree to be hurt, and you would also fall out of the tree. Then the game would be over.

This was a disparate riparian forest. So the game would be complicated here.

However, after I searched for some time, I was able to find a set of trees that reached from where I was standing all the way over and through the woods, deeper into the forest beyond the fence, until they approached close to where I thought the Eagle Tree was standing. If I was lucky, I could actually ride this set of trees all the way to the Eagle Tree itself. It would be optimal to be able to transfer right into the Eagle Tree from the forest.

I would have preferred to climb the Eagle Tree from the ground up—that would have been the best way to go. Of course, I knew there were other considerations that might prevent me from climbing the Eagle Tree from the ground. After all, if it was a true old-growth giant, then the lower limbs would all be gone by now. The first actual limbs on the tree might start at twenty or thirty feet high. Which would mean I would have to have Forest Service tree-climbing gear in order to leverage and lift myself into the tree, and I did not have this kind of gear. My mother has said that she will not allow it until I am at least eighteen years old. I will turn eighteen in three years, seven months, two weeks, and five days.

So for now I would have to play Tarzan to get into the Eagle Tree.

To start the game, it is wise to find a very tall tree, so that all of your subsequent tree transfers can be to trees that are lower than your first tree.

The first tree is a Western Red Cedar, one of the easiest trees for me to climb. As I climb, I carefully watch the adjoining trees, taking note of the limbs I can use to launch myself to the next tree. I take mental pictures of each of the smaller trees that I pass, so that I can track which limbs to land on, in which order.

To play Tarzan successfully, it is necessary to chart your transfers as a series: step one and then step two and then step three and so on. I do not have all my steps charted yet in my head, but I am building a quick catalogue of next steps.

Finally, I reach the highest point in this Western Red Cedar that will allow me to safely jump to the next tree. I have my list of moves in my head. Step one is to jump to the Western Hemlock. From there, I will go to the north side and find a limb that will allow me to jump to the Douglas Fir. That is step two. Step three will be to jump from the Douglas Fir to another very tall Red Cedar, but on a lower limb of that tree. Then I'll climb up the Red Cedar, high enough to transfer to the Bigleaf Maple. Steps four, five, and six involve transferring to the east several times on a set of Red Alders growing close together. Then I will backtrack once, jump to the next tree—another Douglas Fir—and climb again, to get height once more. Then I will be within two leaps of a tree that has limbs reaching over the fence. Steps nine through eleven involve transferring over the fence. I will have to check all the branches to ensure that they are true.

As I complete step five, I hear a shout: "Hey, kid, what are you doing over there? This is private property."

I am concentrating on the next steps, though, and I do not pay attention. Eventually, at around step nineteen, I hear the voice speak again, very loudly.

"I'm calling the cops."

Sometime after that, when I am at around step forty-five, I hear a far-off throbbing, whooping sound, that at first I mistake for the distant sound of a bird in the woods. There are many different kinds of birds in these woods. It could even be a type of frog that I do not know about yet. Coqui frogs from the American territory of Puerto Rico can hit a sound level that is up to ninety decibels strong.

On the other hand, the Northern Pacific treefrog—*Pseudacris regilla*—which lives here in the Pacific Northwest, has a call that only hits about ten decibels.

The throbbing, whooping sound increases in volume and gets closer and closer. Meanwhile, I am sliding through the air, hitting every mark I set for myself. Since I am not naturally coordinated, it takes a great deal of effort to plan each of the steps in my leaps, and to ensure that I've mapped correctly the location of each limb in the air before I seize it. I must remain very focused, or else I will slip and fall, or—worse—I will damage the tree.

While I am flying through the air, though, I feel like a bird. Perhaps a woodpecker, or an eagle. But those birds need to nest. What if I were a bird who is attached to the trees, and does not ever touch the ground?

There is a bird like this. It is called the common swift, and it has developed the ability to never touch the ground. Perhaps I am related to the common swift, and I fly through the trees all the year long, only touching on tree branches as I fly.

But then the sound is very close and loud, and I cannot ignore it any longer. I also cannot ignore the flashing lights that come in pulses every five seconds. The lights are red and white, and sometimes blue. I have seen these lights before; they remind me of the night that Miss Stevens called the police, after which I had to leave my mother for three days.

When I remember that, I feel that I am about to freeze up. I also feel like I will begin to flap and moan. I am afraid of the loud voices.

I cannot focus on leaping from tree to tree while I am also flapping and moaning. My flapping would not lift me off the ground like a bird. Instead, it would probably cause me to fall. So I simply freeze on the limb of a tree and cling to the trunk, as if I am an afraid cat.

Men are shouting at me. And then there is a long process while one of them goes back to the car, and I can see the car's lights flashing for a moment as he turns the car back on. Then the car lights shut off and there is a screech of static, and then I can hear his voice, low and firm, talking on the radio.

The man below me is still saying words to me, but now my eyes are shut and I am moaning and my arms are beginning to flap a little bit, and I hope I don't fall off the limb and crash on the ground.

No, I think. *No. I cannot fall. No.*

A long time seems to pass, and the voices are not as loud. They are talking to each other and don't seem to be shouting at me anymore. I open my eyes, and I do not see the lights anymore.

Someone is saying my name. I almost shut my eyes again before I realize that I recognize the voice.

It is Ilsa's voice. She is talking to me quietly but firmly, and she is asking me to come down out of the tree.

I turn my head from side to side. *No. No. No.*

Finally, after Ilsa talks to me for a long time, I find that I am able to move again, and I create a path in my mind down out of the tree.

The police officers let me go from the tree directly to her car, because I knew her car. I knew Ilsa.

I sat in the front seat of her car while Ilsa talked to the police officers. Then she came to the car and sat in the driver's seat. She was wearing a special badge she had shown to me before that says "Police Chaplain."

She took off the badge. She put the badge on the dashboard. She closed the door, and rolled up her car window, and gave a long, deep sigh.

I thought of the wind moving in the top limbs of the Eagle Tree.

12

In Ilsa's car, my flapping gradually decreased. The thrumming sensation in my chest faded. My moaning became softer and softer, until I could hear it only in my head.

Now I could see Ilsa's hands holding the wheel. She was wearing one gold ring on her left hand and one silver ring on her right hand. The silver ring had a design on it, a design of leaves and branches. I watched her hands carefully.

It takes a conscious effort to reduce my flapping and moaning. That therapist, Rhonda, she started to teach me how to do this by listening to my own breath, but it is very difficult for me, and I was not able to get my breath and my hands under control before I got to the car, so I was not able to hear what the police officers said to Ilsa before I got in her car.

"Peter," she said. Then she said nothing for a long time. Then she said my given name again: "Ah, Peter March."

Ilsa is the only one who calls me Peter all the time. She cannot seem to remember that I now am called March. But I do not correct her, because it seems to me that she has an inability to understand the name. Of course, Ilsa was also the one who baptized me, and so she said my full name—Peter March Wong—when I was a baby, so I don't mind too much.

Ilsa is a little bit like a tree, in that she does not move very fast, and she does not make me feel anxious or strange. After a while, Ilsa moved her right hand with the silver ring down to the gearshift, and the car started moving. I could feel the engine purring underneath my feet, and I worked my sounds to be in tune with the engine. But I did this very quietly. It took effort, but I knew effort was worth it if I wanted to hear what Ilsa would tell me about what happened here in the forest.

I like Ilsa's voice, even though she says many things I do not understand, or that I do not believe. Ilsa talks about things that she considers true, such as magic stories in which God plays a part, or miracles, or other things that are written down in the books put together into the Bible. When she says that things are true, I do not think she means they are true in the same way that I mean.

The limb of a tree can be true—and that means that the limb is solid and can bear enough weight to hang from or stand upon. That particular branch of the tree is not rotten, infested with insects, or otherwise weak or unreliable. I learned from Uncle Mike that *true* can also mean that something is straight and level, according to standard measures of straightness.

That is what *true* means. It means reliable, and as straight as you can make it.

The stories that Ilsa tells me are true to her, but they do not make logical sense. They are not straight. But they seem to be meaningful to Ilsa in some other way.

I do not tell her this, and I especially do not say to her that her stories are not true, because my mother has told me that when I am so clear on the factual evidence, for some reason it can upset many people.

I do not know how to be any other way than factual or blunt, so sometimes I simply do not talk. The energy therefore sometimes comes out of me in moans and flaps, but not in words out of my mouth.

I like Ilsa, and I was glad she was with me; I didn't want to upset her, or make her distrust me. So I simply didn't say anything about the word *true*.

After a while, Ilsa started talking. I thought she was talking to me, but I did not know. Then she said my name, but my given name, so I guessed that she was almost certainly talking to me.

"You know how lucky this was, Peter? If I hadn't been on call this Friday, you might've sat in juvenile detention or even jail—you're big enough now to be booked as an adult—and no one would have known where you were. You understand how serious this is, Peter?"

I did not say anything. I had to maintain equilibrium with being in tune with the engine and listening to Ilsa's voice. Also, my stomach was growling. There was only one thing I wanted now.

"You're lucky I was on call," said Ilsa. "And that the police officers were willing to release you to me. And that the property owner did not press charges. Many other things could've happened here that would've been much worse."

"Pizza," I said. "Pepperoni. I am hungry."

Ilsa did not answer me. She was still talking about something else. "I called your mother," Ilsa said. "She's okay, now that she knows where you are. I'll take you to her, and then I think we should talk about this some more."

"Did something happen to my mother?" I asked. "Why did you say she is okay?"

"Let's see, Peter March," said Ilsa.

I was trying very hard not to moan and flap loudly. But it was difficult, because the way Ilsa was talking was starting to feel loud in my head, and I do not like it when Ilsa talks to me this way. And now the thrumming in my chest was back.

"Your mother waited at your bus stop for an hour, then she called the school, then they called the bus company, then they called the police and the fire department. They started checking all the trees near the school. Your mother has been waiting for you to get home for two hours. During most of that time, she was sure that you were either trapped in a tree or had fallen and hurt yourself."

"I have never been trapped in a tree," I said. I looked out the window of the car. We were passing a grove of small Red Alders. They leaned into one another, as if to hold each other up.

"Yes," says Ilsa. "But you have fallen. You must admit that you have fallen many times. The police said you were jumping from tree to tree. If you are tree transferring, falling is always a very real possibility, and if no one knows that you were up in a tree, if you fell again, it could be serious."

"I was serious," I said. "I wanted to go see that Eagle Tree." I turned to look at her hands again. I could see a shadow on her hands, moving back and forth. Then I figured out where the shadow was coming from. Ilsa was shaking her head. *No. No.*

She spoke again. "I wish Pierre had never talked to you about that tree. It's not useful for you to be obsessing over that old-growth patch."

"I thought it was very useful," I said.

"God's grace was on you, Peter."

"I do not believe in God," I reminded her.

"Well, God must believe in you." Ilsa laughed. Then she lifted her left hand with the gold ring and pushed back her hair from her face.

"You've got some bridges to repair with your mother," Ilsa said. "You were making good progress, Peter. But I think she'll feel this is a setback in terms of normalized engagement with other people." Ilsa's voice swelled in my head, and my chest thrummed and throbbed. "I just want you to be aware of that, Peter. You've definitely got some bridges to mend there."

I did not know what she meant. But I did know that Ilsa was not being the friendly person I usually know. Maybe, I thought, there was another Ilsa, who was driving me to my house but who was not the Pastor Ilsa who talks very quietly and gently to me.

Or perhaps she did not know what I had seen in the LBA Woods. So I named every tree that I had seen. I talked about the Douglas Firs, and I explained that they could also be called by the Native American name *sk'aelk* or the Latin name *Pseudotsuga menziesii*. I also saw Red Alders—*Alnus rubra*. And Bigleaf Maples—*Acer macrophyllum*. I stood in a grove of Western Hemlocks, which Native Americans call *mulu-mulhp* and whose Latin name is *Tsuga heterophylla*. And then there were the Western Red Cedars—*Thuja plicata*. But I still hadn't seen, up close, an old-growth Ponderosa Pine—*Pinus ponderosa*—which Pierre said might be the species and variety of the Eagle Tree. I was unable to get close enough to examine the tree closely before the police officers told me I had to go to Ilsa's car.

In the car, I talked very loudly for a long time. But Ilsa didn't seem to have anything useful to say on the topic of the trees.

I talked faster and faster, because I was sure that at least one of the trees might be of interest to Ilsa. If I could get through describing the trees fast enough, before we got to my house, then maybe Ilsa would talk to me, but not in that cold and unnatural tone. Maybe she would talk to me in her normal voice.

I like to hear her normal voice. It is soothing to me. It is like the sound of water gurgling along through the forest floor, leaving pleasant echoes in my head. But she did not talk that way in the car—she did not respond to what I said.

After we had driven for a long time, and I had talked the entire time, Ilsa finally spoke to me again.

"Well," she said. "Yes, the Eagle Tree—if it is a Ponderosa Pine, it probably grew here originally when this entire region was prairie habitat and it was burned regularly. As the riparian forest grew up around it, this particular Ponderosa somehow survived the change of habitat. The Ponderosa had to have been here first, but it somehow outlasted everything else."

"Does that mean that Ponderosa Pines could survive climate change?"

Ilsa rubbed a hand over her eyes for a moment. "That's quite a leap, Peter. Perhaps this one survived here because it has some sort of genetic variation that is adapted to less arid climates. The woods there are probably the last remnant of a much larger old-growth forest that grew all around Olympia. But how Ponderosas would have even come to live over here is a mystery."

I did not get to hear anything else that Ilsa had to say on the topic of the Eagle Tree and its history, because we arrived at the house with the blue mailbox.

13

It was a Tuesday, and I was in the office with the gurgling bowl of water and the miniature Japanese Maple tree. I was stroking the branches of that little tree very gently. Rhonda is all right with me touching her tree, and it is soothing for me. I didn't understand what she was talking about, though.

"We talked last week about the Ponderosa Pines," she said, "and your conversation with your father, and how that went sideways for you."

"I don't understand."

"We talked last week," said Rhonda slowly.

"Yes," I said. "We talked. I did not see anything go sideways."

Rhonda made a long sighing sound, the air coming out of her nose. I could see the tiny hairs in her nose flicked by the rush of air. "What I meant, March, is that you were unable to explain to your father how you were feeling. That you were feeling afraid of not being able to climb a Ponderosa Pine."

"Yes."

"I am just providing an introduction, March, to our conversation today. I am reviewing what you said last week, up front, so we can remind ourselves of what was said last week."

"I don't require that," I said.

Rhonda sighed again, but this time she seemed to be holding some air back in her lungs. I wondered why she was not sighing as strongly this time. It is interesting, how she varies her breath depending upon what I say.

"I know," she said. "I know, March, but sometimes it is useful for me. Is that all right with you?"

"All right," I said.

"I have a follow-up question about your fears, March."

"I can tell you more about the Ponderosa Pine situation," I said. "There are some steps that we can take. See, what may be happening in climate change is in fact an explosion in beetle populations, but there is the faint possibility that we could change—"

"Wait a minute." Rhonda held up her hand. "I want to ask about something more directly pertinent to your day-to-day life, all right?" She continued without giving me a chance to answer this question. "I want to know how you felt on the night you moved into your new house."

I replied immediately. "I did not like the new house with the blue mailbox. On the first night, I could not climb the trees."

"Right." Rhonda made a sighing sound again. This time it was long and slow. "But how did you feel about being taken away from that house for—let me see, it was a seventy-two-hour psychiatric hold—how did you feel about that?"

"I don't know," I admitted. Uncle Mike has told me to be truthful, and I honestly did not know how I felt about that experience. However, I did feel as if I might want to moan and flap. The memory of that experience is charged hot like electricity, and the energy building up in my chest was painful. It was something that I did not want to have happen again. I gave a small moan.

"All right, that's fine. That's fine. It will be all right," said Rhonda. But her tone had changed, and somehow I got the feeling that she was talking to another person. A small child perhaps. I wondered if this other person was somewhere in the room, or if she imagined this other person. I considered looking behind me to see if there was a small child who had crept in while I was not looking. But then she spoke again.

"Why don't we start with this then? Tell me what happened that night, in your own words. Do you remember what happened on the first night you moved into your new house?"

I remember what happened the night we moved into the house with the blue mailbox. It is all there, inside me, and no one but me has seen it. I closed my eyes and saw it again.

On the night the police officers came to our new house, I was very upset. I did not have a schedule or a system for the new house, and my mother had not managed to explain to me clearly what we were doing there.

It was one month after my father had moved to Arizona, without me or my mother, and my schedule had already changed several times, and that was very hard for me to keep track of.

Then some men put our furniture in a truck while I was at school. When I got home from school, my mother had already put all my clothes in the red suitcase, and we drove across town to a new neighborhood and a new house. My mother told me that this house would be our house now. The men had already put all our furniture into this new house, and my new room was different from my old room. The window that looked outside looked in a different direction, and the light from the sun on the wall of my room was different, and it was all very upsetting to me.

Because we were in a new place, I waited for a new plan. But my mother did not give me a new schedule for after school and for dinnertime and for what we would do after dinner. She said there was no change to our schedule, but I could not see how that could be, because we were in a new place, and I did not know the old schedule in the new place with the light from the sun coming in the windows of the house in different places. The sun was different. The clocks were different. Even the floors were different. The shadows were not the same, and I could not recognize the shapes in these shadows. Time was different. I was lost in dark woods, and there were no friendly trees I recognized around me. I could not identify anything I was seeing.

For example, after school, when we got to the new house, I needed to use the bathroom, but I could not immediately see the toilet. The toilet at our old house had a white handle with a small silver line around it, and the toilet at school also has a white handle with a small silver line around it. I went to every room in the new house and I looked for the white handle with the silver line, but I could not find it.

My mother asked me, "What are you doing, March?" And I told her that I was looking for the toilet.

She took me into the second room I had explored, and she told me that the thing in the corner was the toilet. She showed me that it flushed just like the one at our old house and at school. I went over and looked closely at the handle. The handle was a brass metal color. There was no white and no silver line around it.

I could not understand it. I did not know if this was a toilet. I had to go to the bathroom really badly by this time.

Eventually, after I told her about the problem with the toilet three times, then my mother got some tinfoil and created a silver line around the handle, and then I felt all right about using that toilet, and I was able to go to the bathroom, and I was relieved.

Because I did not want to pee on the floor again. I did that once at school, and many people became very loud, and even Mr. Gatek became loud. I do not like it when my mother becomes loud either, but this time she was very calm.

After I used the bathroom, we ate dinner. I did my homework. My mother unpacked some suitcases.

"I had no plan in the new house," I told Rhonda. "I had no schedule in this new place with different light and different shadows coming in different windows. So I went into the backyard, and I saw that in our new backyard there were three trees. Two of them are small trees, unsuitable for real climbing. But one of them is a large Bigleaf Maple with branched radial symmetry, and it stands approximately fifty feet tall, and there are handholds eight feet and then thirteen feet from the ground."

And then I stopped talking and remembered again.

"Do you like it, March?" said my mother. "That tree is part of why I chose this house to move into. I figured you love trees so much and we'd finally have a tree here that you could climb without any problems and without me worrying about you. It seems like a safe tree."

"Yes," I told her. And I went toward the Bigleaf Maple and started to climb it.

"No," said my mother. "It's dark. It's late. Please don't climb any trees now. Wait until tomorrow. It's Friday tomorrow, and I'll let you stay in the tree as long as you want after school tomorrow. But tonight, let's just leave the trees alone."

"I'm climbing this tree," I said.

"We don't have time right now," said my mother. She took hold of my sleeve, where my hand held on to the first projecting limb of the tree, and tugged.

I looked up at the branches of the tree, beckoning me to climb. The shadows in the yard that were different even in the dark continued to tell me that I was in an alien landscape. Nothing was the same here—even time was different—so why could I not climb this tree that was so clearly asking me to climb it?

My mother pulled on my sleeve again, and I lost my grip on the tree. I began to moan. And then that moaning turned into a very loud sound coming from my mouth.

My mother took my arm and walked me back toward the house, but I did not know the house. And everything was different. And by this time I was making such a loud sound that I was covering my own ears, but the sound roaring out of my mouth was like a wind pouring through the high branches of a tree in a tornado, and I could feel it rushing out of me with every breath. It was a storm coming out of me, filling the world with pain.

And my mother got me into the house and locked the door. But I would not stop making that loud sound, and then I flapped my arms so much that the back window broke and there was glass on the floor. And I think I cut my hand, because my mother took me to the bathroom and tried to put a Band-Aid on it, but I was still flapping my hands and arms, so she could not do that for me, and there was blood everywhere all over the floor and my shirt and her face. The pattern was interesting, and I began to flap more when I saw it.

And then a little while later, there were flashing red and white lights from outside our front door, and there was another very loud sound happening in syncopation with the lights, but I could hardly hear it, because I was still making my own loud sound, and also I had my hands over my ears. And then my mother left me alone and went to the front door. And when she let go of me, I tried to climb out the broken window, and I cut myself some more when I did that.

But when my mother opened the front door, there were two large men wearing dark-blue uniforms, and they came in the house, and one of them took hold of me. And he was talking to me, but I was still making the rushing sound and I could not listen to the words coming out of his mouth.

I had used many words to tell Rhonda some of what happened, but my words were not enough to describe the sounds and that pattern of red on the floor and the different shadows and how I could not breathe when the man was holding me, and now I could feel my cheeks were wet and I was moaning.

There was now only the sound of the water in Rhonda's office. I opened my eyes and looked at the water and at the little Japanese Maple. I had clenched the fingers of my right hand too tightly. I used my other hand to unclench the fingers on my right hand, and I saw in my palm a leaf. I had pulled off a leaf from the little tree. I felt bad about this.

I looked down at the leaf on my palm, and I opened my mouth and kept talking.

"One of the men who came into the house touched me. He held on to my arm for a long time, and after a while, it felt like his fingers were burning me. He said many things to me that I could not do. So I shut my eyes and waited for him to go away, and I was moaning and flapping."

Now with the memory, I was flapping and moaning again. I do not like the memory of the man with the black hair. He was big and tall and had a very loud voice, and he said that we should be arrested, for disturbing the peace. He put his hand on his gun twice when I flapped too close to him. He had been yelling at me for a long time before the man with the red hair sat down beside me.

The man with the red hair and mustache did not say to me, "Look me in the eye," or "Speak when you're spoken to." He sat down next to me on the floor against the wall. He did not try to touch me. He said words in soft, soothing sounds; he spoke so quietly that I had to slow down my moaning and flapping so that I could hear the sounds he was making.

When I was finally able to hear him, I could hear that he was singing a quiet song. It was so very quiet. It started with the words "Somewhere over the rainbow."

The hair on his head was very bright red. The hair on his arms was red and brown, like Western Red Cedar bark.

He said to my mother: "My cousin's son is like this. He's on the spectrum, right?"

"Yes," said my mother. "But I honestly don't know what I'm going to do. My God, my God, how did I get so much blood on me? I just, I just—"

"We'll take him in," said the first man, who had stopped holding me.

"No," said my mother. "I just— Just give me a moment. It's just all too much."

The man with the red hair spoke up then. "Since he's injured, I'm afraid we're obligated to take him in for an evaluation. I don't believe there's any need to arrest him, or to arrest you either. It's a statutory obligation we have. It's classed as potential to self-harm and harm to others. That's an automatic seventy-two-hour hold in Washington State. Don't worry—he'll be evaluated in the hospital, and his injuries will be taken care of. All right? He won't be in the juvenile detention center."

"But, but I—" said my mother. "Look, can't you just—? I just don't know how to do this all the time. I just don't know if I can do it anymore."

The man with the red hair was very nice. I could talk to him. But he was also very mean, because he took me away from my mother, and the new Bigleaf Maple, on the first night in our new house with the blue mailbox.

I was put into the backseat of the car that the men had come to our house in, and the flashing lights stopped moving, and the sound stopped moving too. And eventually I stopped making my sounds. But by that time we were in another new place. And someone took hold of me again in a way I did not like, and they put bandages on me. Several times, because I kept taking them off. And then after I took them off the third time, they tied me up in a bed, which I also did not like.

And the lights in the hospital room flickered—very bright, very fast. I could see them flicker over and over, a pattern of lights that was very disturbing. It was like lightning in my head, close to my eyes. No one listened to me, and no one else seemed to notice the terrible lights.

When the doctor came into my room, he said to me, "Why are you covering your eyes?" and, "Is there something wrong with your eyes? Are they injured?"

"The lights," I said. "The lights are wrong."

The doctor had them turn down the lights that flickered. And then I felt much better. But my mother was not with me, so I could not stop flapping and moaning. And I was there for three days, and could not leave that place until Monday.

People talked to me, but I did not know them, and they did not know me. I flapped and moaned, but no one knew what that meant. There was no one to stop me or help me. I was alone.

Then on Monday, Uncle Mike and my mother came to get me. And I had to sit at a big table in a room where a woman wearing very white pearls talked to me and my mother. And my mother explained about the tree and how I cut myself. And there was more talking, and then my mother had to sign some papers, and then the woman with the pearls had me sign them too.

Then I was able to go home. But not to our home. To the house with the blue mailbox. And the lights and the shadows and the time were still different.

But then I was able to climb the Bigleaf Maple for the first time. I usually would go to school on Monday, but my mother had taken the day off work and I took the day off school. And that is when I climbed the Red Cedar next door and saw the Eagle Tree.

"The reason all of this happened," I told Rhonda, "was because Miss Stevens, who lives two doors down from our new house, heard all my very loud sounds and the glass breaking, and she called the police to come to our house. And it was not good for my mother, and it was not good for me. And my mother does not like Miss Stevens, because that was our first night in our new house. It was not a good night."

"All right," said Rhonda, after a long time. I was not talking anymore. I was done talking. But what was interesting to me is that this time all of my hot energy came out of me in words, instead of in moaning and flapping. I did not feel like moaning and flapping, but I felt empty, as if I had been hollowed out.

People have said to me that time will heal wounds or that memory will fade with time. Mostly people have said that to me in regard to my great-uncle dying or my father moving to Arizona.

But I do not have anything that fades. All of what has happened to me remains in my head, like photographs or movies of the past; it is all precisely present in my head, and it never fades at all. Not even the edges of my memories fade.

But it is interesting to me that telling Rhonda about what happened helped me to understand the events in a new way. I did not see them all again the same way. I was able to see them as a series of events that I could have changed. I could have waited for my mother and explained to her how important it was that I climb the Bigleaf Maple that night. I could have climbed the tree earlier, before it became dark outside. My mother could have introduced me to the trees prior to the day we moved into the house.

"It would have been better if those things had not happened," I told Rhonda.

"Yes," said Rhonda. "I agree. How could things have changed?"

I was not sure how to answer her question. Because that was a dynamic system. The night was chaotic; there were too many things happening that night. And for that reason, these things happened. I now wish that those things had not happened, because perhaps I would not have been taken by the police officers to the hospital and then to the place with the bad lights where I had to stay for three days until my mother and Uncle Mike came to get me.

"How could things have changed?" asked Rhonda.

I feel now like that evening was like the fall of a tall tree. Like a Douglas Fir.

The interesting thing about a tree falling is that it is rare for a single event to cause a tree to fall. Human beings tend to think of a tree falling as a single event. Someone took an ax and chopped a tree. Or someone took a chainsaw and cut the tree.

In the natural world, however, the fall of a tree is part of a complex system. There are many questions to be answered to determine what causes a tree to fall: How solid is the soil that holds up the tree? How much clay and how much sand? How much organic matter? Answers to these questions can tell us how deep the tree's roots can penetrate, and how strong and well-founded the tree's roots can be.

And a tree's fall is not just dependent on the tree itself. The tree is part of an overall ecosystem. Are there burrowing animals that have destabilized the ground the tree stands on? Are there termites eating dead wood underneath the tree, or even inside the tree? Are there other creatures who have dug or changed the composition of the ground around the tree?

Then there are still more factors about what makes a tree fall. The tree's overall weight is a contributing factor. And the tree's outstretched limbs, and its balance among those different limbs. What holds the tree balanced? Is there any imbalance caused by the loss of a limb or a shift in the hillside that holds up the tree, or perhaps a misalignment in the tree's growth circles, so that one side of the tree is heavier than the other side?

And the ecosystem around the tree includes the other trees and plant life. Smaller plants can create a network of roots around the tree's roots, a fine mesh which makes the soil both stronger and more absorbent of rainwater and flooding. This is why open fields flood more easily than forests or wildland. The forestland can absorb water, and it is stronger than human-constructed landscapes stripped of vegetation.

Shorter trees can shield a taller tree from wind and other weather effects, and can deflect some of the wind shear that can push a tree off balance. A group of trees creates a microenvironment that can sustain a tree during a period of drought or flooding. The trees create a safety net of healthier climate around themselves, no matter what poisons are in the air.

That is how I feel about the night the police came to our new house—that there were poisons in the air. I was unable to find solid footing for my roots in our new house—the ground had shifted under me. It was like an earthquake. I felt that there was no one who could shelter me or keep me, except the other trees in the backyard. It was very distressing. And for those reasons, I fell down, like a lone tree in a windstorm, and was taken out of my life and deposited in an alien place.

No one there knew anything about trees.

Most trees, when they fall, can in fact be used in the rest of the ecosystem. They are able to become part of the overall ecosystem and immediately nurture other plant life. Some trees, in fact, keep living on the ground for some time after they fall. Depending on the way that they fall, their upper limbs—the ones facing the sun—can continue to collect good things from the air and from the soil. Eventually, their systems fail, as they are invaded by other species, and by that time, their cells are being used by other creatures.

But when I fell, I felt as if I was not living, not living at all, and I was unable to be of use. Instead, I fell onto hard ground, into a place of flashing lights and being tied up in a bed. And then my mother and Uncle Mike came and got me out of there, and got my roots back into fertile soil and good water, and I was able to thrive again and talk again. I was beginning to be firmly rooted in my new house. And this was a good thing.

14

When I am not climbing trees, I read many books. Most of them are factual books. In these books, people sometimes describe things in big ideas, and sometimes they talk about trees as a concept. I do not see trees as concepts; I see individual trees that I know very well. I can see the Bigleaf Maple behind my new house, and the American Sycamore that stands on the corner in our old neighborhood, and I can see in my mind the Western Red Cedar in the yard next door.

Whenever someone asks me about trees, I think about each individual tree that I have known. Including their species, the characteristics of their bark, and the specific shadows made by their branches on my face. I think of the small sapling Douglas Fir that I climbed when I was five years old at a campground. It was the first tree that I climbed. But I've never been able to climb that particular tree again, because I never saw that tree again. I think of the Engelmann Spruce I climbed with Uncle Mike, the one by Mount Rainier that I fell from. And I think of the first time I saw the vast and powerful immensity of the Eagle Tree.

I think about the Eagle Tree every fifteen to eighteen minutes every single day. It is always in my mind.

Some people like to watch movies. Sometimes I go to see movies, but it is very frustrating for me to watch most movies, because I do not understand what people are doing or why. I like the old silent movies, where it tells you what people are going to be doing.

I also like documentaries. They are factual, and most of the time you can understand what is going on. I especially like documentaries about plants growing. There is a special documentary about the largest trees in the world, and another about a woman named Julia Butterfly Hill, who sat in a tree for 738 days. That is my favorite movie. I have watched it 117 times.

But instead of movies, I prefer to watch shadows and light. I have read about how movies are made, and how all movies are a series of individual pictures projected on the wall by a light-projection system. Perhaps I am watching my own kind of movie, but it is very slow and maybe without any human beings in it.

I am especially interested in shadows and light that are changed by branches or leaves.

So that is mostly what I watch when I am up in the trees. I watch the shadows, I watch the lights, and I watch the leaves move in the wind.

On this Saturday, though, I did not look up at the leaves. I looked down at the ground, where the houses are, and people. The neighborhood is another type of ecosystem; the roads connect to one another, and branch off from one another like the branches of a great tree. From the Bigleaf Maple, I can see the routes of people walking and driving along those limbs, like liquids and carbohydrates moving in capillary action.

I can see people in their backyards, stretched out in the Northwest sunlight, soaking up the energy of the sun. They are spread out like leaves, partaking in the great process of photosynthesis.

And I can see the buildings, like rooted things, dug in across the landscape. I imagine the plumbing and wiring underground, connecting these buildings, like the capillary ruts in the soil that spread out seeking moisture in the environment.

The problem, of course, is that I am not part of this ecosystem. I stand apart. But people seem to have removed themselves from the natural ecosystem anyway. They take from it, but there is no direct connection. The feedback loop is all negative.

My mother allowed me to spend the whole of Saturday morning in the Bigleaf Maple. In the four hours that I was there, I saw many different events happen. It is a different kind of movie to watch, on the street on which I live. But I didn't understand some of the things I saw.

I saw the cat from the corner house sneak into the yard of the blonde woman next door and kill a fish in her pond. I saw two teenage boys come out the back window of the newly painted gray house with a flat-screen TV. Then I saw those same two boys two hours later in the woods, smoking something from a long jar with a round bulb at the end. From very high up in the tree, I saw someone lying close to somebody else deep in the woods, and then they started to take their clothes off. And then I climbed down from my tree.

The next day, Sunday, I climbed a different tree. And on that day, I also watched the houses instead of the leaves. I saw a boy hit a ball over his house, and it bounced against Miss Stevens's car, leaving a big dent in the side. I saw the ball roll out of sight underneath the bushes.

The boy came with another boy to the front yard and looked around, and then they left very quickly. They did not find their ball or take it home.

I knew the reason they went away quickly. It was because Miss Stevens is mean. That's what my mother says.

I could also see Miss Stevens in her backyard from up in this tree. She has a long braid down her back that looks, from a distance, like a snake. Perhaps a brown tree snake, like the type that lives in rain forest canopies. Miss Stevens sat down with her little dogs in her backyard while I was watching and fed them little doggy snacks for a long time before she went inside and turned off the lights and went to bed. I was watching her for a long time because I would like to know what makes people mean.

I could see from how she acted toward her little dogs that she is not mean to them. Maybe she is only mean to people. Maybe that is what people think about me too.

The first day I was here, I got upset, and it was no different from other times before when I got upset, but this time in our new house, someone called the police. We did not know who that someone was at first. Eventually, our next-door neighbor, Mr. Clayton, told my mother that it was Miss Stevens.

The afternoon, I climbed the same tree, and I watched Miss Stevens's house again. And this time I saw something I did not expect to see.

I saw Uncle Mike drive into our neighborhood, and I was about to climb down from the tree to be with Uncle Mike, and then I saw that he was not coming to our house. He parked his truck around the corner from our house, under a small grove of Western Hemlocks that lean out from the corner. I could not see the truck anymore. It was out of sight.

Then I saw Uncle Mike walk down the street. I saw him go to Miss Stevens's house.

He waited for the front door to open. And then Miss Stevens came out of her door, and she held on to Uncle Mike for a long time. Her braid swished back and forth as she talked to him, and then she pressed her face to his face.

He reached back and touched her shoulders and her back and her braid. I wondered if her braid felt like a coiling snake to Uncle Mike.

And then she closed her front door, and she went with Uncle Mike back to his truck and they drove away together.

That night, after dinner, Uncle Mike came to our house. When I saw Uncle Mike in our living room, then I was reminded to talk about what I saw from the tree.

"Uncle Mike is kissing Miss Stevens," I said.

"What?" said Uncle Mike. "What did you say?"

"You went to Miss Stevens's house," I said. "You went to her house, and you kissed her, and you went away with her."

Then my mother dropped a plate on the floor. There was food on the floor now. I watched the cat who lives next door come in through our open window to eat some of the food. I reached down to get some of the food too.

"March," said my mother. "No. Stop that. Come here, and tell me exactly what you saw."

Uncle Mike started to talk. "Now, Janet," he said.

But my mother stopped him. She used the same words and the same sounds that she used with me: "No. Stop that."

She petted me, and she said again to me, "March, explain exactly what you saw."

After I was done, my mother reached down and cleaned up the pieces of the plate and the food on the floor. Then she turned to Uncle Mike. Her face was mottled with different colors, mostly red and white. It did not look like a human face anymore at all. I wondered if she would stay that way.

"How could you?" she said to Uncle Mike. "After what she did? Our first week in this house, after we had that fight and he just up and left for Arizona. It was a hell of a week for me—and that woman just made it worse. And now you're, what? Sleeping with her? Dating her? What am I supposed to think?"

"Look," said Uncle Mike. "I was as surprised as you are. I didn't know who she was when I first met her. I didn't know she was the woman who made your first week here miserable."

Uncle Mike took his hat off. He twisted it in his hands. I do not like it when he twists his hat. I am afraid he will lose his hat, and then I will not recognize him as Uncle Mike anymore. Then he put his hat back on his head. "I think it was all just a misunderstanding," he said.

"Yeah, she entirely misunderstood how wrong it was to call 911 just because Peter here was a little upset after moving into a new house, in a new neighborhood, and I wouldn't let him climb the effing trees at nearly midnight!"

The breath felt hot in my mouth. I moved my hands in front of my face, but the light in the house was not like the forest light at all. Instead, it felt like I was underwater, and I was going deeper into the water, and I could not get out. I flapped my arms, trying to get out.

"Well," said Uncle Mike. "Like I said, it was a misunderstanding. Mostly on her part, I will admit, but it might've been a little bit on your part as well."

My mother gently pushed me out of the way, taking care not to touch my flapping arms. I was moaning now, and I didn't like how it felt to be deep underwater. She stepped to the front door, and she opened it very wide.

"Mike, I love you—you're my brother—but you've got to leave right now. I don't care what else you have to say, or what other excuses you have to make for her. You need to get out before I freaking disown you—and cut yet another person out of Peter's life." My mother twisted her hands together, as if they were roots seeking water. "I thought you, of all people, would have some understanding, some compassion, for him."

"It's not about him, though," said Uncle Mike. "It's just about the fact that the two of us are falling for each other, and I was trying to find the right time to bring it up, but that never seemed to—"

"Yeah, and it never will be the right time for that bit of rotten news. You can take your little tramp and shove her where the sun don't shine."

Then Uncle Mike left the house, and my mother slammed the door. She slammed it so hard that a picture fell off the wall. I watched it hit the floor. The frame and the glass cracked across the front of the picture. It is a picture of me, and I am holding my favorite animal toy. It is a squirrel, from when I was six years old.

Now there was a broken slice right through the middle of my face, so that it looked like my face was made of two different people joined together. The squirrel was not touched by the crack in the glass. I wished I still had that toy squirrel.

The water was gone. I didn't feel like floating or flapping anymore. But I had something inside that had to come out.

"Can I climb the Bigleaf Maple?" I asked.

"Sure," said my mother, but her voice was so soft I could hardly hear her. I thought her eyes were leaking again. I was about to ask her once more, because I was not sure if I had heard her correctly, when she spoke again.

"Sure, March," she said. "Go climb your Hemlock or Maple or whatever. You just knock yourself out back there."

I ascend twenty feet up the Bigleaf Maple, and the wind is blowing. The leaves are shaking, back and forth, back and forth. I look at the leaves vibrating back and forth, the light of the setting sun refracting off them, and I think of the process of photosynthesis, that conversion of light into chemicals in cells. This is how leaves fix carbon into compounds that store the energy for later.

There are two parts to photosynthesis—the light reaction and the dark reaction.

First, the light comes into a cell, and the green chlorophyll absorbs it. The power of the light raises the electrons from the chlorophyll molecules. Water in the cells breaks apart into oxygen and protons and electrons. That's how we get oxygen into our atmosphere—the light breaks it off the water molecules. And then the electrons and protons create other chemicals in the cells of the leaves. That's what breaks apart in the leaves.

My mother breaks things too, but she doesn't make new things out of them, like leaves do.

Because the leaves have a way of putting things together again. The leftover chemical energy is used to make carbohydrates from the hydrogen and from the carbon dioxide from the atmosphere. The energy from the light is stored in these carbohydrates, and the equation for this whole cycle of energy is $6CO_2 + 12H_2O + light \rightarrow C_6H_{12}O_6 + 6O_2 + 6H_2O$.

The sun's light allows the leaves to break things and then to bond new things together.

But maybe breaking things, like my mother does, can create a new type of bond too. Maybe she can break enough things that Uncle Mike will stop visiting with Miss Stevens, and Miss Stevens will stop being mean. Maybe it is possible to make new things out of the broken things.

I do not know if we can be as strong as trees, though. A tree does not care if something else in the forest is moving. A tree does not care if a deer walks by it.

I am a tree in the forest, moving very slowly, only barely touched by the wind. Everyone else just moves past me, and I watch them go, because I cannot be moved from who I am, and what I am, and what I know. It makes me special, unique. My knowledge is a secret that only I possess.

I am like a tree that looks dead to the world, but when you climb to the very top, you find bright-green limbs sucking sap one hundred feet from the ground. And you discover that the tree is very much alive, and is keeping its secret of life from the world.

In the future, perhaps I will simply watch the patterns in the leaves when I am up in the trees, instead of watching people. Trees do not change.

15

On Saturday, we drove down the freeway from Olympia to my grandparents' house, in Centralia. They live approximately twenty-six minutes from our house in Olympia. As we drove, I looked outside the windows of the car to spy out new trees.

I feel entirely calm only when I am in a tree, or when my mother is petting me. My father never petted me, and I do not know why this is. I never bit him when he petted me. I once bit my mother when she petted me, just to see what it would feel like. She did not pet me for a week after that, so I promised that I would not bite her again. But I never bit my father.

I was thinking about my mother and how it feels to have the skin on my shoulders petted by her. I felt like I was watching her, even though I was only watching her hands on the steering wheel, and occasionally her chest and her shoulders, and the hair from her head that touches her shoulders. She has dark-brown hair, but there are also some gray hairs in with her dark-brown hair. It is interesting to me that older trees do not have gray needles like humans have gray hair as they age.

I did not pet my mother, although I felt that perhaps this is something that she would like too. She did not seem to be calm, but I did not know how she was feeling or what she was thinking. I had asked her if Uncle Mike would be at my grandparents' house in Centralia, but she said, "No, he is not invited. Please do not ask again."

As usual at this time of year, the sky was filled with fog and the air all around us was misty. My mother had the windshield wipers going, to wipe away the accumulated mist. But it was not really raining. If you stepped outside of the car, you would only gradually get damp, and only after a few hours would you actually be soaked.

I am merely explaining this because I have seen that people write about the Puget Sound region in the Pacific Northwest having a lot of rain. And this is not technically accurate. We do not have large amounts of rain that fall on us. Instead, we have a constant very low level of precipitation. It is as if we live inside of a cloud for nine months of the year.

In the cloudy mistiness that surrounded us in the car, the trees beside the freeway looked like one massive spiky block of vegetation, reaching high into the sky until its tips disappeared in the cloud cover. They looked like one great organism. And it was interesting to me that although I knew, intellectually, that those were trees in that great mass, I did not have the hunger to climb them. I only feel that way toward a tree when I see it in isolation, or separated out from the rest. As when I saw the Bigleaf Maple in our backyard or when I saw the great rising tower of the Eagle Tree that first time, where it emerged from the forest canopy of the LBA Woods.

So although I enjoyed the sight of these green massed objects that I knew were trees, I did not need to leap from the car and run over and climb each of the individual trees. Because I did not see them as individual trees at that moment.

It is interesting to consider that most people think of human beings in the opposite way. We are expected to consider human beings as individuals, and each person we encounter we are supposed to treat as an individual. I am even supposed to learn a name for each person! I don't learn those names, most of the time. I don't even know faces or voices.

But now that I have had some experience in dealing with people, and trying to communicate with the broader mass of people, I can see that they are like the trees in the mist here—we are all connected; we are all part of one ecosystem.

I felt my hands rising from my lap, and sounds coming out of me, a distant hum. This is what happens when I see something new. And this is what I saw: We are not truly—or only—individual people. It seems to me that we are like aspen groves. We are actually connected to one another underground, and must rely on one another for sustenance, and for the ability to continue to thrive in this world.

But even with this knowledge, I did not know how I could continue to make connections with other people. It is difficult for me to care about people. But I believe it would be useful for me to keep in mind the idea that we are like trees—all connected at the roots, all touching each other all the time, even though we may not consciously feel those connections or those touches. This was a new idea for me.

Eventually, we exited the freeway, and we drove slowly through the town of Centralia. The trees here were not part of an undifferentiated forest. I was trying to identify each individual tree I saw, and this required concentration, as there were many trees on this side of town that I had not previously encountered.

In the car, my mother broke my concentration.

"Peter, the sound you're making is bothering me," she said. "The hands flapping too. Could you stop that, please?"

"March," I said. "That is my name."

"All right," she said. There was a note in her voice that I am familiar with. Sometimes her voice does this before her face twists up and her eyes leak. "March, would you stop that moaning and the hands? The sound is too loud. It makes it hard to drive."

She was still talking to me, even looking at me from time to time—I could see her head shift—but it was just sound to me, because I could see the trees approaching and going by outside the window. The car had sped up, and this made it harder for me to concentrate. My hands moved faster, and I opened my mouth and made the sound louder so I could think better, and focus on the approaching trees.

"Goddammit, March!" came a sound from next to me, but I was not disturbed by it. I just ensured that my own sound and motion was a counterbalance, so I could concentrate.

I counted them as they came by the window. One Douglas Fir. One Western Hemlock. Another. Three Red Cedars. One Western Hemlock. One Oak. Good limbs, easy ascent on the Oak and on the three Red Cedars. Eight trees.

"March, can't you listen to—?"

Then I turned my head forward. I could not think anymore of the three solid Red Cedars and the ascent of the Oak, because there was a flurry of new, smaller trees coming my way, from behind a backyard fence. Two stunted Apples—maybe Pears. And a strange mislocated Eastern Redbud, from the Atlantic region, in someone's front yard. All trees I could easily climb.

I felt something on my shoulder, and I turned my head. It was my mother's hand, holding my brown shirt in a strangely tight grasp. "March," she said, close to me. I could smell her breath—it was a little sweet, with an edge of something citrusy underneath. And I could see her teeth and her tongue. Her voice was very loud. "You've got to stop that sound, honey. I can't hardly hear myself think. It's not safe to drive when you're wailing and flailing like that."

I closed my mouth, but my hands still twitched. The trees were gone behind the car now, and I let them go. Her hand moved away from my shoulder, and her fingers shook as she put her right hand back on the wheel. Her voice was low and husky. Her eyes had leaked on her cheeks, but she did not seem aware of this. She just looked straight ahead at the road, and not at the trees behind us.

I looked away from her and back at the trees, trying to calculate the distance back to the trees I could climb if we stopped moving now. But it was hard, because we were moving forward at a variable rate, and this intermittent velocity made it almost impossible to reach an accurate assessment of how long it would take me to get back to the trees, to climb them.

Next to me, my mother made another sound, and then she shook a white piece of soft paper from her purse. I watched it closely, for it blossomed like a butterfly out of the package. I have seen butterflies before; this one was beautiful. But my mother used it to blow her nose.

Afterward, her fingers were no longer shaking. She glanced at me for a long moment, and I knew that she would want me to not turn away. So I tried, for approximately six seconds, to hold her gaze. Then I turned away, and I was struck in that moment by the similarity between my calculations about the trees behind us and her face.

I could not accurately assess the distance to the trees, because the distance was variable, changing all the time. This is also my problem with faces. Faces are hard, because they change all the time, and people expect you to understand what is happening on their faces, even as their faces change continuously, and when sometimes they do not even know what is happening themselves.

The Oak would have been the best tree to climb of the eleven. I opened my mouth and hummed a bit, so that I could think more clearly about the Oak and define its dendritic structure in my mind, and commit the image of this structure to memory. But then she glanced sideways at me, so that I saw only half her face. Her eyes were white from this angle, with only a bit of pupil showing. I closed my mouth again, but my hands rose from my lap, inscribing an arc that matched some of the branches of the tree.

I wished that I could pet my mother and make her feel like I feel when I am petted, but I did not know how to do that. So I turned from looking at her, and I made the hum under my breath, and the heavy branches of the Oak came clear in my mind, flowing out of the central trunk like arteries growing from a solid heart.

When we visit, my grandfather often shows me photographs of when he was a boy growing up on the East Coast. He talks about the people in the photographs, and I talk about the trees that I can identify in the background.

My grandfather reminds me of a snag broken by many windstorms. He has no hair left, and his ears look like torn branches on his head, spotted dark and light with age. He talks about old trees with me, and I like to hear him talk.

I wish I had been there to see the old trees. My grandfather was there, but he did not care about trees then. He did not know as much as I know about trees. He often says to me, "I guess I just didn't have my eyes open, eh, Peter?"

From what I can see of his photos, there used to be much larger trees in the United States. For example, I have read about the first-growth White Pines of the North Woods, in Minnesota—they were 220 feet high. That is the height of a twenty-story building, and there were thousands of these trees, in every direction. They were chopped down.

In my grandfather's photographs are several pictures of American Chestnut trees. One hundred years ago, the vast expanses of American Chestnut were beautiful things to see. Some of my relatives are standing in front of Chestnut trees in their black-and-white photos. I have also seen pictures and drawings of Chestnut trees.

The American Chestnut rose over one hundred feet from the forest floor and had soaring boughs that stretched out like a huge umbrella.

Because of the great span of its foliage, each tree created the equivalent of its own forest canopy; each tree held nearly an acre of leaves.

The Appalachian Mountains were covered with these immense trees. A full-sized Chestnut could be measured as twenty to twenty-five feet all the way around—if you measured straight through, that would be ten feet through. And there were thousands and thousands of these trees. Even in my grandfather's photos, people are like little dwarves next to a Chestnut.

But my grandfather's photos are very old, and now there are no more of those trees in the wild, especially not at that size or in those quantities. In 1904, all of those American Chestnuts started to die. It was a fungus from Asia called *Endothia parasitica*.

And unfortunately, that fungus soon got into the Appalachians and infected the trees there. Four billion trees died in one generation. Imagine if they were people—that would be like half the people on Earth dying in ten years flat. So now, we don't have very many American Chestnuts left at all. And the only ones remaining are hybrids, or special germ-resistant versions of the tree.

I am a member of the American Chestnut Foundation. This is a group of people who want to restore the Chestnut to the Eastern Woodlands. These are the people who have created a blight-resistant version of the tree. But it is very difficult to restore a tree that has been entirely wiped out.

In fact, right now, we are killing *all* the trees. My grandfather does not believe this. Every time I talk about this, he puts away his photographs and he laughs. "It's impossible to kill *all* the trees, Peter," he tells me. But he is wrong.

Most of the trees are already dying. All across North America from Mexico to Alaska, forests are dying. Seventy thousand square miles of forest—that's as much land as all of the state of Washington—that much forest has died since I was born. What if I am growing up in a world that will not have trees anymore by the time I am my grandfather's age?

There are many causes of trees dying off. In the Southwest, there is the engraver beetle that has killed the Piñon Pine, and the spruce beetle and the fir beetle and the mountain pine beetle. It would be easy to blame the insects. But the truth is that all of this insect activity is coming from warming temperatures and increased stress—all of which can be directly attributed to human activity. The beetles and other insects are just our little soldiers, following in our footsteps to kill what we have given them.

For example, the Canadian province of British Columbia, just north of Washington State, used to be famous for its Lodgepole Pines. But in the past ten years, 80 percent of the Lodgepole Pines have died. This is just one example of how beetles can thrive during global warming and turn forests from carbon sinks to carbon sources.

By the time I am twenty years old, British Columbia will no longer be a forested province at all. What if this happens to Washington State as well? What if I am growing up in a world that does not have trees any longer?

Extinction is what is going to happen to the Ponderosa Pine too. I had already explained the story of the American Chestnut to my grandfather. This time, I started to tell him about the Ponderosa Pine, but when I started talking about the ponderosa pine beetle, my grandfather did not want to talk about trees any longer. He put his photos away and picked up his old ball gloves.

"How about a quick game of catch, Peter?" he said to me.

I do not mind throwing the ball to him, even though my throwing is erratic. But I cannot catch the ball. He knows this. He rolls the ball to me. And then I throw the ball back in his direction. But usually I hit the house instead of his glove. He does not mind. And I like to be outside with my grandfather and the trees.

When we left my grandparents' house, the light had changed. The fog and mist were not covering the whole sky anymore. There were shafts of light coming down from the clouds above. In the Pacific Northwest, we call this time when the sun comes out "sun breaks." And on the radio, they will even tell you when the sun might break through the clouds.

After the mist in the morning, when the clouds were gone and things were no longer half obscured by fog, the light reflecting off everything seemed to give it a bright glow. I felt as if we were submerged in a great ocean of light.

The Pacific Northwest feels like a very different place when this happens. As my mother drove, the light transformed everything I can see. In the bright light, the green land looked like a picture of a tropical island, even though it was not as hot—or as beachy—as an island like that.

It was also hot, though; it was almost sixty-five degrees that afternoon! That is very tropical in contrast to the rest of the year, when the average temperature is around fifty and everybody wears sweaters and fleece all the time.

I imagined that the trees were soaking the light up, eating greedily at all of the energy that pours down upon us.

Sometimes this is how I feel about information and facts. The facts, the knowledge, the information, it is all around us, pouring down upon us in an unquenchable flood all the time.

But sometimes I end up being the only one who is soaking up the truth of things that are around us—identifying the true name of each tree, measuring the distances among trees, estimating the length of the roots, calculating the effects of climate change upon each one, and estimating the amount of time it would take me to climb each and every tree in my vicinity.

Why am I the only person I know who seems capable of doing these things? Am I the only one who cares? Am I the only one who can feel that sunlight of knowledge soaking into us at every moment?

There is an ocean of light around us. We are surrounded by it. We swim in it. We move through it every day. But I am the only one who seems to have my eyes open. I am the only one who can see it.

Sometimes, this is very lonely.

When we arrived at home, I told my mother that I was going to climb a tree. I did not tell her which tree I was going to climb. I cannot lie well, but I can choose what to say and what not to say. This can be very useful.

I realized that I know the route from our house to the LBA Woods, where the Eagle Tree stands. I looked at a map too. The LBA Woods is only 2.1 miles from our house, but it is a circuitous route. Because I had looked at the map, I had a precisely detailed route in my mind. It was like climbing a tree, but walking instead of climbing.

I knew the fence would be there, and I did not intend to play Pat Tillman's Tarzan game again. But if I could get close enough to see the shape of the Eagle Tree again, I could see for myself whether or not it was indeed a Ponderosa Pine.

I felt the bark of the trees on either side of me as I walked. It was very soothing. Here in the LBA Woods, the trees grew very close together, and when I did not walk on the path, I could reach out with my fingertips and touch their bark as I passed. The skin of the trees was warm in the sunlight, and rough, and I imagined that each tree contained a soul. Like an Ent. I knew that this idea was not a true thing, but I still I felt good that the trees were here.

If the Eagle Tree were an Oak, it would be closer to other trees. It would not be so isolated. Oaks grow in groups called savannas—their root systems touch one another. My mother read about this in one of my books. She called it "living in community," and I didn't then know what that meant. It is something she would like to do—with other people, though, not with trees. If I lived in community with anything, I would live with trees.

I reached out my hand now, and I touched the long branches of the trees and watched the leaves tremble at my touch. The tree might know I was here; the tree might not know I was here. My presence did not matter to the tree either way, and I liked it that way.

Then I came across a woman in the woods. She did not see me at first. That is because she had binoculars in her hands and she was pointing the binoculars at the tops of all the trees, as if she were looking for something. I watched her for a long time. She seemed somehow familiar.

That was the only time I had watched another person do something for a long time. It was not dissimilar to watching a deer, or watching the progress of a squirrel in the woods. She was not as quiet and still as a deer. But she was not as fast and flighty as a squirrel. She was somewhere in between. She was a human being, like me. And that was a very odd thought. That we were similar to each other, that we were connected in that way, just like two trees of the same species.

After I watched her for a while, I kept walking through the woods. Then I saw her again. The second time, she was walking in the woods and cutting off small pieces from each patch of the underbrush. When she cut off a leaf, she placed the cut leaf in a small bag. Then she wrote something on the small bag, and she put the bags one by one in the backpack that she was wearing.

When she saw me, she waved her hand in the air back and forth.

"Hi, March!" she called. "Do you remember me? Are you naming trees again?" I must have met her before, although I did not remember her name, and of course, I did not look at her face.

"Yes, I am naming trees," I said. "But today I am here to look at the Eagle Tree."

From my vantage point, I could now make out the great bulk of the Eagle Tree, past the fence, on the other side of a rising hill of foliage. I pointed.

This woman walked closer to me, and she also looked up at the rising heights of the Eagle Tree.

"That's what they call this one, isn't it?" she said. "Have you seen what people leave for the tree?"

"No," I said. "What do you mean?"

"Come over here," she said. She walked to a small hollow on the other side of the hill, which was as close as we could get to the base of the tree from this side of the fence. We were only about seventeen feet away. And here I could tell for sure: the faint smell of vanilla in the air told me that this was a Ponderosa Pine. There were other confirmations as well: The orange of the bark, glowing faintly in this afternoon light. The great sheets of outer bark shearing away. The bored holes of the ponderosa pine beetle, each one cut as tightly as a bullet hole in the bark. My pulse thrummed with this knowledge.

But then the woman called to me again. I turned toward her, and there was another surprise. Below the base of the great tree, there was a hollow. The hollow was a natural indentation in the hillside, but it looked a little bit like the altar at Pastor Ilsa's church. There was a base and something that looked like a little table with a cloth, but made out of a wood stump and pieces of bark.

In the hollow, there were groups of colored feathers tied together by pipe cleaners. There were stones with writing on them that looked like Celtic runes. And there was a silver necklace, around several bright-blue broken robin's eggs.

"See?" she said. "Offerings to the spirit of the tree."

"Why do people leave these things?"

"Ha!" She laughed. "Only in Olympia! My dad says when the sixties ended, the whole Earth tilted, and all the hippies in the country fell down to this coast, and now they all live in Olympia, Eugene, and Portland. Know what I mean?" And for a moment, she sounded like Pierre.

Then she started talking again. "Did you know that they're going to log this last remaining patch of old-growth forest?"

"No," I said. Then my mouth became too dry to talk. The thrum in my pulse was gone. A bitter taste clogged my throat. "Log?"

"Oh, yes," she said. "They plan to cut down all the trees and build condominiums. It's like that old song, where they cut down paradise so they can put up a parking lot?"

I did not know what paradise was, and I did not know what song she was talking about.

"Yep," she said. "They're going to knock down all of these trees, inside and outside the fence." Then she hummed the tune of a song, the song I did not know.

"Go back and read the sign if you don't believe me," she said.

So I walked through the woods until I came to the yellow sign. I did not close my eyes this time. I opened them wide, and I read the yellow sign. The woman in the woods was right about what the sign said.

After I read the yellow sign, I turned to leave the woods. But as I moved through the forest toward my intended route, I felt the trees had changed. In a moment, they seemed to have gone from bright and vibrant and comforting to very dark, and every blackberry vine seemed to catch at my skin and tear.

The leaf shadows on my face no longer felt inviting and playful. Instead, they felt as if they were performing the opposite of photosynthesis; they were performing the dark process by which matter decays.

Energy was leaching out of the dead trees. Energy was draining out of me, faster than I could replenish it. I thought maybe I should just fall down on the forest floor and decay myself. Maybe a tree would grow from me. Maybe I could do good that way. Maybe I could become a nurse log.

I felt already that a shadow was stripping away flesh from my bones. It was the words on the sign; it was as if they had penetrated to my core and infected me. I could not get enough air in my lungs. I reached out my hands to touch the trees on either side of me, but now the trees were cold and corpse-like, a standing forest of the dead.

Despite this feeling, I walked forward. I walked to the road and turned right, and then walked again and turned left, and walked for one more mile before I arrived home.

16

After school on Tuesday, my mother took me to see Rhonda again. I also got to see the running water in the bowl and the small Japanese Maple again.

Since I last saw Rhonda, I had read about Japanese bonsai. So I told her what I had learned about these miniature trees.

"This is a Japanese Maple bonsai, *Acer palmatum*," I told her. "Native to China, Japan, and Korea. But I think this one is a cultivated variety—perhaps 'Atropurpureum,' for the reddish leaves. Do you know if it is 'Atropurpureum'?"

"I don't know," said Rhonda. "I'd like to ask you a different question. Is that all right with you, March?"

I did not say anything. I waited.

"Why do you want to be called March?" she said.

I did not say anything.

"All right," said Rhonda, after a long pause. "What makes you different?"

I could tell her the answer to this one. "I can understand things faster than other people."

"Ah," said Rhonda.

I looked out the window of her office. There was a fruit tree outside that was approximately eighteen feet high. It was a grafted tree, probably between ten and fifteen years old. I wondered what fruit it grew from the grafts. You can graft churches, like the United Churches. But I do not think you can graft human beings.

"Also, I can climb very well," I said. "But many people can climb. Did you know that most people stop climbing trees after the age of nine years old?"

"How old are you now, March?"

"I am fourteen years old. I will be fifteen years old in six months and thirty days."

"So, that is also something different about you," said Rhonda.

"Yes, of course. This is why I said that most people stop climbing trees when they are nine years old. I am not most people."

"Well," said Rhonda. "You have said something very true there, March."

Then she started talking about trees. Most of what she said I already knew. But I appreciated that she was using words and terms I understood, words like *riparian* and *ecosystem* and *epicormic branching* and *xylem*.

Then there was a very long pause, nearly four minutes long. After some time, I played back the words she had said just prior to the pause. It was then that I realized she had asked me a question.

"How did you come to be interested in trees, March?" she had said. So I told her.

"When I was four years, three months, two weeks, and one day old, my mother and my father and I went to the Hands On Children's Museum in Olympia. There was an exhibit on trees and fluid dynamics. I spent fifteen hours learning how to control the flow of water."

"Wait, how long?" said Rhonda. She looked up from the notebook on her lap.

"Fifteen hours. My mother made me stop twice and eat. Once she made me stop and use the bathroom. So overall, I believe it is more likely that I was focused on the flow system for only fourteen hours and sixteen minutes."

"Why in the world did you need to spend—?"

"They had a system that would allow you to control how colored water would flow through different channels. I asked many questions of the people who worked in the exhibit about what caused fluids to move in different things. And most of the examples they used were examples of trees and plants. There was a large model of a tree's internal vascular system there, with explanations of how fluids move up from the ground in a tree."

Rhonda clicked her pen with her teeth. It was very distracting. I stopped talking. Eventually, Rhonda stopped clicking her pen. "Did you go back to the museum at all?" she said.

"Yes," I said. "I went back to the Hands On Children's Museum every day for twenty-two days until the fluid dynamics exhibit was gone. I did experiments with celery, and I watched for two hours as the xylem and phloem in a piece of celery used transpiration to draw fluids up into the stalk. Then I spent approximately ninety-two hours in the tree exhibit."

Rhonda clicked her pen once, but then she stopped, as if she had realized it was not a sound I enjoyed. "What did you learn in that exhibit, March? What kept you going back?"

"Phyllotaxis," I said. "And the Fibonacci sequence." I paused then. I was beginning to feel the need to flap my arms.

"Tell me more," said Rhonda. I shut my eyes. When I could not see her, it was easier to talk. I talked loudly, and my arms moved in rhythm with my words. With my eyes shut, it was as if my branches were moving in an unseen wind.

"Phyllotaxis is about how leaves are ordered on a stem. Leaves on plants are staggered. They grow in a spiral pattern that optimizes sunlight exposure. Fibonacci numbers occur in nature everywhere, in shells and in animals. But I am only interested in plants. In trees, in particular."

"How do plants know to grow this way?" said Rhonda.

My arms moved in furious circles. It was very frustrating to talk with her interruptions. "Trees do not *know* about this sequence—they just grow in the most efficient way. And the Fibonacci sequence naturally occurs through their growth patterns. Anyone can see the sequence, if you keep your eyes open. You can see the Fibonacci sequences in the arrangement of the leaves, in pinecones and sunflowers, or in branch growth in many coniferous trees. But the most obvious one is on the Palm, in the number of rings on its trunk."

I could feel my arms slowing, the flapping growing more mild. I had managed to explain the basics of the Fibonacci sequence in tree growths. But there was much more I could say.

I could explain the continuous water column that is the xylem— the great conduit that extends from the roots up through every leaf. What draws the water upward is the process of evaporation through stomates in the leaves or needles. That evaporation pulls the water up by creating negative water pressure. All of that negative water pressure created by the tree acts as a vacuum pulling water all the way up from the water table into the leaves.

When I was younger, I would sometimes cut a notch into a tree at the highest branch I could reach and watch the sap seep out of it, knowing that it came from deep underground. Tree roots follow the macropores in the soil and use hydraulic lift to pull water from hundreds of feet down.

I also used to cut my fingers or my wrists and then hold my hands up in the air, to watch the sap seep out. But my mother became upset when I did this. And I was taken to the hospital for stitches six times, and then I stopped doing this, because at the hospital they would tie me in a bed, and I do not like to be tied in a bed.

Then Uncle Mike taught me to climb, by showing me carefully on a jungle gym how to move and place my legs and arms and hands. Then he taught me how to plan a route up a tree and execute that route. When I found that I did not have to act like a tree, that I could simply climb a tree, everything calmed down inside of me. So then I began to climb trees every day, for as long as I could.

Now, as I talked to Rhonda, my hands were calm against my side again, my branches quiescent.

"You do these motions because they make you feel calm," said Rhonda. "They are soothing actions."

During our first meeting, Rhonda taught me how to do check-ins on my hands and my sounds. She practiced the check-ins with me now. I told her that it was not easy to do check-ins, but I also knew that it was a valid method of understanding what was around me, and what my body was doing. This is very challenging for me. Also, my hands and my sounds are comforting to me. I like the wind that moves my branches.

"The problem with doing these things all the time, though, March, is that they are distressing to other people," said Rhonda. "Other people do not find them calming. Quite the opposite."

"Quite the opposite," I said. "Quite the opposite. Quite the opposite."

I liked the way it sounded, the way Rhonda put a little accent on the word *quite*. As if it were a word in another language. One that I do not speak.

"Yes," said Rhonda. "Other people can find your motions and sounds distressing."

"Quite the opposite," I said again.

Rhonda paused. She looked at me, and I was caught off guard, with her eyes staring straight into my eyes for a moment. I looked away from her face.

"You understand what I am saying, though?" she said.

"Affirmative," I said. "Yes, I understand."

But I was not sure that it was true.

Ilsa had taught me that sometimes it is important for people to hear what they want to hear, regardless of whether or not it is precisely true. Maybe this was one of those times. I did not know.

Rhonda kept talking to me, so maybe I had said the right thing. But then she asked questions that had no meaning to me. For example, she asked whether or not my mother had ever hurt my feelings. I did not know what that meant. Sometimes I feel fear or anger, but I did not know how my mother could hurt these feelings in me. This I told Rhonda.

"All right," said Rhonda. "So you know you can feel fear, March, correct?" She generally tries to not look at me, because she knows this makes me uncomfortable. But at the next sentence she turned her face toward me and leaned forward, as if to force me to see her face. Then she asked another question: "What are you most fearful of, March?"

I had been told that I must answer Rhonda as truthfully as possible. But I felt like I needed to hold on to my flapping. She was right that it can be distressing at times.

Once, I climbed to the very top of a small snag. It was only thirty or forty feet tall, but on the top was a nest. The nest was concealed from everything around it, but it was open to the sky.

In the nest were two baby chicks. When they saw me, one of them stood up and flapped its wings. So I stood up and flapped my wings too. Then I fell backward out of the tree. That was the time I broke my ankle.

My mother said I was lucky I did not break my back. I do not believe in luck. People like to believe in crazy things, like luck, and they like the idea that we can keep changing the natural environment—for example, so it is hostile to trees—and that our activities will not have long-term deleterious effects on human life on this planet. I do not understand why people believe in crazy things, but I have grown up some now, I guess. I no longer fight against crazy people or crazy ideas.

I just try to be clear in what I know to be true. And I am supposed to be truthful with Rhonda. But the answer to her question conflicted with a suggestion that Uncle Mike had given me on the way to her office. He said, "Try not to talk about trees too much. Rhonda wants to know about other things in your life." So the first time she asked the question, I did not say anything at all. I shut my eyes.

But then she asked the question again. "What are you most fearful of, March?"

To answer her question truthfully, I had to first ensure that she had a complete understanding of the topic. "Do you know about the Ponderosa Pines and their situation today?"

"No," she said. "Tell me more."

I opened my eyes.

"I would like to climb a Ponderosa Pine. But most of them are in drier climate regions. They have very deep root systems and powerful abilities to store water. For decades, if necessary. British Columbia and Montana have been covered by Ponderosa Pines for many centuries."

"All right," said Rhonda. "And this relates to your fear because?"

"That is about to change, because all of the Ponderosa Pines are dying. In fact, most of the forest of British Columbia is now dead. And the trees in Montana are all dying. And the reason for this is what we have done as human beings."

"All the trees in Montana?" said Rhonda. She made a noise. "That's a big claim, March. I was asking you about—"

"We released a lot of carbon—mostly through burning it—and so we warmed the planet."

"Climate change," said Rhonda.

"I still think it is more accurate to call it 'global warming.' We can call it 'climate change,' but it is really just us heating up our own little greenhouse, and wondering why it is so hot inside."

"March, I understand you care about climate change and about Ponderosa Pines, but I'm interested in your own day-to-day feelings. I want to know your truth. I wonder . . ."

She wanted to know the truth about this. So I kept talking. This time I raised my voice, so I could ensure that she understood all of the salient points about the Ponderosa Pine.

"See, for trees, this is problematic in a couple of ways," I said. "The ponderosa pine beetle is native to the northern forests. And it typically can chew on trees for two to four weeks a year. The rest of the year, it is killed off by frost, or it is just getting out of the larval stage, or it is in some other stage of its life cycle. Because the ponderosa pine beetles are killed off by frost every year, they have to lay eggs and hope some of those eggs survive the frost. So the population is kept in check by weather cycles."

Rhonda opened her mouth as if to talk again, but I took a deep breath and continued talking before she could interrupt.

"However, when those weather cycles started changing, because of what human beings did," I said, "then the ponderosa pine beetle could just keep eating Ponderosa Pines. And it did. There was not enough bad weather to kill any of the beetles off, so they laid eggs, and then the adults just kept eating, and the eggs hatched, and more kept eating. So instead of about fourteen to twenty-four days a year when they can eat trees, they instead can eat trees three hundred and sixty-five days a year. And that's what they did. And so now all the trees are dying."

"Is that what you're afraid of, of the trees dying? Is that it, March?"

"And we did it to them," I said. "The ponderosa pine beetle is native to the forests. It is not an invasive species, so there is little we can do to hurt it, unless we want to hurt the whole forest. And we have already done that. It is too late for me. It might be too late for me."

Rhonda sighed and shook her head. "I'm afraid I just don't follow what—"

"I might never get a chance to climb a living Ponderosa Pine. I'm afraid of that. I'm very afraid of that." Just the thought of it is a problem for me. I started flapping and moaning then.

"Ah," she said. She stood and looked outside the window at the grafted fruit tree. "So you have knowledge about this, and you feel that you cannot act."

"Yes," I said, but I was moaning so much I did not know if she could hear. "Yes. I am afraid of that. I am afraid of that. I am afraid."

She turned back to me, and then she gently petted my shoulder, just like my mother does. "Well, here's another question for you then, March. What action can you take to influence the world? What can you do that doesn't hurt you or the people around you? What can you do that takes all that powerful energy you have and does good in the world?"

"For trees?" I asked. Her fingers on my shoulders felt like branches, like leaves, like wind.

"For everyone," she said. "For trees, and for people. For yourself."

17

Every year, on the Saturday closest to Earth Day in April, there is a parade in Olympia called the Procession of the Species. People dress up as animals and plants and pretend to be other parts of the ecosystem. For example, there is an ocean part of the parade, and everyone in that part is dressed as a fish or an ocean mammal. People pretending to be jellyfish hold big decorated umbrellas with brightly colored streamers all around them, like jellyfish tentacles. One year, someone made a whale that was of accurate dimensions—the whale filled up the whole street.

This parade is distinct from other parades. There are no signs and no writing and no cars and no floats, nothing that represents human civilizations or culture. It is a parade of only handmade costumes and handmade rolling things, and everything in the parade is dressed up like an animal or a plant.

The whole idea started in Olympia, for Earth Day, and now there are parades like this, for all the species, in many cities all around the world. But it began in Olympia.

The goal of the Procession of the Species is to have all the species and regions on Earth represented in one parade. When I last saw the parade, I counted the animals and plants, and I identified 142 unique species among 607 marchers. This number is only a tiny fraction of the more than eight million species of flora and fauna that scientists estimate constitutes life on Earth. But 142 unique species is many more than you usually see.

When I was small, I went several times to the parade, but I was too loud when I was counting species, and my mother and father had to take me home early. When I was eight years old, I also tried to run out and join the parade, which would have been all right, I guess, except that what I wanted to do was be an unmoving tree in the middle of the parade, and if you are in the parade, not moving is not allowed. Nevertheless, I succeeded in running onto the parade route and standing as a tree for a short time, until my father picked me up and took me back to the car, and then we had to drive home, and I was screaming and moaning and flapping for a very long time that day. I think I even was screaming when I went to bed that night.

I remember the Procession of the Species that year very clearly, though. I remember every animal I saw before we left the parade route. And every year after that, I have begged to go back. But I was not allowed to go. Not until this year.

Now that I am older, I understand that if you do not move, other parade people in the Procession of the Species—like the salmon band and the huge whale—cannot move past you in the parade route, and this is why you must move forward in one direction during a parade.

And at fourteen years old, I was old enough to be able to look at things like a parade and not have to participate. So, for the first time in six years, we were going to go back and see the Procession of the Species again. This time, I promised to do my best to stay on the side of the parade route and watch the other people act as animals and plants. I knew it would take some effort, but I was going to stay on the side and watch and count species quietly.

These are the people who went to the Procession of the Species together: me, my mother, and my mother's new friend. My mother's friend is a man she works with at her office. He does not wear a Sounders cap like Uncle Mike, and he does not have Albert Einstein hair like Mr. Gatek. Without those things, I thought I would have a hard time remembering him. But then when he moved his arm, I saw that underneath his shirtsleeve is a tattoo that covers his entire upper arm. It is a tattoo of ocean waves, and it goes all the way around his arm, covering all the skin on that part of his arm. If I can see the edge of his wavy tattoo, I think that I can always remember that this is my mother's friend and that his name is Ted.

The Procession of the Species is split into different regions of the world, and all the species for that region come together into their areas. This year, near the beginning, there were dandelions, big huge ones. These dandelions were actually people, and they were dressed in green and wearing huge headdresses that looked like dandelions about to be blown apart by the wind.

Following the dandelions were many tulips, most of them made of adults. But one flower was a little girl on a tricycle, and she was dressed up not as a tulip flower at all, but instead as a very small pink flamingo. Her mother was a flower, but the little girl looked like a flamingo. This was disruptive to me, because flamingos do not live in the part of the world where tulips grow.

So I was momentarily distracted, and I almost missed the beginning of the African savanna. In the savanna part of the parade, there was a musical band of many people all dressed up as elephants. Each person playing an instrument was wearing big gray ears and a trunk. Around them were wildebeests and small giraffes.

There was also a female giraffe who was so tall that she had to duck her head under the telephone wires across the road. She was at least eighteen feet tall, and that is as tall as the wires on the telephone poles. There were twelve people holding the giraffe up. One person on each leg, and many people in the middle, and more people holding up the neck.

The giraffe was very exciting—my mother asked me to sit back down after the giraffe. And I did. But there was also a lion molded out of paper that was on a little cart being pushed by people. The lion was very realistic. And a rhinoceros too.

After the savanna came some other animals I do not know as well. There was a woman who was a dung beetle pushing a big black ball that was supposed to be a ball of dung. Everyone around me laughed at this woman, but I liked her, because her costume was precisely accurate: the beetle was pushing with its back legs, just like I saw in a documentary on the BBC. Next were some jackals on skateboards and a pair of dragonflies running from side to side with huge eyes and even bigger wings.

Then came the Pacific Northwest region. In this section, there were people dressed as flying squirrels and fish and deer and bears from our forest. The band in this section was dressed as pink salmon, all wearing fish heads, with the trumpets and other instruments sticking in the fish mouths. But in this section, I was very disappointed to not see anyone dressed as a tree, even though we are surrounded by trees here in the Pacific Northwest. There were tree frogs, though, and I was gratified to see that the lines and spots on their skin looked very technically accurate.

My mother's friend Ted is also interested in the Pacific Northwest biome. He works for the Washington Department of Fish and Wildlife, and he told my mother and me all about the animals in the Pacific Northwest section of the parade. He commented on the flying squirrels, and then came some otters, and he mentioned that he had worked to restore otter habitat. Then came a pair of eagles, pretending to catch salmon from the band and then fly back to their big nest, which was on top of a moving cart, and a lot of little kids were in the nest, dressed up as fluffy little eaglets. Everyone laughed at the little kids, and I did too, because one of the eaglets did not look like an eaglet at all—one of them was dressed as a chicken, which is an unlikely bird to find in a bald eagle's nest. I have seen many bald eagle nests, and I also have seen eagles like these fly over me.

But then came a bird that was different from the eagles. It was very large, like there were two people inside this costume instead of one. The proportions in comparison to the eagles were therefore wrong, because it seemed to me that if this was a seabird, it should be smaller than the eagles. At first I thought, because of the curved bill, that it was a great auk, which would be unusual because the animals in the Procession of the Species parade are supposed to be living animals. The great auk is extinct.

It was not streamlined like an albatross, and it was colored gray, only it also had stripes on the side—curved stripes of white and black.

My mother's friend Ted recognized the bird before I did. "Wow," he said. "Now that's pretty neat—that's a marbled murrelet. It's an endangered species, you know. Incredibly rare."

"I guess I've never seen one before," said my mother. "Do you know this bird, March?"

"Yes," I said.

"Great," said Ted. "Then you know the marbled murrelet is unique to the Northwest forest. A diving ocean bird that only lives inland on an old-growth tree. If its tree goes down, then it dies with the tree, all too often. And no one knows how it selects a tree or how it lives. I've studied this bird. It's an odd duck."

"It is not a duck," I said.

"That's true, that's true, March," said Ted. He looked at my mother, and then I realized he was explaining to her, not to me. "It's not a duck at all. It's related to the auks, and it's unique because it's a seabird that nests far inland and leaves its young on inland old-growth trees. How the little birds know how to get from those trees back to the ocean is a mystery. It's a very rare bird indeed. I'm happy to see one in the parade. Aren't you, March?"

But I was not really listening to him any longer. I knew how I could save the Eagle Tree. I knew now what I had to do. But I had to confirm one thing. And so I had to examine the limbs of the tree. Very carefully.

So I stood up, and I began walking. From here, the tree was approximately five miles away. I thought the correct route would be to walk up Capitol Way, and after four miles, take a left on North Street near the line of Box Elders planted by the city. Then I would travel past the line of Vine Maples near Olympia High School, take a right at the large out-of-region Sequoia on Cain Road after another three-quarters of a mile, then take a left at the Red Alder grove near the corner of Boulevard and walk to the end of the road at the bus stop, where I would be .53 of a mile away from the Eagle Tree.

I did not know how long it would take me to walk there. I knew I would need to confirm this soon.

When I started walking away from the Procession of the Species, my mother was getting her sunglasses from the car. So she was not there and she did not know what I was doing.

My mother's friend Ted said something behind me, but I kept walking. Then Ted caught up to me, and he put a hand on my shoulder. "Does your mother know that you're leaving?"

"I need to go look at the tree," I said. "I need to check the limbs."

"Okay," said Ted. "I'll tell her that's where you went, okay?"

I didn't say anything to him. I just kept walking.

I was walking in the opposite direction from all the animals and plants in the Procession of the Species, so as I walked up the parade route, I was surrounded by herds of make-believe antelope, and then there was a set of barking coyotes that scared me at first, before I remembered that they were really people. Then I barked back.

For a while I was underwater, surrounded by flowing blue silk and waving underwater ribbons. In the ocean part of the parade, there were people who represented giant sea kelp but looked like walking stalks of broccoli, because they could not trail five hundred or six hundred feet into the ocean depths. Rushing back and forth in between the strands of kelp were many people acting as different kinds of jellyfish. They had tentacles of all colors. The tentacles were made of fabric and balloons and plastic, and many other colored materials that I could not identify. There was a giant sea turtle on a cart chasing one of the jellyfish around. I liked the sea turtle's beak. It looked very authentic.

Also, dolphins swam all around me. Some of them looked like ocean dolphins, like bottlenose dolphins, while others were colored like Amazon river dolphins. In real life, these dolphins would not be swimming together. But this was a parade.

Next, I was surrounded by a swarm of bees and wasps, who were all riding bicycles and buzzing around in big circles. They had with them a beehive, made of coils of rope painted yellow. It was a great-looking hive. Inside was a small bee, who was really a little kid dressed as a bee. But there was no honey in the hive, which I thought was a failing.

Finally, I reached the end of the parade. The Procession of the Species ends with a big picture of the Earth held up by four people. Then people gradually drained away down the street as I continued up Capitol Way. I stumbled as I left the people, and my ankle twisted, but I kept moving.

After about a half mile, I passed the Washington State Capitol building on my right. It reminded me of the big beehive that was carried on the cart with the bees on bicycles. I was thinking of what I was going to do to save the tree. Maybe I needed to go into that big building, where they make all the laws, and have them make a law to not hurt the tree.

But then I stopped thinking about the building, because I was passing through the very old part of Olympia. This is where my father used to live before he moved to Arizona. Now I am the only March Wong who lives in Olympia. There used to be two of us: my father's name is also March Wong. But now there is only me.

And my father used to live with my mother and with me before we moved to the house with the blue mailbox.

On the corner ahead was the out-of-region Black Cottonwood—*Populus trichocarpa*—that I used to climb every morning when my father lived with us. I felt the hunger in me to climb it again. But I pushed that feeling down and I kept walking, because I had to save the Eagle Tree.

After I passed the Black Cottonwood, I realized that this was one of the first times I had ever pushed away that feeling of needing to climb a tree.

And it was all right. I was still standing. I was still walking. I could feel like climbing a tree, and not climb it. And not get upset.

Now, somehow, for some reason, I felt that my feet were lighter, and that I did not need to worry about things so much. I felt like I was floating a little bit off the ground as I walked forward.

But then that feeling went away. My feet were very tired.

I made it to North Street, and at North Street I took a left, and then I sat down for a while on the curb to rest.

When I stood back up, I realized that my legs were shaking a little. I started to feel that I might begin to flap and moan. But I didn't want to waste time before seeing the Eagle Tree, so I kept walking, even though my legs were shaky and my ankle hurt, as if I had bent it badly when I stumbled on the way up Capitol Way.

I kept moving forward.

I remembered what I saw when I climbed the Western Larch in the LBA Woods to see the heights of the Eagle Tree. I remembered the vast unshakable weight of the tree above me, and high, on its highest limbs, the small gray fluff of a nestling marbled murrelet.

18

Uncle Mike's White Elm–colored truck was at the corner of North Street and Cain, right next to the Box Elders. I was surprised to see him. He did not look surprised to see me. He rubbed his hand through his hair, as if he were very tired.

Uncle Mike had pulled his truck to the curb in such a way that it formed a fifty-five-degree angle, so it was misaligned with both a true right angle and a parallel relationship to the curb. It seemed out of line, out of order, to my eyes.

Then he came around the truck, and he almost hugged me before I flinched back. Then he must have remembered that I do not like to be hugged, and instead of hugging me, he stroked my skin on the shoulder and he talked to me. But I was too tired to talk to him, and my legs were too shaky, and I did not listen to what he said.

Uncle Mike had Miss Stevens with him in the truck. I recognized her because she was wearing the same long braid that goes down her back like a snake. I felt I would like to touch it, because now that I was close to her, the braid really did look to me like a brown tree snake—*Boiga irregularis*—which is an arboreal rear-fanged colubrid snake native to eastern and northern coastal Australia.

Miss Stevens said some words to me, but I was not paying attention, because I was thinking of the brown tree snake and wondering which trees the brown tree snake likes to climb in the rain forest canopy in the South Pacific, where it lives.

We drove to the house with the blue mailbox. The new house, where I live now. My mother's eyes were leaking again, and I looked away until she wiped her face. And then she wanted to hug me, and she asked me first, so I let her do that. And then I sat down on the couch and she gave me a snack, and then she petted my shoulders the way I like.

"Ted was useless," said my mother. But she was not talking to me. She was talking to Uncle Mike and also to Miss Stevens. I was still thinking about the tree snake. *Boiga irregularis.*

My mother was still stroking my shoulders. "Can you imagine just letting March walk right up the street and leave, in the middle of a big parade?"

"Well," said Miss Stevens. Her braid looked different in the lights inside the house. "I'm not sure I would've known what to do."

"Okay, maybe not," said my mother. I could tell my mother was not happy to say this.

"But I agree with you," said Miss Stevens.

I turned from looking at the braid now coiled on Miss Stevens's shoulder to look at the Bigleaf Maple in the backyard. The wind had caught at its leaves, and as the leaves moved, they called to me.

"Even if I didn't know what I was doing," said Miss Stevens, "I wouldn't allow him to walk up the street unaccompanied. I probably would've at least tried to walk with him."

"See?" said Uncle Mike. "Samantha isn't so bad."

Miss Stevens and my mother both laughed. I am not sure why they were laughing, but then Miss Stevens was talking again. "Look, I can only say I'm sorry so many times. But I am really sorry for what happened. I just heard—"

"I know, I know," said my mother.

I did not think my mother thought Miss Stevens was mean any longer.

They talked about how Uncle Mike knew where to find me, and how Miss Stevens helped him to choose the right route from the Procession of the Species. But I did not wait for them to finish, even though my mother had told me before that I have to wait for people to finish talking. I did not wait because it was still important for me to go to the Eagle Tree. And now that I had eaten a snack, my legs were no longer shaky, and I was closer to the tree, so I thought maybe I should go there right away. The Bigleaf Maple had reminded me what I still needed to do. So I started talking.

"I need to save the Eagle Tree from being knocked down," I said. "I need to do this now."

"What's that, March?" said Uncle Mike. He was getting a drink from the refrigerator, and I could not see his head.

"To save the Eagle Tree. From being knocked down for the housing development. There are several methods that I could use."

"All right," said Uncle Mike. His head reappeared, and he brought several drinks in bottles back to the living room. He pointed a bottle at me, which was strange. I do not drink these drinks. I did not want one. But he was talking to Miss Stevens and my mother.

"Okay, listen up, folks. March here has a proposal for us," Uncle Mike said to them. To me, he said, "So, tell us more."

I was glad that Uncle Mike was listening to me. For the last few days, I had been thinking about these methods. I had been thinking about sitting in the Eagle Tree and refusing to leave. My favorite movie is about the woman named Julia Butterfly Hill who sat in a Redwood for many days, to prevent it from being cut down.

I told them about her, but I also said I did not think this was viable for me. I could not be a Julia Butterfly Hill. Julia Butterfly Hill stayed in a tree for many days. My mother's rule requires me to come down after a maximum of twenty-seven minutes in a tree.

"Thank God for that!" said my mother when I told them I had decided against this possibility.

There was another option. I could go to the capitol and ask the state lawmakers to pass a rule that no more trees could be cut down. I told my mother and Uncle Mike and Miss Stevens about some people who worked on a team that tried to do this in 1990. It was a very good idea, to preserve the majority of the Redwoods in Northern California. This is the only place on Earth that Redwoods grow.

"Earth First!, eh?" said Miss Stevens.

"I read about their story in a magazine article that Uncle Mike saved for me. I would have supported their idea." But then I rushed ahead to explain the bad part.

Someone who worked for the police department, or the FBI—which is a branch of the federal government—put a bomb in the car of the people who worked for Earth First!, and blew them up. One of them was hurt for a very long time, and she had to stay in the hospital, and she could not climb trees again.

Then the government lied about what they did, and they said that this lady had created the bomb herself. Fortunately, she was able to sue the government, and she won millions of dollars when they proved that the government had lied about her. Uncle Mike found this article for me last year on May 24, which is the anniversary of the date that the government bombed this group. It is very distressing to me to hear that people who wanted to save trees were blown up.

Unfortunately, the government succeeded in blocking the rule that would have made it impossible for the Redwoods to be cut down. Also, the article said that this group—Earth First!—became associated in people's minds with bombs. That is the reason that my mother recommended against me joining this group.

"That's not the only reason," my mother said.

I spoke up louder. "Even though it was proven to be untrue, and even though it was proven in court that the government did the bad thing, not the people protecting the trees, people still believe this lie about Earth First!"

"Well, that's kind of debatable," said Miss Stevens.

"No, it is not," I said. "I do not understand how people can believe untrue things." And then I went on.

If the government was going to destroy the people who ask for change, I told them, maybe talking to the legislature about the Eagle Tree would not be effective. I did not want to have a bomb put in my car by a government agent.

Miss Stevens shook her head, and her braid twisted from side to side, like the movement of a brown tree snake, but I was not distracted this time. I kept talking. I explained the sign.

When that woman in the LBA Woods told me to look at the sign, I looked at every word very carefully. This means I have an exact picture of the sign in my head, and I can read it at any time I choose.

The yellow sign clearly said that the property will be developed if the city gives permission for development. I have never heard of a city putting a bomb in someone's car. Therefore, I thought maybe I could talk to the people who are in charge of the city of Olympia. I could tell them, and they could decide not to give permission for the Eagle Tree to be knocked down for the development. That was what I proposed now.

"I don't know," said Uncle Mike. He had his arm around Miss Stevens, and his skin was touching her braid again. I wondered how it felt.

"I don't know if this is a good idea," said Uncle Mike.

I told Uncle Mike and Miss Stevens and my mother all about my plans to talk to the city. "I will go talk to the mayor of Olympia. I will talk to all of the city council members. I will tell them what I know about trees. They will listen to me. Then they will save the Eagle Tree."

Then I was done talking.

So I went in the backyard and selected a new route on the Bigleaf Maple. I planned the route, and then I climbed the route. Then I stayed on the ground for the requisite three minutes between trees, and then I climbed the next tree, the Cherry.

I felt that I was in a good rhythm, and I knew what I was going to do next about the Eagle Tree. It was getting dark, and I had climbed my five trees for the day.

I climbed back down the last tree, and I went indoors.

It was darker outside now, and the lights inside the house at first hurt my eyes. I fluttered my fingers in front of my eyes so the light would look more like the light through the leaves on the trees. Then, gradually, I slowed them down until the light was not as strong on my eyes. When I looked through my fingers, I could see my mother turn toward me.

"March, please shut the door," said my mother. I did that. Then I came into the kitchen to get a glass of water. Miss Stevens was gone. It was just my mother and Uncle Mike.

Uncle Mike talked to me. He said, "Okay, look."

I did not know what to look at, but I thought he meant that he wanted my attention. So I stopped near to him and looked forward, waiting for what he would say next.

"We've discussed your idea of talking to the city. We don't really think this is a good idea for you, March. You're uncomfortable talking to people. You've never done anything like this before. It's challenging, even for adults, to do something like this, and—"

I started to make sounds. I started to flap my arms and talk very loudly at the same time. But my mother talked softly, and I had to stop talking so I could hear her, in case what she had to say was important.

"March," she said, "we think you've done enough regarding the Eagle Tree. We think you should leave that tree in the hands of the experts now, all right?"

A hot thing rose in my chest, and my heart was pounding very loud. I was moaning so loud that I could not hear anything else. But my arms were tired from climbing, and I could not flap the way I wanted to. My mother came close to me. She stroked my shoulders and she petted me until gradually the hot thing in my chest curled up deep inside me and went to sleep and I felt that I could stop moaning. When I was done moaning, my mother spoke to me again.

"All right, March, please go to bed. I'm glad you're safe and sound, and I just want to know you're safe in bed now. All right? Please, March?"

I think my mother was surprised when I went to bed very quickly. But I go to bed quickly sometimes because I need to think, because no one can control me in bed. After I was in bed, I was going to plan how to save the Eagle Tree. So after the lights were turned off, I lay there for a very long time, with my eyes open, making a plan.

It was like making a climbing plan—you must list one step and then another step, and then you can achieve the precise height you want to achieve. I stared into the darkness, and when I concentrated hard enough, I could see very small lights in the corners of my eyes, black and red swirling dots of Brownian motion. They are real things, but no one else sees them unless they focus for a very long time like I do. And I can focus.

The last step in my plan was to save the Eagle Tree. And after it was saved, I would wait three years, six months, two weeks, and five days until I was eighteen years old. Then I would climb the Eagle Tree.

19

On Monday, I woke up early. The light in the house looked blue and dim, as if the entire house were covered in tiny gray snow. I blinked several times, and slowly the light changed until it was only faintly blue, as if I were in a blue forest. I thought of the ocean part of the Procession of the Species, and what it would be like if I were underwater. There would be giant kelp all around me, and jellyfish, like in the Procession of the Species, but they would be real.

But I was not underwater; it was just early in the morning. The clock said 4:17 for a long time, until it changed to 4:18. I had to talk to the city council about the Eagle Tree. How could I learn how to talk to the city?

I knew one person who worked for the city.

I picked up the phone, and I dialed 911. That is the number that you dial.

"911. What is your emergency?" said a lady.

"I just want to talk to a policeman," I said. "A man I met before at my house."

"Not an emergency?"

"No," I said.

"All right, sir. But the nonemergency number for the police department is 360-704-2740."

"I already called the police," I said. But maybe I was being loud, because the next time she talked, the lady sounded like she was not very happy with me.

"All right, all right, calm down. I can transfer you."

"Hello," said a man's voice. "This is the Olympia Police Department. If this is an emergency—"

"This is not an emergency for me," I said. "This is an emergency for a tree."

"A tree emergency?" said the man. "At four thirty in the morning?"

I explained: "I am calling for a policeman. One man who works for the police."

"Any particular man?" said the voice. He made a sound, and a moment later I realized that he was laughing. "We've got a few working the night shift. I mean, we've got a lot of policemen here—we've got white ones, black ones, Chinese ones, redheaded ones . . ."

"That one," I said.

"Which one?"

"The one with red hair. He also has freckles."

"Uh, okay, I actually think I know who you're talking about," said the voice. He laughed again. I did not know why he was laughing.

"I think you're talking about Officer Griffon," he said. "Does that sound familiar?"

"I do not know his name," I said.

"Clearly," said the man. "Well, is this regarding an open case? Something he's working on?"

"He did not arrest me," I said. "I want to talk to him about that."

"Okay, sounds like you do have something to discuss." There was a long pause. "Well, it's your lucky day."

I did not tell him I do not believe in luck, because he was still talking.

"Officer Griffon happens to be on-site. He worked the night shift. I'll put you through to his desk, young man."

The phone rang for a long time. Then Officer Griffon picked up the phone, and I recognized his voice, even though he was not singing. I shut my eyes so I could hear him more clearly.

"I am Peter March Wong," I told him. "You did not arrest me when I was cut and bleeding in my new house with the blue mailbox."

Officer Griffon still did not know who I was, so I explained to him again. Finally, he remembered me. "But I don't know why you called me," said Officer Griffon. "I don't even know how you found me here. Why did you call?"

"You are the only person I know who works for the city. You were helpful to me."

Then I explained that I must talk to the city. I told Officer Griffon all about the Eagle Tree, but he did not know about the development of the LBA Woods, and there was too much to explain to tell him everything before my mother woke up. So even though he did not know what I was talking about, I asked him my question anyway.

"I need to talk to the mayor of the city. How do I talk to the mayor?"

He asked me why again, but I could tell he did not understand my answer. But then he told me something useful.

He told me that the city council has public comment sessions every Tuesday night, and that maybe what I was talking about would be addressed at a public comment session on the development of the LBA Woods.

But he also said that no one wins those discussions at city hall unless there is already public consensus—and that *public consensus* means that there is a very large group of people already gathered behind an idea.

"You know, if there was a big protest the city council would probably see it as a sign that public opinion has shifted, that many people care about this. And then you might have a chance," he said. "But as it is, if it's private land, I doubt any statement by someone like you would have much impact."

"What would show that many people are protesting?" I asked him. "What would be the sign that many people care about this?"

"Well, I dunno," he said. "I mean, if a whole group of people surrounded the tree and pushed down the fence, and made a big stink, I guess the city council would have to take some action. But that's unlikely to happen. And I don't recommend it. You'd have better luck taking it up with the owner of the property."

"I do not believe in luck," I told him.

And then he said that his work shift was done and that he had to go. Then we were done talking. I hung up.

"Who were you talking to on the phone, March?" said my mother. I opened my eyes. The light had changed in the room. It was no longer like being underwater. Now the light was bright and white, and it came in the windows sideways, and it hurt my eyes. I fluttered my fingers in front of my eyes, like leaves, until I could bear to look at the sunlight pouring in the windows.

"I called 911," I said. "To talk to the police about the Eagle Tree."

My mother did not like this. She talked to me all the way to school about why I should not have called 911. She said things that I have heard her say before, so there was no need to hear these things again. But some of the things she said made new demands upon me and created temporary rules. She said things like "Listen to me when I'm talking to you" and "Acknowledge what I am saying to you, March." Which made it hard to identify the trees on the route to my school. I was forced to say the names of the trees very quietly under my breath while my mother talked to me.

But I knew what to do next. I would find someone who could help me. Someone who had very strong arms. And then I realized that I had already met someone who could help me.

I was climbing a route, and this was the next branch in my climb plan.

In my classroom that day, it was necessary to watch the other people in the room and to determine who was there and where they were located. This was a task I had never done before. Usually I ignored the other people in my classroom. There was no need to know these people. But now, I needed to know where each person was, and where everyone was sitting, and how I could talk to one of them, to ask for what I needed.

I was sitting in my desk at 8:17 a.m. At 8:22 a.m., Mr. Gatek came into the classroom and began to sort papers. The flipping of the papers on Mr. Gatek's desk, back and forth in the light, caught my eye. The papers reminded me of the white undersides of the American Sycamore and Bigleaf Maple leaves in the forest around the Eagle Tree, moving in an unseen breeze in the canopy far above.

The world's tallest tree canopies are in the temperate conifer forests of the Pacific Northwest—forests full of Douglas Firs, Western Hemlocks, Redwoods, and Sequoias that often grow taller than one hundred feet. Boreal forests like those in Europe—those composed of Spruces, Firs, Pines, and Larches—usually reach less than 70 feet into the sky. In the middle are the temperate broadleaf forests of Europe and the United States, and the undisturbed tropical rain forests, which average 80 feet tall. But we have the largest canopies here. I like living in a place that is so hospitable to large trees.

While thinking about canopies, I had forgotten to watch other people come into the classroom. I scanned the classroom carefully for people who had already arrived. I decided to count them first. There was a girl at a desk immediately to my right. She was drawing. I did not know her name, although I thought she sat there often. Behind me there was a boy who was smaller than me. I did not know his name either. And then to my left was the boy I was looking for, the boy with the yellow corn-silk hair. Stig. I found him.

Three people. One person located among those three.

But as I was thinking about standing up from my desk and going over to talk to him, other people from the morning bus that I do not ride came into the classroom. They were like a stream of moving salmon. There were eleven more of them, and I counted them as they passed, but they filled in the space between me and Stig, and it made me nervous to stand up in front of so many people and cross the room. And then while I was thinking about this, the 8:30 a.m. bell rang, and then I could not get up from my desk. It is a rule.

I could not talk to Stig in the classroom. Mr. Gatek will not allow talking in class. That is one of the rules too. And I could not talk to Stig at lunchtime, because I have my lunch outside, and he always eats inside. I cannot change where I eat; it is what I do every day. Instead, at lunchtime, I looked at the trees around the playground.

At school, I am prohibited from climbing trees. In the first month of my first year at ORLA, there was a special talking time with my mother and with the school principal and with the firemen who took me down from the biggest tree on the school property. They said it was a safety issue, and they have continued to say it is a safety issue, even though I have proven multiple times that the trees on the school property are very safe and have no unsound limbs. But they do not listen to me, and the rule clearly states that I cannot climb trees on school property.

I have not yet been able to find a loophole in the rule that would permit me to climb a tree here. I asked about ownership of the trunk of the tree, but the principal was there, and he claimed ownership over that part of the tree. And then I asked about limbs which may not be on the school property, but the fireman outlined the city's rules about tree climbing on city property. And then my mother put her own rules in place.

It is very irritating. It is like the Road Runner in those cartoons when Wile E. Coyote ties him up in so many interlocking layers of rope that he looks like a bundle of ropes, with just his beak and his legs sticking out. I am tied up in rule-ropes that people have wrapped me up in so that I cannot do what I must do. But the Road Runner always breaks out of the ropes, and I was going to do the same if I could find my way out. My plan to talk to the boy with the corn-silk hair was a way to break out.

Finally, one hour and forty-three minutes later, at the afternoon recess time, I was able to find and talk to this boy again.

"Stig," I said to him. "I need to talk to you."

"Why do you call me that?"

"Corn-silk hair," I said. "*Stigmata maydis.*" But he did not really care about his hair. I would care about my hair if I had corn silk on my head. I would touch it all the time. But I do not have that hair.

"You can push things very hard," I said. "I need you to push a fence down."

Stig is taller than me. He is very tall. I have to bend my head back to look up at his hair. I told him about the Eagle Tree. I told him that it was important for him to come with me. Stig did not want to go with me to the Eagle Tree. But I brought something with me that I knew Stig would like. I held out the insect book that my father sent me. "You can have this book if you go with me," I said.

After he looked at the book, Stig agreed to come with me after school that day if I would give him the book of insects. He agreed to come, to push the fence down. And to get the book from me.

We took the same bus I always take. This is also Stig's bus, but I did not know that fact before. I had never noticed that we ride the same bus.

This time, when we got off the bus at the earlier stop, I remembered to tell the bus driver, "We have a note."

It was not just me getting off this time; it was both of us. And it felt good to have him with me. Stig being with me was different from my mother or Uncle Mike being with me. I have not determined how it was different or why, but it was different. And it was good.

Stig told me what he knew of ponderosa pine beetles. He knew some things about the beetles that I did not know. He knew the exact life cycle duration during cold winters, which I did not know, and this was interesting to me. Then I started to tell him about the life cycle of the Ponderosa Pine itself.

Then Stig stopped walking. We had passed three trees and had entered into the LBA Woods. The edge of the canopy was just over our heads, and the patterns of the leaves were on his face and my face.

"Look," I said. "The Eagle Tree is ahead." I pointed at the rising bulk of the tree—it seemed as big as a skyscraper from here. And I kept walking.

But Stig did not move. I needed him to push the fence down, and I came back to him and said again that I needed his help, and I reminded him about the fence.

"I like looking at trees," said Stig. "But I don't like touching them."

"That's okay," I said. "All you have to do is push a fence."

"But I will have to go through the trees to get to the fence," he said. "And on the way, some of the trees will probably touch me."

"Trees don't move," I said. "It is the other way around. You will touch the trees. They will not touch you."

"Whatever," said Stig. "I don't want to be so close to the trees. They kind of freak me out. I like insects. I am not into trees the way you are."

Stig took two steps backward. He said he did not like the patterns of the leaves on his face. And he talked about the trees being too big. He does not like to be in the forest alone.

Then I came close to him, and I talked very loudly, and he acted as if he wanted to push me again. I was about to push him too, but then I stepped back, and then I tripped over a root, and then he tripped over me. And then we both fell down.

He helped me to stand up after I fell down.

After he helped me up, Stig told me about fire ants, *Solenopsis invicta*, who use their bodies to hold each other up and build bridges across waterways and big roots, like the one I had tripped on. He said he learned about this when he was watching a Bill Nye program.

"I like Bill Nye," I said. "He's a science guy."

After we stood up, and after we were done talking about Bill Nye, I realized that we would not be going to push the fence down now, and we would not be going to see the Eagle Tree.

But that was okay with me now. And I was hungry.

I gave Stig the book, and he liked the book. Then I told him I was hungry, and he told me he was hungry too. So we walked from the woods to where I live.

We talked more about the ponderosa pine beetle's nesting patterns and the pitch that the Ponderosa Pine excretes to try to cover over the beetle, and how sometimes that works to save the Ponderosa Pine tree, but with too many beetles it does not work, and the tree ends up looking like it is covered with oozing bullet holes made by beetles.

And finally, we arrived at the house with the blue mailbox.

"Who is this?" said my mother. "And where have you been, March?"

"This is Stig," I told her. "We go to the same school."

"Hello," said my mother. "It's very nice to meet you . . . Stig?"

"Hello," said Stig. "My name is Thomas. Only March calls me Stig. See, I went with March to see the tree, but then I didn't like the forest, so we came here."

"Stig is my friend," I said.

"That's nice to hear," said my mother. "So what is your plan now?"

"Do you have any snacks?" said Stig. "I like Doritos, and I like milk. Also Popsicles."

"Well, we have some of all those things," said my mother. "So you are in luck."

My mother gave us glasses of milk. Then she gave us Doritos. And she asked Stig for his phone number, and she wrote that down. We sat at the counter, and we had our snack, and then Stig's father came to pick him up.

"This is the first time he's ever gone to anyone else's house," said his father.

"First time for both of us," said my mother. "This is the first time March has had anyone over."

"We did not get Popsicles yet," I said.

My mother got us Popsicles then.

Stig told his father what we tried to do. "I can push things really well," Stig said to his father.

"I know," said his father.

"So, March wanted me to push over a fence. A fence around a tree."

"Push over a fence?" My mother's voice grew loud. "Are you going onto private property? Typically, fences are owned by somebody. It's not legal for you to simply push over a fence."

"But then I decided not to," said Stig. "Because the tree was so big. The tree is the Eagle Tree. So then we came here."

"Wait a minute," said my mother. She stood closer to me than I prefer. "March, pay attention—you took him to see the Eagle Tree? That's two miles away from here."

"Yes," I said. "It is. Two point one miles, actually."

"So you boys walked several miles, and then you tried to push over the fence at the Eagle Tree?"

"I wanted to do that," I said. "But Stig did not do what he said he could do."

"That is true," said Stig. "The tree was too big for me. I got scared. And I didn't get to see if there were any ponderosa pine beetles there."

There was a long pause. We ate our Popsicles until they were done. Then Stig's father said it was time for him to go.

"Thanks for having him over," said Stig's father. He shook my mother's hand. "We'll see if we can do this again sometime. Hopefully, the next time won't involve miles of walking and illegal pushing of fences."

After Stig left, my mother wanted to talk to me. She called up Uncle Mike, and after dinner he came over to our house.

20

A tree is a vast thing full of heavy mass. But that mass is mostly inert. The real life of the tree happens in three very thin layers—the phloem, xylem, and cambium. These thin layers are just beneath the bark and they are the envelope of life around the heartwood at the center of the tree.

The life of a tree is really found in just this thin three-layered membrane of cells that encircles the tree—a layer that forms a living bridge between the roots and the leaves. These few pounds of living organism lift thousands of pounds of water out of the earth every day and create lignin and cellulose, tannin, sap, gum, oil, and resins.

This layer takes the solar energy gathered by the leaves and converts it into chemical energy and carbohydrates and sugars so the tree can keep growing. No human beings know how to do this yet, although scientists are starting to use cellulose models to split hydrogen and oxygen.

Most of the time, I feel like I am deadwood moving in the world. Most of the time, no one pokes at my living xylem and phloem cells, the ones inside me that generate the hot throbbing in my chest and the flapping and moaning, and everything else that makes me move differently in the world.

But this night, Uncle Mike and my mother were asking me questions and telling me things that felt as if they were peeling apart the layer just under my skin. Miss Stevens was there too—she came with Uncle Mike—and it did not feel good for all three of them to be asking me questions. It did not feel good at all.

"March," said my mother, "I think we were very clear that you should not be taking actions involving the Eagle Tree. Am I correct?"

I did my best to explain to them what I was thinking.

"You said I should not go to the city to talk to them about the Eagle Tree. And I should not call any more policemen. But I still have a plan to save the tree, and I will climb my plan."

Uncle Mike gave a long sigh. "Please, March, remind us of what you wanted to do."

"So, I thought if I was not going to talk to the city, I could try to get the fence pushed down, so that other people can see the tree. Maybe those people would go talk to the city, or talk to the people who make laws."

"Seems logical to me," said Uncle Mike. He laughed. He laughed very loudly.

"Well," said my mother. "If you're going to take action anyway, maybe we should just have you go and talk to the city council. That police officer said there were public hearings every Tuesday?"

Uncle Mike shook his head, and as the light touched his hat, the light above it seemed to move too. I watched a faint green shadow move, like a reflection of his movement; it flashed back and forth on the ceiling.

"I just don't think that's a good idea," said Uncle Mike. "The timing is really atrocious, Janet. Really atrocious for you and for him."

"I looked the hearings up online," said my mother. "And it turns out there is actually a public comment session on this specific development. It's a public invitation. It wouldn't be out of bounds for March to make an appearance. See, I printed out the page from the city council."

"Let me see that," said Uncle Mike. He read the printed-out page for a long time. I wanted to see it too, but he told me to wait.

Uncle Mike started talking to my mother after he read the paper, but I did not listen to what he said. I was reading.

The paper said that there was a meeting to ask for public comment on the development of this land. Any citizen of Olympia could show up on May 20 and put their name in to give a public comment to the Olympia City Council. Written comments were supposed to go to the city council by April 23, and then there would be a hearing to talk about the comments on May 20. People could come to that hearing and speak at that time.

It was now April 28.

That means that I had missed the deadline for submitting written comments. However, I still wanted to tell the city council why they should save the trees.

So, I decided I would attend the hearing on May 20. Although I have never spoken in front of anyone, not even my class, I would go there, and I would talk in front of everyone. It would be very difficult for me, as I do not like to talk to people, and I do not like to talk to people I do not know. I especially do not like to talk to more than one person. But I was going to save the Eagle Tree.

I told Uncle Mike and my mother and Miss Stevens this fact.

Uncle Mike shook his head again, and there was the green shadow on the ceiling moving again.

"I still think it's a better idea for him to write down his thoughts, and send them in as part of the public record," said Uncle Mike. "Why can't he just write this thing down?"

Uncle Mike tapped his hand on the paper, and it shook like an Aspen leaf in a high wind. "After all, it says here that when you come to talk on May 20, you can turn in a copy of your written comments at that time as well. It even says you can submit drawings. No media, no videos, but you can turn in a drawing. I mean, look, that's easy—just turn in a drawing of the tree, March!"

"No. I do not draw. And my handwriting is hard to read," I said. "Mr. Gatek said that to me. He said it four times. I do not draw, and I do not write."

"So type it then," said Uncle Mike.

"I do not type," I said.

"Gosh, March, I'll help you type it up," he said. "You talk, and I'll write down what you say. Heck, maybe we should start teaching you how to type."

"The deadline for public written comments has passed," I said. "That is what the paper says."

"Well, he's right about that," said my mother. "The city website says that the only way for March to submit a comment at this stage is to appear in person and make a statement."

"Do you really think he can do that?" said Uncle Mike. "I mean, have you ever seen him willingly talk to someone else?"

"I can talk to people," I said.

Uncle Mike threw his hands in the air, and for less than one second he looked like a tree. Then his hands came down again. "Yes, but you never do," said Uncle Mike. "That's my point."

"Shouldn't we let him try?" said Miss Stevens.

"I don't know if this is a good idea," said Uncle Mike. This was the third time he said these same words.

"Well," said my mother. "We can talk about this more later, but for now, March, I just want you to know that it is possible for you to go and talk to the city council on May 20. We'll give you permission to do this. We would prefer you to do this instead of calling the police and doing things like pushing fences down."

"All right," I said. "I will go get ready. I have research to do, so that I can present a comprehensive set of data to the city about the Eagle Tree, and also—"

"The city council hearing on this topic is in three weeks," said my mother. "That's twenty-one days away."

"I know," I said.

"All right then, March," said my mother. "Then with the agreement that you can go to the city council, I want you to go to bed, please. I know you'd like to stay up later. But we've done all we can right now. For now, no more climbing, no more preparation, no more big ideas. We can talk more in the morning."

I went to bed.

Later that night, I went downstairs to get a glass of water. But when I was about to walk down the stairs, I heard Uncle Mike. He was still in our living room, talking to my mother. I looked downstairs very briefly. I could see that Miss Stevens was gone. Then I stepped back. Uncle Mike was still down there, talking with my mother. But I did not think he had seen me. This is what I heard them saying:

"I just don't know if this is a good idea," said Uncle Mike for the fourth time.

"Well, I think it's something we should help him with," said my mother. "This is one of the first and only times he has ever initiated actual contact with the society around him. He actually wants to go and talk to a group of people. I say we should encourage him in that."

"Yes, I agree it's a great ambition. It just seems so far out of his reach to address the city council, since he won't even look his own teacher in the face. It's like saying you're going to go from learning to walk to climbing Mount Everest. I mean, it's a pretty tall order for anyone—any teenager—but someone in March's shoes?"

"What are you most worried about?"

"Well, it could be traumatizing for him. What if he gets up there and simply freezes, and then he feels like he himself has failed to save the tree in the LBA Woods? He could close down even further than he's already closed down."

The hallway at night was like being up high in a tree, close to the top of a canopy. I moved my fingers in flutters, simulating leaves again. But it was not the same as being outdoors, and somehow I found this caused my breath to speed up, my pulse to accelerate, and my head to hurt. I stopped moving my fingers, but still I was breathing faster, my heart pounding in my chest.

"I just think we should let him try," said my mother.

"Okay. I'm willing to help," said Uncle Mike. "But if he hits the wall on this, it could affect the other hearing. It could make him nearly catatonic if he tries and fails. We've seen it before, Janet."

I did not understand what Uncle Mike was talking about.

"And the self-harm hearing is on May 29," he said. "Only a month away. And that's only a week after the city council thing."

Uncle Mike sighed. "I just think the timing is atrocious. This could have a terrible effect on his long-term capabilities. And if he acts out or breaks down in public, it could be cited at the other hearing. Could affect you, and your perceived ability to be an effective parent to him."

I did not understand, but I could feel a faint vibration in the walls of the hallway from a distant train, and I could hear the sound of a mouse climbing somewhere in the attic; it reverberated through the wall when I really listened. And outside, the wind was blowing the leaves of the Bigleaf Maple. Back and forth, back and forth.

"You know what?" said my mother. "At the end of the day, I need to do what I think is best for March, as his mother, rather than considering my own needs, or whether or not I will be pilloried in a hearing on my capabilities as a parent."

The leaves moved in my head, back and forth. Sometimes I wish it was not so hard for me to make myself understood. I wish I could plug an electric cord from my brain into someone else's ears, so that they could hear how I think and I could understand how they think. I wonder what that cord would look like. Would it be a black cord? Or a white cord?

"If I'm not providing him with this kind of opportunity, when he has stated clearly that he wants to do it, I couldn't respect myself," said my mother. "Ultimately, that matters more to me than what a hearing says about my suitability to be his parent."

Maybe it would be a green cord, like the cord that I saw on December 24 last year, lighting up our Christmas tree. Sometimes my brain feels like a Christmas tree, with sparks of light that illuminate all over the world, but only I can see them.

The leaves moved faster and faster, in a storm in the wind.

"But this hearing could result in March being taken away from you!" said Uncle Mike. "I mean, you don't want to have March act out in public just beforehand, do you?"

"I don't know that that's going to happen, Mike. I don't think he's going to lose it. I really think—"

"The state could make him a ward," Uncle Mike said. "Or you could lose custody to his father. Then March would be in Arizona, without your say-so at all. He'd have no voice in that decision, and neither would you. He'd just be gone."

Arizona. I shut my eyes tightly, and I tried to stop listening to the sounds in the walls and the leaves outside the window. I did not know what hearing they were talking about.

Why were they talking about whether or not my mother is suitable to be my parent? She is my parent, and right now she is the only parent I live with.

The leaves moving in the wind seemed to move in my head, and I gave a soft involuntary moan of fear. This was not a sound that I had planned to make; I was trying to hold my breath. But my mother heard the sound, and she came up the stairs, and she found me standing there, facing the wall and moaning, the leaves in my head moving back and forth.

She petted me on my shoulders until I stopped moaning. Then she got me a glass of water and helped me go back to bed. In the morning, I thought as I fell asleep, the leaves would stop moving.

21

On Wednesday afternoon, it is time for history. Mr. Gatek always teaches the history of human beings in North America. There are many things that human beings have done in North America, but I do not care about most of them. Why were we studying human beings' histories in North America, when we could study other species in North America instead, like trees? Why should we be studying one kind of history instead of another kind of history?

After all, without the trees that cover the largest portion of the land mass in North America, we would not have the ability to breathe or have an ecosystem we could survive in. So during history on this one day, I began to talk about the history of trees in North America and how the tree cover was once very great, and then it was all cut down, and now it was coming back. But it was not old growth anymore; it was newer growth. And some trees—like the American Chestnut—probably weren't going to come back to the same degree.

I also told Mr. Gatek about how trees do not necessarily come back when you kill them all, and I reminded him of the wonderful forests that used to be in Arizona and New Mexico. My mother read a book by a man called Jared Diamond in which he explained that those areas used to have vast acreages of forest. If Arizona were still the way it was eight hundred years ago, I would move there to climb trees and play Tarzan like Pat Tillman. I would like to be with my father, and then we could be two March Wongs together again. But the trees are gone, and ever since they died, those kinds of trees have never come back to Arizona. I will not see them, ever. And my father moved to a place without trees, and I do not understand how he could do that.

I will not move to Arizona.

However, Mr. Gatek interrupted me, and he made the point that we *are* human beings, so it would make sense for us to study the history of human beings. He also said that at some future time he would let me talk to the class about the history of trees in North America. So I let him talk about human-being history in North America, and I did my best to listen for a while, but it was very boring to hear about people who moved here and there, and fought wars and built houses and established institutions. It was so boring I wanted to scream. Or at least moan.

After history, we have math. Sometimes I enjoy math, especially when it involves charts and graphs and measuring things. I do not enjoy math when it involves equations and arithmetic, like addition and subtraction and multiplication. The numbers mix themselves up in my head, and I find myself tracing the shape of a number over and over and yet I have lost the sense of what it is supposed to mean.

My experience of confusion when I look at numbers reminds me actually of my experience learning to read. For a long time, my mother and my father and my teacher at the time, Miss Pattison, worked with me to help me to read. And I could not read. And I found the idea of taking letters and trying to sound them out very frustrating. They would point at a shape—such as the letter *A*—and they would say, "This makes the sound *ah* or *ay*," and I would stare at them, because clearly the shape on the page did not make that sound.

It was a shape on a page. It could not make a sound at all.

Eventually, I realized that they wanted me to make that sound when I saw that shape. But the shape and the sound were not connected in my mind, and no matter how hard I tried to make that connection, *A* continued to be an acute angle with a horizontal line across the middle. I could think of a tent when I saw it, because the lines were almost identical to an orange tent I had seen when I was six years old, when we were camping at a campsite near the Mima Mounds, south of Olympia. So when I saw that shape, I sometimes said, "Tent." My father became very frustrated with me when I did that—I guess because the word *tent* does not have any of the sounds he wanted me to associate with the letter *A*.

However, my mother had a good idea. She wrote down the word *tent* and then she drew a picture of a triangle-shaped tent on the same card, right next to the four letters that made up the word. She was about to color the tent a green color, but fortunately I caught her in time, and I told her that the tent should be colored orange. She draws very precisely, and I was grateful that she drew a picture that matched almost precisely the tent that I remembered from our camping trip. I could see the picture and remember the tent.

Then she turned the card to me and showed me the card and pointed at the letters and said the word *tent*. She covered up the picture and said the word *tent* again, and because all the images I see are stored like pictures in my head, of course I could see a picture of the tent right beside the letters, even though she was covering up the picture. And so I said the word *tent*. I had memorized the entire word as a sequence of letters to represent the idea of a tent.

After that, I did this with every word. They showed me words and told me what they meant, and if I had difficulties, they showed me a picture beside the word, and then I was able to mentally make the connection between the letters and the picture. That was how I learned to read. I still cannot sound out many words, because I do not know what sounds individual letters make, and I do not care. Words are what matters, not the individual letters.

For me, learning letters would be like trying to learn about a tree by looking at an individual leaf. Why not just look at the whole tree?

I do not know how many combinations can be made with the twenty-six letters in the alphabet, but I can read my books anyway, because I know most of the words in them. And that is how I read now, by identifying words that compose sentences, which are groups of words I know together in a set. Kind of like putting individual trees together into a grove; they can grow into a forest of words.

I turned to look out the window of Mr. Gatek's classroom. There were trees outside that I wished to observe. But then I remembered that beside the window there was a piece of paper. On the paper was a tree. It was a beautiful tree, with scaly bark that I could almost taste, and leaves that were turning in the wind, and branches that twisted and turned in the air against a pale-blue sky. It was very similar to my favorite tree outside, the one I used to climb when I was younger, before the rules against climbing trees on school property.

A girl in my class drew this picture of the tree, and then she gave it to me, so that I could put it beside my desk at the window. I did not know who she was, though.

I could not take the city council to the Eagle Tree to show them how amazing it is and to make them realize that they cannot hurt the Eagle Tree. But the website said that you could submit drawings with your oral statement. I thought perhaps if I took them a picture like this, a picture that feels so alive and real, they might begin to understand.

I carefully removed the tape. I took the picture down from the wall. I stood up. Mr. Gatek was talking, and I heard his voice stumble and stutter to a halt. Then he spoke again, a moment later, and his voice had a little bit of rusty sharpness to it, like in the old knife in our kitchen that is rarely used.

"March," he said, "we are in the middle of math. Is there something you need?"

"I need to know who drew this picture," I said.

"Sarah drew that lovely picture," said Mr. Gatek. He pointed at the person in the chair to my right. "You know Sarah. She has been seated at the desk next to you for two years now."

"Sarah," I said. I sat down again. I looked down at the picture of the tree in my hands.

After lunchtime, it is free-reading and drawing time. I was sitting at my desk, looking at the picture of the tree again. I put my finger on my tree and traced the limbs up from the main trunk. In the crook of the tree's branches is the figure of a boy in a blue shirt and a gray sweatshirt and black pants. I wondered who it was. Maybe it was supposed to be me.

"You like the picture, March?" said a voice.

It was a high voice, and one I did not recognize as speaking to me very much, and at first it made me uncomfortable. I began to make a moaning sound.

"You like the picture of the tree?" said the voice.

The voice was talking about the picture I was holding.

"It is the best picture of a tree," I said. "It is very accurate."

"I am glad you like it, March. I'm sorry you forgot my name."

I did not tell this girl that I had never known her name.

"My name is Sarah," she said. "You can see it right there." She reached out a finger and tapped on the black letters written in the lower right-hand corner of my picture: *S-A-R-A-H*.

I did not like her finger on my picture, but I needed to talk to her. If I pushed her hand away, she might not talk to me.

"Yes," I said. "I like the picture."

"Good," she said. "I gave it to you in September. We were supposed to draw pictures of each other. I drew you climbing your favorite tree."

Then she said, "We were taking turns."

"Oh," I said. "Did I draw a picture too?"

"No," she said. "You didn't draw a picture of me. You didn't draw anything at all. You just sat there and looked at the trees outside until art was over."

"Oh," I said. "I was thinking of a picture, though. I was thinking of a picture the whole time. You drew a good picture. You should have gotten the picture I was drawing in my head."

"Thank you," she said.

I have learned from watching movies that some people do not mind looking at each other's faces. And they do not mind touching each other. And there are times when you should say something to someone else, even if you do not understand what they want from you.

I remembered what I had learned from Rhonda the therapist. I also thought about what my mother has told me about how to ask for what I want from other people.

I turned my head toward the girl, I squinted my eyes almost shut, and I looked up into her face. I saw her eyes flutter and blink open and shut, open and shut. Breath was coming out of her mouth, and I could see her lips and a little bit inside of her nose, where I know it is slimy. But her skin was smooth, and there were none of those red spots that I have seen when I have looked at some other people's faces. I thought back to what my mother had said in the past. I remembered the last time that my mother tickled me and made me laugh—and I used that memory to smile at Sarah.

She smiled back, and I could see her teeth glisten. It was not pleasant to me, but I did not turn my face away immediately.

"Can you do another picture like this?" I asked.

"Just like that one?" She pointed at the picture in my hands, and I turned my face quickly back to look at the tree on the paper. Now I had a reason to look away from her face.

"No," I said. "I know of another tree, a bigger tree, and I cannot climb it. Could you draw a picture of that tree?"

"I would have to see the tree, March," she said.

"I will ask my uncle to take us to see the tree," I said. "Then you can draw a picture. And then I will show your picture to the city council, all right? Everyone will see it."

"Yes, I guess so," she said. "Okay."

"Thank you," I said. Then I remembered to say her name. "Sarah," I said. "Sarah."

Later that night, I remembered to tell Uncle Mike he would be taking Sarah and me to look at the tree, and Uncle Mike said that he would help me make a list of things to say to the city council. He said this was an important step in learning how to talk to people.

I can see the forest and the trees, and I can name each tree I have ever seen in the forest by its scientific name and subspecies. If they just knew which trees were there, and how big they grow, then I thought the city council members would know not to chop them down. But Uncle Mike said that information was not good enough for the city council.

When Uncle Mike said that information was not good enough, I flapped for almost one hour. And then he told me that I should not flap at the city council meeting, and I tried to shut my ears.

I was not sure he was right. But he explained that he had done this before, at his job, working for the state office of transportation, and that I should listen to him. And my mother agreed with him.

So he helped me make a list of reasons why people should not cut down trees like the Eagle Tree. There are many reasons, but most of them concern things that I enjoy about trees. I made a list of all the things that make trees amazing and beautiful and worthy of saving. Here is the list:

- Fibonacci sequences are found in the growth of cones, foliage, and branches.
- Epicormic branching fills in gaps in tree growth.
- Aspen groves and Giant Sequoias are the largest living things on Earth.
- Trees create microclimates in their environment.
- Trees are the most diverse, most widely proliferated plant life on the planet.
- A single tree lifts hundreds of gallons of water every day.
- Trees are a perfect filtering system.
- Trees are the pinnacle of photosynthesis: no other plant on the planet has reached their level of direct conversion into matter. (Algae is close, but they do not convert as much light energy to solid matter.)
- Trees are the tallest organic objects on the planet.
- Trees are the deepest-boring organic objects on the planet.
- The low albedo of forests causes cooling and fosters the growth of flora and fauna.
- A single tree can contain an entire acre of leaves.
- A single tree can clean an entire watershed, given enough time.
- A single tree, through its offspring, can create an entire forest.

But when Uncle Mike read back this list, he said that there was very little in the list that people would consider important in terms of being worth saving, that people would consider to have intrinsic value.

"What *is* of intrinsic value to people then?" I asked.

"Well, that's a good question," said Uncle Mike. "I would venture to guess that it's things that affect people's lives directly. People ultimately care about themselves." Uncle Mike pushed his green hat back and scratched his forehead.

"People are selfish," I said.

"Yes, I suppose that's one way of saying it," said Uncle Mike. "It's not the way that I would choose, but you make a good point."

"All right. I will think of some selfish reasons to save trees," I said.

It took me six days and four hours. I climbed trees. I walked around our lawn, and I walked around the sofa in our house. I thought for a long time. Then I came back to Uncle Mike, and I said, "I have the selfish reasons."

At first, Uncle Mike did not understand what I was talking about. So I had to remind him of our conversation. It is always curious to me that people do not remember conversations the way I do. For me it is an audio recorder in my head that I can turn off and turn back on.

This is why I like talking to Pastor Ilsa and Pierre. They seem to understand my audio recorder, and they can turn their own audio recorder back on and pick up a conversation right where we left off, in the middle of discussing the leaves of the Bigleaf Maple, or its peculiar spinning seeds, or even the growth cycle of the Douglas Fir—which is a complex topic not usually tackled by nonspecialists.

In any case, I eventually got Uncle Mike to remember our conversation about reasons to save trees. Here is the list of selfish reasons that I told Uncle Mike:

- Trees absorb carbon dioxide (called carbon sequestration), which prevents further climate change and global warming.

- Trees manufacture oxygen, which creates and maintains a viable atmosphere for human beings and other life-forms on Earth.
- Trees help with water filtration and the breakdown of toxins in the soil, which preserves human lives.
- The preservation of biodiversity supports the ecosystem that human beings require for our long-term survival.

"I thought of another one," said Uncle Mike. "This is one you may not have thought of, but it does appeal to forestry people, and industries."

We added his item to the list:

- The creation of additional forest ensures that human beings will continue to have wood to build houses and other structures, as well as furniture and other necessities.

Then my mother typed up these lists of reasons on cards, and Uncle Mike showed me how to read them out loud, and he demonstrated how to look at the cards to remember what to say, and then how to lift my head to talk again.

I was pleased that there was a proper order for the cards, and I could keep them in order. It was a precise list of reasons and things to say, and I thought it would be like climbing a tree. Step by step, card by card.

Two days after Uncle Mike and I took Sarah from school to the LBA Woods, Sarah drew a picture of the Eagle Tree that I like very much. And we were able to make photocopies of the picture to give to everyone at the city council for the night of the hearing. I didn't want to give the drawings away. I wanted them to fill the walls of my room. But my mother made sure that I had the original above my bed, and she told me that one drawing of the Eagle Tree is enough. And so I let them give away the rest of the copies of the pictures.

We put the cards in the precisely right order. And I liked the order, and that they were a list I could hold in my hands, numbered, like a climbing route, and that was good for me.

Later that week and the next, my mother wanted me to practice reading from the cards, and I tried to practice for several evenings after school, but it did not feel right, and I did not like to do it, and so I refused to do it.

And then it was too late. It was May 20, and it was the night of the city council meeting.

22

We traveled in my mother's car to Olympia City Hall. In the car were my mother, Miss Stevens, Uncle Mike, and me. The car was much more crowded than I prefer—it made me feel hot and stuffy and uncomfortable. But then the car doors opened and we walked to the building, and then we walked inside.

Olympia City Hall is a new building made of white walls and glass walls, and large gray beams that look like tree limbs frozen in concrete. It does not look like something that has any actual wood in it, though, and I like it for that reason. Inside there was a hallway, and my mother and Miss Stevens went to sign our names on a clipboard, and Uncle Mike and I walked ahead past the hallway into a big room. This room had a kind of stage with people sitting behind it at a long table. And I think the wood used to build that stage was Western Red Cedar.

At the door to the big room was a man, standing, who shook hands with everyone who was going into the big room. I did not want to touch his hand, so I stopped walking.

"Welcome," said the man. "Thank you for coming to the public hearing."

And Uncle Mike shook his hand. But I did not.

"This is Mayor Stephen Chancel," said Uncle Mike to me. "We have a drawing of the tree for you, Mayor Chancel," he said, and he gave the mayor a copy of Sarah's picture of the Eagle Tree. "We have copies for each member of the city council."

"Thank you. I appreciate your interest and your comments," said Mayor Chancel. I was looking at the hair around the mayor's face. It was unusual.

The mayor was a white-skinned man with white hair and a little fringe of white beard around his face. The fringe looked similar to a white fungus that can kill a tree. Looking at the fringe around Mayor Chancel's face, I remembered the last time I saw that fungus. It is called *Phanerochaete chrysosporium*—and I had seen it high up in the forty-two-foot-tall White Pine on the third street away from our old house.

Fungi like this infect the inside of a tree's trunk. *Phanerochaete* degrade the lignin, and leave the cellulose, deeper inside a tree, alone. When they degrade the lignin, some fungi create a layer called mycelial felt, which goes deep into the tree.

I wondered if Mayor Chancel had mycelial felt inside him. Probably not, I decided, since he was a human being and not a White Pine.

Then we went and sat down, and later Mayor Chancel went to the stage and sat down with the other people there. I was still fascinated by the fungi around his face.

Uncle Mike had told me to pay attention to who was in the room, so before we sat down, I counted the people. There were 209 grown-up people and 2 children. Some of the grown-ups were holding signs that said "Save LBA Woods" and "Save the Eagle Tree!" These signs were interesting to me. I did not know that other people cared about trees the same way that I care about trees.

I also saw people I know. In the back were my mother and Miss Stevens. They were passing out copies of the picture of the tree that Sarah drew. Then there was Mr. Clayton from next door; and Rhonda, my therapist; and even Stig and his father. I also saw Sarah from class, who drew the picture. When I looked at her, Sarah moved her fingers in the air like the leaves of a tree, and she held up a copy of the picture she drew. On the side of the picture it said "Save the Eagle Tree!" I did not move my fingers so that she could see them, but I nodded my head when she waved her fingers. I like Sarah's drawing. Very much. I was glad everyone would have a copy of the picture of the Eagle Tree.

Then I turned around and sat down in my chair. I carefully counted the number of people who were sitting on the big stage. There were seven people sitting at the big table, and all of them were facing me. They were shuffling papers and waiting for something.

I looked behind us. More and more people were coming into the room, and this caused me to start to breathe faster. My skin was hot, as if I were being cooked by all the people. Too many people.

I looked away from them, and then I sat down. But I sat down too abruptly, and the cards fell out of my hands and onto the floor. They scattered like leaves on a forest floor.

I began to moan. But Uncle Mike touched me on my shoulder and said very gently, "Don't worry, March. We can sort them out. Don't worry." And Uncle Mike tried to sort them out, but then he could not find one of the cards. I was hot and breathing very fast, and the cards were out of order.

After a long time of other people talking, they called my name, but they said my other name; they said "Peter Wong."

Uncle Mike said, "That's you, March. Don't worry. I'll stand up there with you, all right?"

"All right," I said.

And I stand up. I walk to the front. And I look down at my cards. They are still out of order. One is missing. The route is not precise.

Uncle Mike speaks first. "Mayor Chancel, members of the city council, and citizens of Olympia, I'm here with my young nephew, Peter March Wong, who is a self-trained botanist and naturalist. Over the past six months, he has engaged in a study of the area around the LBA Woods, with a special focus on the unusual Ponderosa Pine at the center of the woods that is commonly called the Eagle Tree," he says.

"March has a great deal of knowledge in this area, so please listen to him carefully," says Uncle Mike. "However, I would also ask for your indulgence and patience, as March is also on the autistic spectrum and sometimes has difficulty expressing himself clearly. He would like to share some of his observations regarding the environmental effects of developing the forest in that area."

Uncle Mike then turns to me, and he touches me on the shoulder. "March?"

I am thinking of the spreading limbs of the Eagle Tree. I am thinking of how broadly they spread out. After the first hundred years of the tree's growth, the lower branches break off. It is probably not possible to climb the Eagle Tree unless you could start at one hundred feet up in the tree, or higher. I wondered, how could I get that high?

"March, it's your turn," says Uncle Mike.

I step forward three steps to the microphone. I look down at my cards.

Once I am at the microphone, I cannot seem to remember all of the things that I want to tell them about trees. I want to tell them everything I know about trees in the ten minutes that is all the time I will have at the microphone. I wish that I could turn a fire hose on, from my head, and I could splash water across them, and every drop of water would be full of facts that I know about the trees.

I wish that I could give them all of the moments I have experienced, when I have been high up in a tree and I have felt the wind caressing my shoulders, gently, just like my mother pets me. And I wish that they could understand the patterns of the leaves the way I do.

And I wish that they knew that the Wild Fig in Mpumalanga, South Africa, has roots that go four hundred feet deep, and that is the deepest a tree's roots go. And I wish that they knew the wonderful and terrible history of the American Chestnut, whose leaves numbered in the billions before it caught that fungus and all the Chestnut trees died.

I wish that they knew about the devastation of the Ponderosa Pines, and that this Eagle Tree might be the largest Ponderosa Pine found west of the Cascade mountains. Centuries ago, there used to be many Ponderosa Pines on the west side of the Cascades, when this was a prairie, but now there are few. This might be the last one. But I don't know that for sure, because no one has done a genetic analysis of the tree. And that is the only way to be sure.

All this knowledge fills me up until I feel like the sky is a whirlpool that will suck me down into a great river of knowledge that runs underground and disappears from view for centuries, and no one else will ever see everything that I see.

The difference between a living forest and a clear-cut is very simple—it is the difference in one thing. So I try to begin very simply, with the simplest thing I can think of, which is light and darkness. That is where we should start.

"Albedo," I say.

There was a long pause. "I'm very sorry, young man," says the mayor. "I'm afraid I didn't understand what you just said."

"Albedo," I repeat. "When you cut down a forest and replace it with a sidewalk or a street or even a house, you make a surface that has a low albedo go to a higher albedo. From dark to light. Albedo. You know."

In natural ecosystems, there are critical links that cannot be broken. With trees, we are actively destroying those links. It is as if we want the system to crumble. That is the only explanation I can find. There are simple things that we are doing to remove the capability of the ecosystem to function. Obvious things. Albedo, to start with.

"The removal of trees at vast volumes changes the effect of sunlight on the land," I say, "and therefore it changes the weather, it changes the plants, and it changes the weather pattern itself."

Everyone sitting at the long round table is looking at me. I look down, so I do not have to see their faces shift in the light. There is the sound of paper shuffling and the mayor clearing his throat. "Okay, then."

Uncle Mike whispers from behind me. "Explain what you mean, March."

"You have to listen," I say, but the microphone whines, and I know I have spoken too loudly, so I slow down, and I speak more softly into the microphone. "Albedo is the incident light or radiation that is reflected by a surface," I say. "Light-colored land—such as ground covered by snow, or a parking lot—it reflects most of the sunlight that hits it. A dark forest, on the other hand, absorbs more of the sun's energy and so has a low albedo."

"To be clear," Uncle Mike interjects as he leans over the microphone, "this has to do with mitigating the effects of global warming. If you have a forest, it absorbs energy, because of—"

"Low albedo," I shout, but again the microphone whines. I am too loud. So I step back, but I keep talking. My throat is already hurting from talking so much. "High albedo is bad," I say. "And that is what you get when you build streets and houses and such. The light cannot be absorbed. It just grows warmer. Like a greenhouse. We live in a giant greenhouse. Keep the trees for the low albedo."

There is a long pause, and then the mayor clears his throat again, and I realize that I have started to moan; the sound is clearly audible through the microphone. Uncle Mike takes my shoulder and gently pulls me back.

And I realize that I am never going to have time to tell them every-thing about Aspen groves, which are interlocked deep underground. And how trees produce their vast mass merely from carbon dioxide in the air and sunlight; they draw none of their mass from the soil itself, and isn't that amazing? Wouldn't you love to be able to survive just on air and sunlight and water, and produce a tree mass that weighs tons and tons?

I know that I am never going to be able to tell these people every-thing they should know about photosynthesis, and Fibonacci sequences, and epicormic branching, and how leaves and in fact whole trees can turn toward the sun, given enough time and enough sunlight to moti-vate them.

The mayor says a lot of words, and I stand there, pretending to listen, but all I can think about is the way the wind rushes through the higher branches of the forest, and how dark and cool it is in the forest. And so when there is a pause, I move away from Uncle Mike's hand, and then I stride up to the microphone again.

"There is a simple way to know what the effects of cutting down this forest will be," I say. "We need to know exactly how much sunlight the land reflects compared to how much it absorbs. Why don't we just contact NASA and ask them to measure the albedo of the Eagle Tree forest? NASA's Moderate Resolution Imaging Spectroradiometer can measure the amount of albedo."

"Contact NASA," mutters a large woman with blonde hair, who is a council member sitting with the mayor and the other council members. "To measure our forest. Right."

But I am not listening to her sounds, because I am still talking. "See, a broadleaf deciduous tree like an Oak," I say, "has an albedo of zero point one three, and an evergreen forest with Hemlock and Douglas Fir has an albedo of even less, perhaps zero point zero nine, so it's important to know just what the albedo of our forest is."

Uncle Mike puts his hand back on my shoulder, and I stop talking. I hum instead, while the mayor says something about "recognizing" the right of the man in the suit and tie, standing to my left, to talk.

"Yes, sir. Thank you, Mr. Mayor," says the man crisply. "I really would like to acknowledge the passion of this young man, but I feel the need to point out that it's not *our* forest. This patch of trees is, in fact, private property—the property in fact of my client. It is his property in dispute here. Not public property, not the subject of a people's mandate in any way, shape, or form. We don't need NASA involved, for heaven's sake. This patch of lovely wooded area is not the residence of anyone at all, and furthermore, we feel that the council has wasted enough time debating a matter really of private property and individual preference. We have all the permits required, and I would humbly ask that the city just lift the hold they've placed on my client's private concerns, which do not affect any other person in this city, or any wildlife that we can readily identify—"

"Murrelet," I say loudly. I move back to the microphone before Uncle Mike can take my shoulder again and pull me back. "Murrelet."

There is a pause, a dead silence in the room for a minute. I hear a sound and turn my head. A woman with dark hair in the back of the room, in the audience, is now standing up. She is wearing a blue dress and a black scarf on top of the dress, over her neck. *She is standing up because she is going to leave,* I think. *They are all going to leave. Then I will be happier, because I will be alone.*

Then the man standing to my left makes a sound as if something has choked him, or as if he is learning to laugh. I do not look at him, because when people laugh, their faces distort, and that is not a pleasant sight to see.

I squeeze my eyes tight shut. Inside my head, I can see the trees of the LBA Woods. And high in those tree branches, something moving. A small thing. The memory of a bird.

"Mirror-let?" says the man in the suit and tie. "What is that—some new kind of tree? I'm all for saving the trees, sure. But off my client's land, if you understand. These are timber acres, open to—"

"What did you say, March?" says a soft voice behind me. I open my eyes and turn my head to see the woman who stood up. She did not leave the room at all. She has come up to the front, right behind me. She is talking quietly to me. I look at the ceiling quickly, so I will not see her face.

"What did you say?" she repeats. She does not seem to care that I will not look at her face.

"Murrelet," I repeat.

Around us, there is a rising buzz of words: people talking back to the man in the suit, the man in the suit talking loudly, the council members talking to each other.

"You have a confirmed sighting of a marbled murrelet?" the woman says.

I am still looking forward, so I do not have to look in her face, which makes it easier for me to talk to her.

"Yes," I say. "I saw it in the Eagle Tree, on the highest branch with the angle that points northwest, at 1:07 p.m., Monday March 17. I know it was a murrelet because I read about it in my uncle Mike's book, *Birds of the Pacific Northwest Coast*. And I know it was a murrelet because it had the mottled brown and white described in the book, the exact coloring, and I waited for forty-two minutes in the tree until I could see its beak and the kind of small avocado-shaped head that the book talked about, so that I could be sure it was a murrelet. And it was."

The woman sighs, but the sigh does not sound upset. She sounds happy, for some reason.

"You are sure?" she says. "In that tree?"

"Yes," I say. And then I can hear Uncle Mike on the other side of me speaking, and I guess that he has been saying the same words for a while now, but I have not been listening.

"Peter," he says, "you've either got to keep talking, or you've got to sit down. They're asking you to sit down. Do you hear them, Peter? They're asking you to just sit down."

So I step back to my seat, and I sit down.

When I did this, the woman in the blue dress and the scarf stepped forward to the microphone.

"My apologies for the delay, Mr. Mayor, city council members. I'm speaking for the Environmental Defense Council here in Olympia."

The man in the suit opened his mouth, and his face was mottled red and white.

"Mayor Chancel, sir, I'm on the list of people who signed up to talk tonight. Right there—number four on the list, I believe." She nodded at the man in the suit, and then he closed his mouth.

"My name is Maria Elliot," she said. "I'm an attorney and natural-ist with the Environmental Defense Council. I had intended to speak regarding this particular stand of old-growth forest, with the hope that the council might put more time into consideration and evaluation of whether or not federally endangered species were resident in this particular band of forest. However, now I don't have to ask for that evaluation."

"Good," said the man in the suit. "Can we just proceed with the motion to close discussion for my client's—?"

"I don't have to ask for that evaluation"—Maria Elliot leaned closer to the microphone—"because this young man here, Peter March Wong, just confirmed for me that indeed he has definitively identified the marbled murrelet. That was the name he said earlier. The murrelet is a rare seabird, and it is protected by the federal government under the Endangered Species Act."

The man in the middle, the mayor, sighed a long sigh. It almost sounded like one of my moans. "A seabird? Isn't this a long way from the sea, Miss Elliot? I mean . . ." He fumbled with some papers on the table in front of him. "This particular stand of trees is more than ten miles inland."

"Yes," said Maria Elliot. "Yes, it is. And this is a characteristic of the marbled murrelet. It is a seabird, and one of the last of the auk family. The murrelet lays a single egg—perhaps only one egg in five years—on an old-growth tree branch. The chick hatches there, miles and miles inland, and the parents return with fish from the open water for months. Then, one day, when the parents have stopped coming, the small murrelet spreads its wings and flies directly to the part of the coast that is near its parents."

She held up a book with a picture of the marbled murrelet. The book said "*Rare Bird*" on the front, and I guess that is a good description for the marbled murrelet.

A man with a camera in the front row turned around and pointed it at Maria Elliot, and there was a bright flash as she held up the book with the picture of the marbled murrelet on the cover.

"This is a book on the marbled murrelet in this region of the Pacific Northwest," she said. "It describes the local habitat, and environmental considerations regarding the murrelet. We've been working for months now to confirm the presence of the murrelet in the LBA Woods, and with Mr. Wong's visual sighting, I believe we have confirmation that merits further study."

"Now really!" said the man in the suit. "You're crediting that kid with an observation—"

Maria Elliot turned her body so that she was facing the man. "Mr. Wong here has merely provided confirmation of observations that we've documented here for some months and which we have already advised the federal government of," she said. "The murrelet is unique to this region, and it has been listed under the Endangered Species Act. It's a seabird that—"

The man in the suit sat down in his chair. "This is an inland forested patch of development-ready land. With no access to waterways—we've already made that clear."

But Maria Elliot continued talking. "No one knows how it can fly directly to the ocean from deep inland without any guidance system," she said. "And no one knows how the murrelet first started laying eggs in old-growth trees, or why it lays them so far inland. But this is the murrelet's life cycle, and we must preserve its habitat if we want future generations to enjoy the sight and sound and life of this marvelous bird. Mr. Wong here has confirmed what we know to be true." She pointed at me.

There was silence in the room for a long minute. I heard pens scratching as people wrote in notebooks. The camera took another picture, and the flash burned into my eyes.

Then the man in the suit cleared his throat. He coughed a little. "What," he said, "are we supposed to stop calling this tree the Eagle Tree now? Should we call it the Mirror-let Tree now?"

Maria Elliot turned her head and looked at him, and I saw that she had no difficulty looking in someone else's face for as long as they would let her look. The other man, though, the one in the suit, he looked away after a moment, and his fingers twitched as if he had been surprised by something.

"Yes," said Maria Elliot calmly. "Yes, it would be more accurate to call it the Murrelet Tree. If that's what it takes to save the tree and this band of forest, by all means, let's rename it. Mr. Mayor, I will leave a copy of this book about the murrelet with you, for your consideration. Please note that the bird is federally protected—and our organization does in fact expect a response from the U.S. Fish and Wildlife Service, which enforces the Endangered Species Act. I will now add to our report the observational sighting made by Peter March Wong."

She pointed back to me, but I had already stood up. Every time I blinked, the flash was still there in my eyes, throbbing red and white, back and forth. It was distracting.

So I stood up, and I turned, and I walked out of the building. My mother wanted to go with me, but I told her that I was just taking a walk. I wanted to be alone. Uncle Mike followed me, but he did not insist on talking to me, so that was all right.

I walked past the big double doors, and past the cars parked close to the building, packed tight like spawning silver salmon in a black stream, past the two blocks of buildings with neon signs that blinked and burned colors into the darkness. I walked across the two nearly empty streets with their yellow and white markings. A car honked at me as I crossed State Avenue, and it swerved around me, sliding in the rain like a fish in a shallow stream.

Across the wide road, I could see the Hands On Children's Museum, where I had first learned about fluid dynamics and trees, and I could hear the churning sound of the stream that ends in East Bay.

I was walking toward East Bay, and at this time of day, I could smell the brine and the mud, and I could hear the sounds of seabirds across the tidal flats. I wondered if there were marbled murrelets among them, in the open water.

The tide was low, the sun gone from the sky. The sound of traffic faded behind me, and finally I could no longer see the flash in my head. I walked to the center of the open field that lies between State Avenue and East Bay, so that I could hear the faint waves on the shoreline, the gurgling of the stream. I lifted my head and looked up at the night sky. The stars were bright glints of ice in a dark river.

23

The next week, on Thursday, I had to go to a meeting with people in a room in a big gray building near the capitol. The pillars in the front of the building looked kind of like tree trunks, but unnaturally precise. I felt as if they might become tree trunks when I was not looking at them, but that made me oddly uncomfortable.

I was uncomfortable all over. I did not understand why I had to be there, but Uncle Mike said I had to wear a shirt that was not a T-shirt and that I could not wear my gray sweatshirt, even though it is the most comfortable sweatshirt I own and I wear it every day. But not this day.

I had to wear a scratchy uncomfortable shirt, and I was supposed to be wearing new pants that my mother pressed with the ironing machine, but they were too uncomfortable, and after I moaned and shrieked for a long time about the pants, my mother let me wear my comfortable jeans with the uncomfortable shirt. And also I had to comb my hair; my mother made me do that, and that meant I had to look in the mirror, which I do not like doing.

In the room in the big gray building near the capitol, there were four people sitting at a set of big black desks. The person in the center was old and wrinkled and seemed hard and bent by time. His hair was wiry and gray-black. He reminded me of krummholz, the Whitebark Pine thickets that grow hardened and tough on glacial slopes. Next to him was a woman with a dress on that had little images on it that were curled in spiraling shapes. It reminded me of the whirling shapes of the branches I passed as I fell from the Engelmann Spruce near Mount Rainier.

Krummholz and Engelmann were flanked on either side by a man in a gray suit, almost exactly the color of Red Alder bark, and a younger woman in a blouse that reminds me of off-white Paper Birch bark. *Betula papyrifera*. Two of these people were wearing ties, and I do not like ties. I was glad they did not make me wear a tie.

Krummholz and Engelmann introduced themselves first, and then Alder and Birch. But with their true names, not the tree names that I had assigned them in my mind. Then Uncle Mike and my mother introduced themselves, and then they introduced me.

I did not know anything about these Alder, Birch, Krummholz, and Engelmann people. But my mother had told me that this was a very important meeting.

So when Alder, Birch, Krummholz, and Engelmann held out their hands to my mother and Uncle Mike and me, I did what my mother asked me to do, and I squeezed their hands, but I did not think it felt good to squeeze their hands and I told them that. Then my mother asked me to sit down, so I stopped talking.

"Thank you so much for coming," said Krummholz in a deep and grumbling voice. "But you should know that Peter Wong does not need to be present for this hearing. In fact, he may find some of the testimony distressing, so we'd recommend, especially with his disability, that he—"

"This hearing concerns his future," said my mother. "As his mother and legal guardian—at least for the time being—I have made the decision that because this concerns his future, he should hear about it. He deserves to know what is being decided here today. If he cannot be present, then no one from our family will be present. Have I made myself clear?"

There was a long pause while Alder, Birch, Krummholz, and Engelmann talked to each other in voices that I could not hear. They referred to a piece of paper, and they passed the paper to each other.

"All right," said Krummholz finally. "Well, for the record—and for your benefit, Mr. Wong— this is the psychiatric commitment hearing by the state of Washington. One of the possible outcomes is a commitment for psychiatric evaluation for a time period not to exceed one hundred and eighty days. Is this fully understood?"

My mother did not say anything. She nodded her head, but her eyes were leaking a little bit, and she wiped them.

"Just as a further explanation," said Alder, "the potential to self-harm issue previously evaluated by the state during the seventy-two-hour hold is what brought us to this hearing today. As representatives of the state's interests, we are obligated to consider the best interests of Mr. Wong."

Engelmann spoke up then. Her voice was higher and stronger than Alder's and Krummholz's. "Let us be clear. In the event of further parental failings, there is a possibility that the state of Washington will make Mr. Wong its ward, under the permanent care of the state. As a licensed psychiatric evaluator, my responsibility to this board may be to recommend—"

"That won't be necessary," said Uncle Mike. His voice sounded tight and firm and dangerous. The room felt hot and uncomfortable. My shirt itched, and Uncle Mike's voice was all wrong.

"That won't be necessary," said Uncle Mike again. "We've undertaken steps, as Peter Wong's family, to ensure he receives the help and support he needs."

"We understand what you're saying," said Alder. He looked down at the papers in front of him. "But the state must consider the fact that several months ago it was said by Peter Wong's mother—Janet Wong— in the presence of police officers, that she didn't know what to do with him and that she didn't feel that she had the tools she needed to be an adequate parent to him. It seems clear from the police report that Janet

Wong here felt considerably overwhelmed by his needs on the night in question. There were severe injuries to a vulnerable minor." He stopped talking for a moment, and I looked at his hands on the table. His fingers moved like little frogs on the papers. "Unfortunately, the psychiatric evaluation in the hospital of Mr. Wong was inconclusive. But to the officers and to this board, it does not seem that she has been providing a safe environment for young Mr. Wong. When he was removed from the premises, he was screaming and nearly uncontrollable. It isn't clear to this team that—"

"I can speak to that," said a voice that I recognized. This was the voice of Miss Stevens.

"I'm sorry—do we have you listed?" said Engelmann. She was looking at Miss Stevens and holding a set of papers, as if Miss Stevens's voice could not be heard without the papers, as if the papers were a microphone or a loudspeaker. "This is a closed private hearing, under administrative law. Only family, or those designated to give testimony by the state, can—"

"I'm Samantha Stevens, and I came to this hearing as the fiancée of Mike Washington. Peter's uncle. So I claim a family affiliation."

Alder leaned forward and said, "You are his fiancée?"

"Well, not just yet, but I have hopes," said Miss Stevens. Then she laughed, and it sounded to me like something refreshing and strong, like the sound of a waterfall in a dark forest. "I just felt like I should be here, because I'm the one who made the original 911 call about March—I mean Peter—getting injured. It was my fault. And I don't think I should've made that call, now that I know him better. He didn't mean to hurt anyone, not his mother or himself. And so if it were possible to go back in time and withdraw my phone call to 911, I would do that today."

"Well," grumbled Krummholz. He looked at the people next to him. "I appreciate you taking the time to come in and share your experience with us, Miss Stevens. However, we must take the facts that we already have on the record."

Alder cleared his throat. "And although we appreciate your perspective, I'm afraid that the administrative board here is forced to ask you to leave this private hearing."

"All right, all right," said Miss Stevens. "I've said my piece. Thanks for listening to me. Good luck, Mike." Miss Stevens came close to our chairs. She kissed Uncle Mike on the cheek, and he whispered something to her that I could not hear.

"And good luck, Janet," she said. She touched my mother on the shoulder. Then she leaned over me. She kissed me on the cheek too. And I could feel the tiny damp spot on my cheek slowly drying, the moisture wicking away.

"Good luck to you too, March," she said. I told her that I do not believe in luck. But I told her very quietly, my voice whispering. So I do not think she heard me. And that was all right with me. I was glad she was here.

No one talked again until the door closed behind Miss Stevens.

"All right," said Alder. "Where were we then?"

Birch spoke for the first time. "We had just stated that the record shows there have been multiple previous injuries. There is a complete listing here in the case file. The matter at hand is further self-harm or injury to others. The pertinent question is whether there is a danger to the community's well-being, I believe."

A voice spoke from behind us. I turned my head. It was Rhonda, who has the little Japanese Maple and the water in the bowl. She did not bring her Japanese Maple with her, and I was disappointed by this, so I turned back to the front, where Alder, Birch, Krummholz, and Engelmann were sitting.

But Rhonda kept talking. "I'd like to speak to that, if I may. I believe my perspective as the court-assigned therapist to assess injury and mental health can add some context here."

Rhonda explained first that she had talked with me many times. She gave a big stack of papers to Alder, Birch, Krummholz, and Engelmann, and she talked about the papers. And she used all sorts of words I didn't understand. But then she started talking about trees, and suddenly I was very interested. She talked about how much I love trees, and what trees do for me, and how I understand trees very deeply.

I was surprised to discover that she had been listening to everything I said in her office. It is rare that another human being actually hears everything I say and writes it down. She talked about the first time I met with her and about some of the basic information I communicated to her regarding the Ponderosa Pine and the Western Red Cedar. Then Rhonda read from her papers about the Ponderosa Pine trees, and how much I am worried about them and their long-term viability.

Mostly she talked about my feelings. She talked about the first night I had in the house with the blue mailbox, and I wanted to cover my ears, because I do not like to remember that night. But then my mother leaned over to me and told me I could not cover my ears. So instead I covered my thoughts, and I thought of other things.

I began to imagine the four people in front of me—Alder, Birch, Engelmann, and Krummholz—as real trees, growing next to each other in a grove in a deep forest. I wondered what their intertwined root structures would look like.

Root structures look very different, depending on the tree. The Engelmann Spruce has a very shallow root system—in fact, it is kind of a weak, superficial lateral root system. But the Western White Pine has roots that can spread eight meters laterally from the root collar, with verticals that descend from that rooting spread.

Trees communicate through chemical signals, and perhaps even through electrical impulses. I imagined the roots of Alder, Birch, Engelmann, and Krummholz reaching out to each other, sending tendrils of communication to each other, saying "This is my area, not yours."

It gave me a way of understanding some of the things they were saying to each other in the room in the gray building near the capitol, but I didn't really understand many of the questions they asked Rhonda.

They asked my mother questions to clarify things that Rhonda had said, but I still did not understand their questions, or my mother's answers either.

So I went back to thinking of Alder, Birch, Engelmann, and Krummholz as trees, joined together in one single microclimate, which would exist only while we were all in this room. When they departed as separate people, the grove would dissolve.

As I looked at the motions of their heads moving in synchronicity with the wind of people's words, it occurred to me that if they were really trees, and if these four trees were given the task of judging me, or weighing my relationship with my mother—which is what I thought they were doing—if they *were* trees, perhaps they would look favorably upon me.

I like trees. I know how they move; I appreciate their implacable, solid nature. I would like to think the trees and I have something in common. Perhaps these people could see that I had something in common with them too. And that my dream was to climb the Eagle Tree, and then someday to keep climbing trees, when I am grown up.

Could I get those things? Could these people help me get those things? From what Uncle Mike had said, it was clear that these people could at least prevent me from getting these things. And that is why I kept doing check-ins, and I did not cover my ears, and I did not flap, and I did not moan, and I did not take off my shirt. And I did not . . . There are too many *did not*s. I thought I might scream.

I did not scream.

Right at that moment the only thing I desired, more than anything, was to climb the Eagle Tree.

Krummholz was talking now. "And I believe the family was able to request some of the educational facilitators for this young man," he said, "to request their perspective on Mr. Wong's mental well-being and potential for self-harm?"

And at his words, another person walked to the front of the room to sit in the chair to our left. I recognized him by his hair and by his voice. It was Mr. Gatek. But I did not know why he was here. He did not look around the room when he talked; he just looked at his papers.

"I've actually seen enormous progress in March—that's what he prefers to be called—just over the last three to six months," said Mr. Gatek. "His progress in terms of connection with other members of his class, and other human beings in general and his vicinity, has led me to believe that March is being well served by his current educational environment and his current health care situation. Frankly, if this hearing had occurred nine months ago, I might have had a different assessment for you. But as it is, I have seen March have significant breakthroughs in terms of friendships with other students in the class, respect for personal boundaries, and basic self-care."

Mr. Gatek cleared his throat, like he does when he does not know what he will say next. But then he kept going. Maybe he did know what to say. "In the past," he said, "there have been issues with March injuring himself, and not acknowledging this as a concern, and not understanding that self-injury or injury to others is not acceptable."

Mr. Gatek cleared his throat again, as if something were caught there. "This is not true anymore, as I've seen in March's self-expression in our class. I've seen him demonstrate the ability to respect personal boundaries, to acknowledge his own pain, and to acknowledge both his own needs and the needs of other human beings. These are significant points of progress, although we will keep working on critical areas of concern."

Then Alder, Birch, Engelmann, and Krummholz asked a series of questions of Mr. Gatek, and he cleared his throat several times. I did not understand most of the words in the questions they asked. Words like *self-efficacy* and *executive function* and *dyspraxia* and *stimulus response* and *shifting cognitive sets*, and other things that I do not know about.

Mr. Gatek answered some of these questions, but then he went back to talking on his own. I liked how Mr. Gatek's hair moved when he talked.

"I have a class of students who are mostly special needs or on the autistic spectrum," he said. "And I personally find it beneficial to ask people in the class about their experience with others in the class. I would point out that the students tend to be fairly blunt in their assessments. With that in mind, I'd like to share with you two statements by other students in my class regarding March. Here's the first one: 'He is my friend, and he is nice to me. He likes my drawings, and he tells me that.' Now this statement indicates to me a degree of interpersonal sensitivity and . . ."

I thought the person who wrote that was Sarah. She is the only person in our class whose drawings I like. Mr. Gatek talked on and on about that one sentence from Sarah. Then after that, he read another thing by someone else in the class.

"Another one of my students also acknowledges March as a friend, and says this: 'March gave me a book, and he took me to his house, and we have fun talking about insects and about trees, and how they interact. He is my first friend, and he does not mind that I like to push things.' Now this second one is interesting, as the student who said this is relatively solitary and has had his own issues with relational interactions, and so it is positive to note that March has . . ."

Alder, Birch, Engelmann, and Krummholz nodded their heads, trees in a storm. If these four people were actually trees, their tallest branches and their upper canopy would be reaching to a great height, perhaps up into the clouds. At that height, I could not see or understand them.

I got the impression that their upper limbs touched on all sorts of complicated parts of the government and were connected to other trees like them, trees that I would never see, and who would never see me for who I really am.

But the part of these trees that really mattered to me right now was the roots. Those are the parts of the tree that search through the soil for nutrients and water, and slowly discover what is buried deep underground. I was what was underground here. The majority of who I really am is buried underneath the surface, and no one sees it.

I am always connected to the deep river of knowledge, my taproot sliding right into the river's main spring. And these trees were trying to determine who I was from the little bit of me that they could see sticking up above the soil. It hardly seemed fair that they could judge all that I am from the little bit that they could see interacting with other people, because that's the smallest part of who I am.

I was still thinking of myself as a hidden root system, deep underground, when my mother stood up and then Uncle Mike stood up next to her. My mother reached out to my shoulder and tapped my skin firmly.

"Time to go, March," she said, and so I stood up too.

"Thank you for all you've shared, Mr. Wong," said Krummholz in his dark and grainy voice. His hair reminded me of bent twigs, his face of an old stone. "Your family and your therapist have been very helpful. We'll provide our decision to the court system within two weeks." His face wrinkled, and a minute later, I realized he was giving an expression like a smile.

"We have to wait?" said my mother. "We have to wait to know if they're going to take my son?" She turned toward Uncle Mike, and her eyes were beginning to leak. No one was smiling now.

"Yes, I do apologize," said Alder in a smooth tone. "We cannot finalize this case today. Pardon the delay, but we've had a backlog of cases to review. You'll have your answer within two weeks. I'm sorry. You'll have to wait for the final decision."

24

On Saturday, in the morning, I remembered the most important reason that I should have talked about at the city council meeting. Many people think trees grow so big because of soil and water, but this is not true. Trees get their mass from the air. They gobble up airborne carbon dioxide and perform an act of chemical fission by using the energy from sunshine to split the carbon dioxide molecules apart. Then they spit the oxygen back into the air—that's the stuff that humans and animal life can breathe—and they store the carbon in glucose that they use for metabolic growth. Essentially, trees are made of air and sunshine. I never told them this.

I was thinking about what I should have said at the city council meeting at breakfast. That in fact, every life-form on Earth is based on carbon. Human beings are also a carbon-based life-form. But if you burn us, you will not release as much carbon as when you burn a tree.

My mother went to the front yard to get the newspaper. When she came back inside, she gave a big shout, and I had to cover my ears momentarily. But when I uncovered my ears again, she was showing me the front page of the *Olympian*. There was a picture of me there, and Sarah's drawing of the Eagle Tree.

"We won!" said my mother. "It's on the front page. The city council voted to deny the developer the right to build inside the LBA Woods. He says that instead he's going to sell the old-growth area to the city to make a public park. So there will be a remnant of old-growth forest preserved right here, right near downtown Olympia."

Then my mother said, "What you said made a big difference, March. You should read the story in the newspaper."

But I was thinking about how newsprint paper is made from trees. I had seen a video of how the wood is cut down and then shredded into pulp and then churned into a thick slurry before it is pressed into paper. I wondered how much of the carbon fixed by the photosynthesis remains in the pulp wood that is used to make the paper. What percentage of the carbon remained here? What percentage was released back into the atmosphere? I wished I knew this; it seemed like a crucial fact to me at this moment.

"March," said my mother. She flapped the newspaper in the air near my face, and I stopped thinking about the pulping process.

"Listen, March—they are going to save the Eagle Tree. Because of what you said. They actually talk about you in the newspaper. There's a picture of you right there."

I took the newspaper from her hand.

I saw a photograph of Maria Elliot standing next to me. I was the largest human in the photo. But my mouth was open, and I could see my teeth, and I do not like to see my teeth. It appeared as if I was smiling, but I knew the expression on my face was not a smile.

There was also Sarah's drawing of the Eagle Tree printed beside my picture in the newspaper, and I liked Sarah's drawing.

I scanned the words in the article, reading about things different people said about the LBA Woods. Then I came to this paragraph:

A disabled young man, Peter Wong, revealed that during recent excursions to the woods he had discovered a marbled murrelet, an endangered seabird, nesting in one of the old-growth trees on the site. Wong made several strident statements regarding threats to the health of the wooded area and the effects on climate change from cutting down trees. He eventually left the meeting and was not available for further comment afterward.

However, Maria Elliot, representing the Environmental Defense Council in Olympia, said Wong's statements were factual and important. "What Peter Wong saw in the woods is a critical finding in regards to the federal statute on protected species and needs to be considered very carefully by the City Council," she said. "I have seen his work firsthand, and he is a precise observer of natural phenomena. We need to take his observations seriously. We should assign a team of scientists to evaluate these woods and determine if they are in fact nesting habitat for a federally protected species."

After the public hearing, the City Council voted in closed session to restrict the sale and development of the property. The developer subsequently agreed to sell the property, untouched, to the City of Olympia for use as a public park.

"I think it's pretty good about you," said my mother. "But I didn't know Maria Elliot knew who you were. How did she know you?"

"She is the lady who followed me in the woods a couple of times, and asked me all those questions."

"Did you talk to her when she was in the woods with you?"

"I told her about trees," I said.

"Of course you did," said my mother. She put her hand on my shoulder, and I started to feel uncomfortable, but then she began to pet me in the way I like to be petted. I liked the way that she was touching me.

I saw the shadow of the Red Cedar on the grass in the backyard, and that made me think about the Fibonacci sequences I counted in the growth of foliage on that tree. There had been new growth this spring, and it was curious to me that it seemed to go in the opposite direction from what I had expected.

"The only thing I dislike about the article is that it called you 'disabled,' and that's not an accurate description," said my mother. "That's not how I think of you. I wish the reporter had talked to us."

"No one in the article talked about albedo," I said. "I think the albedo consequences are very important. Also, the carbon fixation issues are important. We should measure the carbon stored there, in those trees."

My mother sighed. I imagined, again, that I could freeze her, and I could also freeze her sigh, and that I could hear each little particle of air coming out of her, the little molecules of air colliding with one another, and the moisture coming out of her mouth, like a tree exhaling.

"I know, honey," said my mother. "But those issues are hard to explain, and a bird is easier for people to understand. Especially a rare bird like the marbled murrelet."

"Okay," I said. "Can I go climb the Red Cedar now?"

At school on Monday, we talked about what was written in the newspaper. I also brought my cards from the city council meeting, and Mr. Gatek allowed me to talk to the class using my note cards. And I was finally able to talk to people the right way about the trees, instead of starting out of order like I did when I went to the city council hearing. And then I felt good about my presentation, because I got to give it correctly, and I was able to talk about Fibonacci numbers and leaf growth. And Sarah also came up front, and she did not talk about how she drew the tree, because she does not like to talk in front of people, even more than me. But she drew on the board, and everyone in class got a copy of her picture of the Eagle Tree. And this made me feel very good.

After the talk with the class and after she drew on the board, Sarah said thank you to me, and I do not know why she said that. Maybe she was happy too?

The next day, I was on the school bus going to my new house with the blue mailbox. I was sitting beside Stig. He is the friend I always sit beside now. Sometimes we talk about trees, and sometimes we talk about insects. We take turns.

This day, though, Stig and I were not talking about anything. I looked out the window of the bus, and I saw that we were turning onto Boulevard Road just like every day. The forest was up ahead, and we got closer and closer, and then we were almost passing it by. But as we turned past the LBA Woods I thought of the Eagle Tree, standing unmoved and unknowing at the center of the hill of old-growth trees. I needed to go see the Eagle Tree again.

I did the same thing I have done before, even though my mother made me promise I would not get off the bus at the early stop. I could not help myself. I stood up at the bus stop, and I told the driver I had a note, and fortunately he was a substitute driver, so he did not know about the rules my mother worked out with the usual bus driver. Stig stayed in his seat this time. But the substitute driver let me get off the bus here by myself with the other kid who lives near this bus stop.

The sun was shining on the pavement. This is high albedo; the sidewalk and the pavement reflect the light. But when I stepped into the woods, I could feel the air shift into a different zone around me. The trees created a damp coolness and a thickness of oxygen and moisture in the air. This is low albedo, and it is also the microclimate created by a large number of trees.

Air temperature, relative humidity, and solar radiation are all different in the forest, and I find that I am different too. As I walked toward the Eagle Tree, I felt as if the hot engine that is always on fire inside my chest had slowed to a faint rumble. There was no need to flap or moan or move in any direction. I was with the trees; their energy was in my head.

I walked by the holes in the ground where the fence used to be. The fence around the Eagle Tree was gone, and I realized that the sign was gone too. I did not need to shut my eyes to avoid the yellow sign, and I did not need to worry about running into the fence with my eyes closed. There would be no need to play Pat Tillman's game of Tarzan in the woods to get close to the Eagle Tree.

But when I got close enough to the tree to see the vast height of it stretch above the forest canopy, I saw that on the road that was cut into the forest, there was a truck. I suddenly felt like I might need to flap and moan again, because I remembered the man who was smoking the cigarette, the man who called the police when Ilsa had to come and get me.

But the truck was a different truck. It was a white truck with words on the side that said "U.S. Fish and Wildlife Service." I have read fourteen research papers with the same letters and name on them, so I thought that maybe the people in this truck were here to help the trees, not to hurt them.

There were men and women here, wearing hard hats and in climbing gear. Someone was holding a rope, and someone else was up in the Eagle Tree. I could barely see them high above me.

I walked very quietly around the edge of the road. I could see that these men and women were examining the Eagle Tree carefully. Someone was measuring the tree with a pair of special calipers that I knew were used to gauge tree dimensions and age. I stopped moving, and I stood in a clump of underbrush composed of salmonberry and bracken fern. I knew trees, but these people were tree experts. It was very exciting to me to see tree experts.

Then a man turned his head, and he looked at my face. I tried to turn and move back through the forest, but when I turned, a branch from a low-hanging Western Hemlock limb hit my face, and I could feel that there was blood running down my face from my nose. My nose was hurt by the limb.

The man came closer to me. He had a mustache on his face. It was a sandy color, like the bark of an immature Red Cedar.

"Hello, young man," he said. "You okay there? Looks like you got a bloody nose."

I reached up and felt the blood. I held my left hand over my nose and squeezed it closed.

The man stared at me a moment longer. "I'm Harley Jackson," he said. "With U.S. Fish and Wildlife. So, you're interested in the Eagle Tree, eh?" The man with the mustache held his right hand out in front of my chest. I knew that he wanted me to touch his hand, but that still did not feel comfortable for me.

Now I remembered what Pierre said to me, and I reached out too, to this man, and I gave his hand a small squeeze with my right hand, as if I was holding a hard branch on a tree. I gripped it for a count of two seconds, then I let go.

"Wow, you've got quite a grip there," said the man with the mustache. He shook his fingers a little after I let go. "And I think I even recognize you. You're Peter Wong, the kid who spoke at the Olympia City Council meeting, am I right?"

"Yes," I said. "That is me. But I prefer to be called March."

"Well done, March," said the man with the mustache. "I'm doing my job here today partially because of the testimony you gave. We're evaluating the woods to determine which portion of it is old growth, and which portion may serve as habitat for a variety of nesting species, including the marbled murrelet."

The man leaned close to me, and I could smell vanilla on his breath. It reminded me of the smell that you can sense if you find the right Ponderosa Pine. I usually do not like people to be so close to me, but he was saying things about trees, so I did not mind so much.

"So far, though, I got to tell you, I haven't seen any sign of the marbled murrelet here. And I really find it hard to believe that they would nest so close to human habitation. Now I know you testified to that, at the meeting. And I'm all in favor of keeping more old growth here, but I just haven't seen what you say you saw. So I wanted you to know that, for what it's worth." The man with the mustache reached out to touch my shoulder, and I flinched back.

But then I thought that when I flinched away from him, he might think I did not like what he was saying. So I made an effort to look up at his face. I struggled hard to keep my attention on his face as he blinked, as he breathed, as he moved. It is hard for me to look at faces, because they shift so much; they are disturbing. But it was not as hard as it once was, especially when I imagined the man with the mustache as a tree moving in a windstorm, the leaves shifting back and forth, his eyes like knots in a tree limb.

"Thank you for telling me," I said. "But I know what I saw."

"Okay." The man with the mustache spread his hands out, like branching twigs. "I'm not contradicting you. I'm just reporting the facts."

"Yes, I understand," I said. I took my left hand away from my nose, and blood dripped down.

"Gosh, looks like you just got yourself a real fountain there," the man said. He held out a handkerchief in front of my face, and I took it and pushed it against my nose. The man gave a smile and showed his teeth. They were slightly yellow, and I could see moisture on them, and then I had to look away again.

"Unfortunately," said the man with the mustache, "I also have some further bad news. This particular tree here, the king of the jungle—"

"The Eagle Tree, they call it," I said. "But no eagles nest there anymore."

"That's true, that's true. No sign of recent bald eagle inhabitation."

The man with the mustache rapped his knuckles against a large orangish plate of bark on the Eagle Tree. "Well, this tree here, it's old enough that the bulk of the tree is dead. You know about this?"

"Yes. As the tree grows, the heartwood dies, and the sapwood at the outer extremity continues to grow and change."

"Exactly," said the man with the mustache. He touched the tree again, caressing it, like he was petting someone's shoulders. I liked the way he was touching the tree. I wonder if the tree liked it too. "So if there's a wound to the tree, decay can get into the dead heartwood. And the wounds can come from many sources—"

"Yes," I said. "From birds—say, of the Picidae family, like the sapsuckers. Or from bears. Or more likely in this area, from bark beetles. The decay can start in the living and dead sapwood and spread into the heartwood. Or fire, or storms that break limbs."

"Exactly," said the man with the mustache. "It's a pleasure to talk to you, March. That last one is exactly how it happened here, it appears. Storm injury to the very top of this tree, topping it off and turning it into a snag up there—that's probably what led to the decay of the heartwood. And I'm sad to report that it's simply not a very healthy tree at this point in its life span. The rot inside the heartwood has destabilized it. And after the earthquake about ten years ago, the hillside that it's on doesn't provide much support for its root system."

"It will fall down," I said.

"Yes," he said. His voice sounded sad. "So if we have another windstorm, it's going to come crashing down. We would let it take its course as a natural event if it was in the middle of forty acres of pristine wilderness."

The man waved his hand, as if to point at the other side of the woods. "However, just on the other side of the old-growth part of the woods, as I'm sure you're aware, there are a number of human dwellings. And if it fell that direction, it could kill people."

The man rubbed his mustache with one hand, as if he were not comfortable with the mustache any longer. His voice got softer, and he came even closer to me, as if he were about to whisper a secret. "Therefore, we're going to have to take it down in the next week or two, in a controlled fall. To ensure it doesn't crush any houses or kill anyone. It will still be part of the forest ecosystem, and it will probably become a nurse log, but it won't be standing here for much longer."

"When will you take it down?" I said. My hands were beginning to move in small circles. I could not stop them. The energy was rising in me, sap in the tree.

"Probably next week," said the man. "Assessing tree health and taking down unhealthy trees is a requirement of the city before an area becomes a park. That's why my colleagues from the Forest Service are here with me today. So they can measure the tree and figure out how much work it's going to be to have it fall precisely where they want it to fall."

The air moved in and out of my lungs, and it felt painful, as if it were on fire. The man was still talking, and I worked hard to listen to him.

"But my team from U.S. Fish and Wildlife has to ensure we aren't going to damage any protected species first. There's paperwork to file and such before it happens."

I gave the man back his handkerchief, and I left the Eagle Tree. I walked to the house with the blue mailbox. But when I got home, because I was not holding my nose or the handkerchief, my shirt was covered with blood. And my mother was very worried when she saw me with my shirt covered with blood, and she asked me what happened.

But there was nothing I could say; there was nothing I could do anymore. I had done everything I knew how to do, and the tree would still be cut down. And then I would not be able to climb the tree when I got to be eighteen years old. I would never be able to climb the Eagle Tree.

"What's wrong?" my mother said again and again. "What is wrong?"

But I did not reply to her. I did not know any words.

25

On Saturday, it was raining. I have read poems and stories about June sunshine and how just before school gets out for the summer, it is very sunny. But I guess those poems and stories were written about other parts of the country, or other parts of the world, where it is sunny in June. Because here in the Pacific Northwest, it is typical for the weather to be rainy and windy in June.

I like it. I like it because it is as if the trees are being given a final rinsing of fresh clean water before they are sent off to grow in the heat of the summer. Of course, the summer temperatures here go up to only about eighty degrees, so I guess it's not too much heat. But that's why we have all of the evergreen trees here in this region: the Douglas Firs and the Western Red Cedars and the White Pines. If climate change, caused by human action, forces the average temperature in the Pacific Northwest to rise by three to five degrees, many of these evergreen trees will die forever. They are not designed to survive in hot environments.

Fortunately, the Pacific Northwest is not a hot environment. It rained all day on Saturday. I took a very brief walk out to the bottom of the backyard, where the ferns grow wild. I watched water dripping off the ferns and the needles of the Western Red Cedar next door.

I watched it flowing in runnels down the bark of the Cherry, and I looked at the small droplets of misty water that were accumulating on the broad leaves of the Bigleaf Maple.

I touched one of the accumulated droplets, and instantly it was gone, absorbed into the water on my fingers, or absorbed into the leaf. It disappeared immediately into the larger collection of droplets all around.

I wondered what it would be like to be a droplet like this. What if I could disappear back into the mix of other droplets with just a touch? Wouldn't that be better for everyone? What would a world without March look like?

The trees would be fine without me. I thought my mother would be better off without me. Then she would no longer would have to go to meetings in rooms where people we did not know discussed me. She would no longer have to put bandages on me, or wait at the bottom of a tree for me to come down from climbing it.

I touched another droplet, and then another. Each one disappeared peacefully—no mess, no fuss—and the leaf looked so much better without the dots on its green surface. The light was going, but there was no real sunset; the sky turned from bright aluminum to dimmer tin and then to gunmetal gray before it all went dark.

I went back in the house, and I looked out at the rain. From inside, there were many droplets that spotted the windows. But when I reached out to touch them, I could not make them disappear. From inside they looked like they would be there forever, like little glistening rhomboids, distorting the sight of the outside from coming through. They made it hard to see and understand the world. They erased the light.

The next morning, we went to church. Pastor Ilsa was wearing her white church robe, and over it she was wearing not her usual purple stole, but a new one, a stole that had a picture of a tree flowing down on each side over her shoulders.

I went up to Ilsa before church began, when the rule is that I can still stand up and walk around and talk to people. I went up to Ilsa, because I wanted to know what kind of tree was drawn on her stole. As I approached her, I could see that it was a type of evergreen, with the curved and sweeping limbs of a Douglas Fir or a Noble Fir. It was dark green against a background of light green and blue. It was like a tree in the mist, seen from far away in the morning light.

I could not determine what species of tree the picture was supposed to be. It was a floaty and foggy picture, not as clear as Sarah's drawing.

"What tree is that?" I asked of Ilsa. I pointed at the stole around her shoulders.

"Well," said Ilsa, looking down at her stole, "that's a very good question, March. Pierre gave it to me for our anniversary. But I never thought to check what species of tree it was. I suppose I could ask Pierre, but he's not here today."

We both looked at the images of the tree that fell over her shoulders and down her chest.

Finally, Ilsa said, "I suspect it's an abstract tree—a piece of art—not to be taken literally. Not a precise picture like a photograph. Does that make sense to you, March?"

I looked at the tree. I felt like I could almost make out the species. Maybe if I looked closer. I leaned forward, until the fabric was an inch from my eyes.

No, at that distance, the branches just melded together into one color. Like the droplets on the leaf.

"I would still like to know what kind of tree it is," I said.

"Yes, sure looks like you would," said Ilsa. She laughed, and then she touched my shoulder gently and stepped back. She spoke quietly to me. "March, people are staring at us. I need to go up and start church now, all right?"

"But what kind of tree is it?" I said.

"Well," said Ilsa. "Let's just call it the Tree of Life. That's scriptural, and it's the title of my sermon today. You might like my sermon, March. It's a little bit in honor of you and your success with city council and the Eagle Tree. So listen up, okay?"

"Okay," I said.

Then Pastor Ilsa went up front. She stepped up the four steps onto the stage at the front of the church, and she picked up the singing bell. She rang the bell, and it made that high humming sound that I often try to match, even though I find it hard to hit the exact note.

This morning, I found exactly the right groove, and I hummed along with the bell. I was in tune with the bell. Outside, the rain pelted down on the windows, and I thought of the droplets. What if I were in tune with water and could just fade away?

When Ilsa rang the bell, the other people talking in the church grew quiet. I could hear the wind blowing outside the church. Against the north window, the branch of a large American Sycamore moved back and forth. It swayed in the wind. If I listened very closely, I could even hear the swoosh of the leaves rubbing against each other and against the glass of the window.

American Sycamore leaves are palmate, which means they are shaped like a hand, and they have three to five lobes that look a little like fingers, if you squint. The edge of the American Sycamore's leaves are wavy and edged with little spikes. The petiole, or leafstalk, on the American Sycamore is very long, longer than on other hardwoods like the Maple or the Oak. Another thing that's interesting to me about looking at American Sycamore leaves is that they alternate colors. The top of the leaf is bright green, and the underside is pale green.

The wind stopped for a moment, and I looked back at Pastor Ilsa standing on the stage at the front of the church. Just talking.

Suddenly I realized that if she was just talking there, without holding books or anything in her hands, that meant it was her sermon time. I had missed the beginning of the sermon because I was thinking about American Sycamores. I wanted to ask Ilsa to start over, to start at the beginning again, because I missed what she said about me and the trees. But it is not allowed to stand up and ask Ilsa to talk differently in church. This is one of my mother's rules, which started when I was ten years old. Before I was ten years old, we did not have that rule, and I talked to Ilsa many times when she was talking in front of the whole church. But now that I'm older than ten years old, I cannot interrupt Ilsa any longer. So I tried to concentrate on her words so that I wouldn't miss any more.

"I believe that God's glory comes to us through many things," she said. "Through almost everything, because matter itself is a thin veil over God's rich glory spilling through, like light through every crack."

I was surprised by what she was saying, because it reminded me of water on the leaves. I thought she was going to talk about trees, but I was listening to her talk about water. Then I realized I had stopped paying attention again, and I tried to listen to Ilsa once more.

"I like to think that God has planted reminders of grace everywhere in our world," she said. "And I look around us, here in the Northwest, and I wonder sometimes: Do we really have our eyes open to see the glory of God?"

I looked back at the American Sycamore branch rubbing on the window. I wondered if I went outside if I would be tall enough now to reach the lowest limbs of that massive tree.

The American Sycamore grows little clusters of seeds called achenes, which are packed tightly together. The achenes are like dry and spiky fruit. But the achenes also ensure the survival of the tree, because they can float, and they can be caught by the wind and blown to new locations. Sometimes I wish I were an achene—I could be blown to a new location and take root and grow there.

Then Ilsa said something that made me pay attention again:

"As I mentioned earlier, I chose to speak this morning not only about the sacred text of the parable of the seeds, but also what I felt when I watched our own Peter March Wong and his family step forward to try to preserve the glory of our natural world at the city council meeting a few weeks ago. As you may know, Peter succeeded in communicating some of his vital observations about the wildlife in the woods, and that has already led to the city declaring that the old-growth portion of the woods will become a city park. I think this is a marvelous achievement, and well worth celebrating."

There is a sharp smacking sound. Then another, and another. I look at the pews on either side. Many people here are slapping their hands together; they are clapping for what Ilsa just said. They are celebrating.

"Is the mention of this achievement, and a discussion of our old-growth forest, appropriate to a sermon? I believe it very much is, and I'll tell you why. Many of you know that I studied botany at UW before I went to Princeton to study theology. And most of you know that my husband, Pierre, is a working botanist and professor of botany at The Evergreen State College here in Olympia."

I looked around for Pierre before I remembered that Ilsa had said Pierre was not at church this morning.

"But this is not just about my personal connection to botany. I also see a theological connection. I see a very clear connection between the study of nature and the study of God. Nature is God's vast palette, and through it I believe that we can see fingerprints of grace everywhere we look."

A sudden blast of rain on the stained-glass window made me think of the Eagle Tree and the rest of the trees in the LBA Woods.

For four days, it had been raining. That meant that the soil in the woods must be soaked down to three or four feet deep. The first day, the water would have penetrated only a few inches. But after the second or third day, the water saturation point in the upper layer would have been reached, and then the water would have begun to seep down further in the soil.

Ilsa was still talking. Her voice was a counterbalance to the sound of the wind outside. Her voice rose like a gust of wind itself, high and beautiful, in the arched room of the church.

"Earlier this morning, we read in the scriptures of the parable of the seeds," she said. "And those words tell us of God's glory. But I don't think of these symbols and parables in scripture as the only way that we see God. After all, the great theologian Augustine said that there were two books that show us God. One is scripture, and the other is the book of nature. So let us look at the second book today."

Ilsa's hand moved a paper on the podium, and my eye was caught by the trees on her stole. The book of nature. That was what she is wearing.

"Human beings are on the cusp of destroying all of God's great natural world, which was originally gifted, according to the scriptures, to the human race, who would function as stewards of this great Earth. We have not been very good stewards in the last century. Why is that?"

I thought Ilsa asked a very good question, and I was anxious to know what her answer would be. Her answer was surprising to me, though.

"I believe," she said, "that part of it is that we have lost the connection to the natural world which has been there from time immemorial. We are not looking around with wonder and with eyes wide open at the world around us. The more we do that, I believe, the more we will care about not destroying this marvelous place. The writer Rachel Carson said that when we focus on the universe around us, on the wonders we can see here and now, the less taste we will have for destruction. Personally, I can see no greater sign of God's glory than the wonderful trees around us in the Pacific Northwest. All you have to do is look outside to see God—there are trees everywhere."

I suddenly felt that I liked Ilsa very much, even though I do not believe in God. I felt like standing up and shouting out to Ilsa that she was right. But I tried hard and I resisted the urge to stand up and shout. She was telling people to look at trees. We should all look at trees. All the time.

"A tree starts small and delicate," she said, "just as Jesus came into our world as a baby—something fragile that needs to be cared for. I also find powerful the knowledge of how the large evergreen trees in this area scatter their seeds on the ground. A single Douglas Fir can produce up to forty thousand pounds of seeds in a year. A Ponderosa Pine can produce over one hundred thousand individual seeds. We think of our children as our hope for the future—and I think of every seed borne by a tree as the tree's hope for the future.

"In fact, our scripture reading today speaks of seeds scattered in different soil and growing in different ways depending on that soil. All of us hope for good fruit, don't we?"

The rain gusted outside the stained-glass window, and I saw again the shadow of the leaves of the American Sycamore moving back and forth. That Sycamore has a long, straight trunk, but after the first twenty feet, that trunk splits into several large spreading branches, creating a crown that is perfect for climbing. At the moment, it was too slick with water for climbing, though, and the wind would blow back and forth as the rain hit my sweatshirt with spattered droplets.

Ilsa's voice rose clear over the wind.

"When a tree grows," said Ilsa, "it takes a very long time to mature—sometimes hundreds of years. I feel that God, in the same way, is with *us* for a very long time, looking at the long cycle, the big, big picture. God hopes with us for good fruit.

"God's power shines through everything we see, but it is no more evident than when we see the shining steadfastness of a tree that is hundreds of years old. I look up at the great arching branches of a tree like the Eagle Tree, found in the old-growth LBA Woods, and I think that is what it feels like to be embraced by the everlasting."

I thought of the hillside around the Eagle Tree now. The rain would add instability to any hillside of dirt that is not firmly anchored by a root system. Hillsides covered with grass or with small trees should be fine. But the soil itself would turn into an unstable mass, not a solid object. As I watched the wind push the American Sycamore's branches, back and forth, I imagined the same thing happening in the grove of trees around the Eagle Tree. The smaller trees there would be largely protected from the wind. Their canopy would create a natural wind-break. They would protect each other.

"To know that this tree, this guide, was here before you," said Ilsa, "generations before you, and will be here long after you are gone—doesn't that give you a kind of peace? To know that the grace of God is always there, unshakable?"

But the Eagle Tree stood above the general mass of trees. It rose another fifty to seventy-five feet beyond the forest canopy. That meant the wind could catch it up there. With the unstable soil at its feet, the slides and shallow roots of the Ponderosa Pine would not have a good purchase to hold on to. And if the wind pushed it back and forth, something could happen.

It could fall. It could fall even before they had a chance to cut it down next week. My last chance to climb the Eagle Tree would be gone.

Ilsa moved her hand on the podium. She opened a book. Then she read out loud to us. Usually, I don't like what is read from books in church, but I liked this.

"Annie Dillard writes about grace in nature," said Ilsa. "And in this passage, she writes about a living tree full of wonder and glory, a tree 'with the lights in it.' Let me ask you today, are you looking for the tree with the lights in it? Are you keeping your eyes open to the glory of the world all around us?"

Then Ilsa looked up at us all watching her, and for a moment I looked at Ilsa's face, and in that moment, I could understand why some people like to look at each other's faces. There is something in a person's eyes that you cannot see anywhere else in the world. Something haunting and unsettling.

Ilsa started talking again, and I looked away. The wind pushed the branches of the American Sycamore, back and forth, back and forth, sweeping them like a broom against the glass. Then the rain came, with the rattling sound, and a moment later I could hear water trickling down the roof into the gutters.

The tree would be wet. The tree would be moving back and forth because of the wind. But for the moment, the tree would still be standing. It was probably the largest standing Ponderosa Pine west of the mountains.

"Annie Dillard ends the book with this same vision of the tree," said Ilsa. She put the book down and stepped away. She looked up at the stained-glass window, at the shadow of the leaves moving in the wind, and she said:

"'The tree with the lights in it shines and the mountains ring,' says Annie Dillard. 'My left foot says "Glory," and my right foot says "Amen," and I dance away, dance exultantly—to the twin silver trumpets of praise. Amen, and amen.'"

26

The words that Ilsa said reverberated in my head that night, like the sound of the singing bell still hums in my head after church begins. *The tree with the lights in it. The tree with the lights in it.* Every time I said that phrase to myself, I saw the Eagle Tree, as I saw it on the first day that Uncle Mike and I visited the LBA Woods. A rising tower of wood and needles and branches and great slabs of bark that has grown for hundreds of years. An impossible castle made from air and sunlight, fixed in place by the power of photosynthesis and chlorophyll. Magic. With lights.

With the rain and the wind, it was possible that the Eagle Tree could fall at any time, all through the day. But it was not possible to climb the Eagle Tree during the day. Someone would have seen me, and then they would have told me not to do it. This is the mistake I made on every previous occasion when I tried to climb the Eagle Tree—I did it during the daytime. *But if I do it at night,* I thought, *then no one can see me, and no one can stop me.*

I tried to make a climbing plan, but I also had to make a plan to explain to Uncle Mike and my mother about climbing the tree. I had to work around the rules. Although my mother and Uncle Mike and Ilsa told me the rules about climbing the Eagle Tree or climbing over the fence to climb the Eagle Tree, the truth of it was that they did not own the property around the Eagle Tree, and they could not claim ownership of the primary trunk of the Eagle Tree.

If the owner of that part of the tree told me I could not climb the tree, then I would have to desist. But as it was, I had only heard other people's rules about the tree, and therefore I had found a loophole in the rules that were given to me by my mother and Uncle Mike and Ilsa and the police. They could not make a rule about something they did not claim to own. I had not met the owner, so I could always say that I had not heard directly from the owner that the rule is that no one can climb that part of the tree, or parts of any tree on the property. So this was part of my plan, and it seemed okay.

I wait in my bed until it is very dark and I can hear that no one else in my neighborhood is awake. Then I stand up again. I put on my favorite gray sweatshirt and my raincoat. I put what I will need in my pockets, and I make sure to include a flashlight. It is still rainy and windy. Also, it is dark, and I cannot see in the dark like the northern flying squirrel—*Glaucomys sabrinus*—who lives in the trees of the Pacific Northwest and is strictly nocturnal. I would love to be able to glide between trees and see in the dark. But I cannot. So I take a flashlight.

Then I walk from my house with the blue mailbox to Boulevard Road, and then I take a left and walk for another mile and a half until I come to the LBA Woods. No one is here now. It is perfect.

When I arrive at the old-growth patch within the LBA Woods, the air is filled with that damp mist turning into rain that makes most of the days and nights in the Pacific Northwest so good for large trees. As I get closer to the old growth, my stride changes from that weary trudge that I use on the asphalt road and in school to the little leaps and sideways hops that I use when I can feel forest mulch and miles of roots intertangled deep under my feet.

I walk into the night forest. I reach out my hands on either side. I can feel the smooth bark of the Red Alders and the rough chasms of a mature Douglas Fir, and then I can feel the stringy fibrous bark of a Western Red Cedar. I can push my fingers into the Red Cedar bark; it is like cloth to my fingertips. But here and there I can also feel the lacelike fingers of Western Hemlock and the prickly needles of Sitka Spruce touching my face and my neck.

I know these trees by their feel and their scent. I do not have to turn on my light to know them. The wind blows through the trees. The leaves and needles shake. I almost feel that the wind is sweeping through me as well.

I stumble through the evergreen huckleberry and the sword ferns until I arrive at the foot of the Eagle Tree, and then I touch the bark. It is raining, and it is windy, but I can still climb the Eagle Tree. I have climbed smaller trees in worse weather.

However, it is very clear I am going to have other technical difficulties. On the Eagle Tree, there are no branches close enough to the ground to provide handholds up the side of the tree. Furthermore, the circumference of the tree is so large around that it is convex and nearly flat. I cannot get a grip on the bark.

I step back and evaluate. There are smaller trees—Douglas Fir, Western Hemlock, Red Cedar—close at hand. They are at least fifty feet shorter than the Eagle Tree, but the limbs interlace at about the sixty-foot level. I can climb one of the smaller trees, and then tree transfer to the Eagle Tree.

I shine my flashlight up at the trees around the Eagle Tree, and I take a mental picture of what I can see in the rain and the dim light of the flashlight, for my climbing plan.

The great size of the neighboring trees at one point overshadowed a little Douglas Fir so that its lower branches died out. Later in its life, when some of those larger trees died, the Douglas Fir recouped its strength with epicormic branching—new limbs that filled the lower canopy and made it possible for the Douglas Fir to gather a new bounty of sunshine. This means that its branches reach up at two levels—at the original crown, and at the newer and lighter epicormic branches, most of which stretch toward the Eagle Tree. So these provide a convenient transfer system—a lattice web of branches that I can use to climb.

I make a mental map in the light of the flashlight, and I add up the moves. There are approximately thirty-one moves to transfer, and then many more on the Eagle Tree itself. I will have to figure out the rest of the moves on the tree once I get high enough to transfer. And since it is the middle of the night, I will have to transfer in the dark.

I use my finger to trace the outline of the tree branch I will have to shimmy across at the fifty-foot level to get into position for the sixty-foot branch that reaches out. There will be an interim step I will have to take in empty air before I land solid on the outstretched limb of the Eagle Tree. That is the only genuinely tricky moment. The problem is that if I fall, there are no other limbs below to break my fall, and I will land hard, sixty feet below, on the forest floor. I do not know of many tree climbers who have survived a fall from that height. I have not read of any, although somewhere someone must have done so.

When I get to the sixty-foot level, I will not be able to check the soundness of the limbs by touch or by sight. I will have to take a calculated risk based on my memory of where the limb is, and perhaps from what I can see quickly in the beam of the flashlight before I jump.

I try to check the health of the limbs from down here. I wipe raindrops out of my eyes and look for green growth at the tips. Each limb seems okay. Fresh needles and bright green greet me, instead of overgrown moss and dead decay. The branches seem true.

I stare upward into the canopy as the dampness of the rain increases. Lines of falling drops cut across my vision and trickle down past my hood and into my collar. I hitch my raincoat tighter around my shoulders and turn to the smaller Douglas Fir. I grip the closest limb, and it seems to bend down toward me for a split second in the wind and the rain, as if in welcome. I pull my left leg up, and then my right. My hand clenches a needle-strewn branch, and I slide up against the wet trunk before swinging myself higher into the adjacent limbs.

At forty feet, the sky is entirely black, but now starlight bleeds faintly down into the forest from between rushing gray clouds. The wind is picking up as well. I can feel it catch at my coat as I twist above the branches. Along with the wind pushing me, it also pushes the branches I am relying on, in one direction or another, back and forth. That means that when I reach out with the clear memory map I have kept from the ground, the limbs I reach for have moved several inches in the wind to the right or the left, so I must fumble in the air before I can grip them again. And because of this movement in the wind, I am uncertain sometimes if the limb I am gripping is in fact the one I want. By taking hold of the wrong branch, I could be drifting out of my defined course, and I could end up leaping from the wrong branch into thin air instead of catching the next limb from the opposite tree.

The wind gives a mighty gust, and my feet slip out from under me, so that I'm hanging by only my arms. I scramble back onto the limb, but now I don't know precisely which limb I am standing on. When I almost fell, had I landed on move number eleven, or move number twelve? How far ahead is the transfer point now?

I attempt to concentrate on the mental map that I carry with me. Inside my head, it is bright and clear—like a 3-D puzzle constructed on a computer. I adjust the map ever so slightly to align with the reality of the limbs as they are pushed back and forth in the wind. I give the imaginary branches variability and wind shear instead of absolute position, and I think I am still all right. Still on course. I close my eyes and reach behind me, testing the map in my mind.

Yes, the twelfth branch is there, where I thought it would be. I keep a tight grip on the branch in my left hand, and I reach my right out into the darkness. This is what Uncle Mike calls a death grip. Thirteen is right in position, although it trembles in the wind. And if I lean far forward, I can touch the needles of the hold ahead of that one—fourteen. I release my left hand, and reach for thirteen, then for fourteen. I move forward, up into the tree.

But when I reach the final hold in the sequence, I wait. I breathe. This is the moment in my plan when I have to drop down to stand suspended on a lower limb of the Douglas Fir and then let go with my arms, balancing on the slippery branch for a moment before I leap across the void onto the projecting limb of the great tree in front of me. In the dark. What if that branch is misplaced? What if I am facing the wrong direction?

The wind blows, and I can hear a creaking from the Eagle Tree itself. I remember that the man from the U.S. Fish and Wildlife Service said that the tree is hollow inside. And with every creaking sound now, I remember that the canopy above is feeling all of the force of the wind. If the wind hits the right resonance frequency on the right points of weakness, this great tree could crack and fall.

I look up. Clouds are above me, moving apart. The moon shines down through the broken clouds.

I look back at the tree branches. Now I can see the limb I've been waiting for. It is about six inches closer than I expected. If I had jumped on plan, I would most probably have overshot it. I might have been lucky enough to catch it with my hands as my feet slid past, but the statistical odds on my ability to catch the limb are not good. I would have fallen.

I swing myself down. I stand on the slippery bark of the Douglas Fir branch, and I let go. I balance against the gusts of wind, and I bend my knees, and I launch my body across the gulf.

My feet hit, land, and slip. My body is pushed backward by the wind, and I scramble to hold myself up. My right hand lands on the projecting knob of a cone on the adjoining branch. I steady myself, and I stand tall on the branch.

The wind gusts again, as if to knock me off my perch, but I have made it. I am on the Eagle Tree.

I can feel everything now. I bend my fingers and I grip tight to the sharp cone in my hand. Every single one of the tiny scales presses against my hand; each one is imprinted on my skin. Needles touch my neck, and I know each one of their individual triangle shapes, precise in their formation, sharp and green. And underneath my feet, I can feel the branch bending ever so slightly in the wind.

I pull myself higher and higher, hand over hand, moving up against the rain as it blows against the tree. Then I stop.

I am on the top of the broken crown.

Years ago, the top of this tree snapped off in a strong wind, and now the broken edges rise around my feet. Around my feet are also the ancient scattered remnants of an eagle's nest. The branch that I grip is the only way of accessing the very top of this tree.

I step down onto the branch I stood on before, so I am just beneath the snagged peak. I lean backward against the trunk. The deep furrows of the bark are vibrant wrinkles, bending and unbending over centuries, cracking and melding with time's vast passage.

The tree's presence is overwhelming. I want to spread my arms and allow the sound that is building in my chest to come out of my mouth in one unending scream of joy.

But there is one more thing I want to see here, so I do not scream. I swallow the sound in my throat.

Now I do not spread my arms. I do not move at all. Just like Rhonda taught me, I do a check-in on my hands and my sounds, and I make myself be absolutely still. But I remember to breathe, so I won't lose consciousness and fall out of the tree.

I am still for forty-five minutes by the count I am keeping internally, and after forty minutes, I see a small movement on an adjoining limb. It is what I expected to see. There is, in fact, a creature there. It is a bird, about the size of my hand. It is the marbled murrelet, the bird they could not find. It is here with me.

In the sky now, I can see faint sunlight rising, and there are colors that I have read on crayons: vermilion, cinnabar, maroon. The sky beyond the forest looks like the bark of the Rainbow Eucalyptus, all colors bleeding together as the light seeps over the forest. The wind picks up around me and the small shape of the crouched murrelet. I can feel the branches begin to shake and tremble again. The sky is shot through with gold. There is a rending creak from the depths of the Eagle Tree, a deep and profound groan.

The murrelet stretches out its marbled wings, and then it launches itself forward; it flies away from the creaking Eagle Tree. It is leaving me alone here, flying out toward Puget Sound and the distant ocean.

After the murrelet is no longer in sight, I stand up tall on the broken crest of the Eagle Tree, and I raise my arms in the growing sunlight. The wind rises.

I am standing at the highest place that can be reached within five miles, a broken eagle's nest above me, a single limb under my feet. The sun is shining on the craggy shattered top of the tree, and it makes the dark-reddish Ponderosa Pine bark glow like orange mica, with deep furrows concealing the gleam of sap in the depths. Broken dead branches stick out into the air all around me, like broken ribs over the forest canopy.

And then the tree begins to fall.

The wind is blowing hard around me, the sound is rising in my chest again, and I feel I can fly.

And then the branch has shifted under my feet, the deep furrows of the bark have left my back, and I have no time to spread my arms. I am not flying. I am falling.

I fall forever. I remember where the Eagle Tree came from as I fall.

First, sunlight touched this hillside, and buried inside the earth, a seed stirred, turning slowly in the deep soil like a tadpole in a dank pool. In the timescale of the growth of a thing that lives for centuries, the next part happened very fast. In only a few early years, the seed sent out shoots for water, deep underground, perhaps hundreds of feet down. At the same time, this seed used its storehouse of nutrients to reach a tendril up through the layer of decomposing wood and needles and biomass that make up soil, and found—finally—the great treasure of sunlight shining on that knobby outcrop.

The tiny plant breathed in deeply from the rich atmosphere and used the burning power of the sun to split that atmospheric carbon dioxide into carbon it could use to build new cells and grow new minuscule branches and miniature needles to gather yet more sunlight and breathe in more carbon. It drew water from deep underground and split the water into hydrogen and carbon dioxide. The tree fixed the carbon in place, expanding day by day its empire of growth.

Gradually, the hunger of the seedling brought it the power to surpass the smaller trees beside it. The Red Alders at its feet fell away into irrelevance, topping out at forty or fifty feet, yet the Eagle Tree kept growing, outlasting a fire that burned to char many smaller trees. The Douglas Firs and the Western Hemlocks kept up for perhaps two hundred years, but slowly this Ponderosa Pine outstripped their ability to reach higher and higher into the atmosphere, and eventually the great tree stood as if alone on this forest knob.

There were windstorms. There were setbacks. Decay set in deep in its core. But the Eagle Tree persevered.

After all these hundreds—perhaps thousands—of years, the center of the great tree had grown unstable; there was a weakness in the heartwood and the roots. The wind found these weaknesses, and it turned and twisted the tree, bending it, back and forth, until there was no strength left, no way to keep up the centuries-long struggle.

Now, the great tree is accelerating downward, to begin the cycle over again, to form the forest floor that will be the bed of origin for all future seedlings on this hilltop. The trunk is cracking as it falls, breaking under its own weight. The limbs themselves are bigger and heavier than many other trees, and as the branches strike, the smaller surrounding trees give way, snapping in sudden defeat. The tree is clearing a path through the canopy, opening up a chasm in the forest itself.

I can see the forest floor approaching. We are plunging toward the earth, where the nurse logs still bear memories of woolly mammoths and ancient riparian wilderness before human civilization.

We are completing that vast cycle of time. And as we approach, I see a Douglas Fir branch hurtling toward me, attached to a smaller, unmoving tree. And as if in a dream, I reach out my hands, talons stretching for flight. And I seize hold of the Douglas Fir branch, or maybe it seizes me.

I think for a moment that I am safe, and my body bends, and the great trunk of the Ponderosa Pine crashes past me, and I am hanging in the air like some abandoned squirrel.

And then I am slipping, limb after limb catching me on my way down. I am falling again.

When I first saw that Eagle Tree rising above the forest to the west, I had a sense of hope in me. A sense of future possibility.

Now I feel like I have come to some sort of great summit and I can see beyond the dark forest I was in. It is true that I am still afraid that I will grow up in a world without trees. I am afraid the trees will all die.

But I am also able to see the life around us, and the possibility that trees will survive. That we all will survive. We still have trees with us, and each individual tree that I see is proof that the ecosystem can survive and thrive. I have hope.

After all, I survived the fall of the Eagle Tree. I rode the tree part of the way down, and then I jumped from the falling Eagle Tree, which was snapping trees like little toothpicks as it fell through the forest. I seized onto the Douglas Fir branch, and I decided in that moment that I did not want to fade away like the water droplets. I wanted to stay there on that window. I wanted people to see the things I saw on the Eagle Tree. I wanted them to see the vast cycle of time, and the way the tree worked so hard to grow, and the way it stayed alive for all those centuries, and the way it embraced the forest floor in the end. I wanted them to see the glory and the pain. I wanted them to see everything.

I broke my collarbone in one place and my left arm in two places when I landed on the ground, and no one found me by the Eagle Tree for three hours and eighteen minutes, according to my watch. And I was in the hospital for two days. But I survived. I was all right.

And after all that, despite the fact that I broke my collarbone, my mother received a special letter that said that I would not have to go somewhere else for 180 days, but that I would have to keep seeing Rhonda. That is fine with me. I like Rhonda. She listens to me. Also, we are not going to move to Arizona. That has been finalized, and I am very happy with that.

The newspaper and the online articles say that I was climbing in the grove around the Eagle Tree before I jumped over to climb the Eagle Tree itself. That part is true. I did climb the Eagle Tree, in the end. I climbed it to the very top.

But then everyone wants to talk about *why* I climbed the tree.

Some people say that I climbed the Eagle Tree to save the marbled murrelet. In fact, it is all over the news on the TV, how I climbed the tree to save the murrelet before the tree fell down. But that rare bird did not need saving. It would have flown away on its own, and anything I did in the tree would probably have hurt the bird or scared it, if I had tried to capture it or interact with it. Don't people know that wild birds are not the same as pet birds?

And then my mother told me that someone else wrote that I climbed the Eagle Tree because I wanted to do a tree sit, like Julia Butterfly Hill, and save the tree from being cut down by the Forest Service. This is probably because the movie about Julia Butterfly Hill is my favorite movie.

The idea that I climbed the tree to stay there is not true either. Again, I do not understand how people can believe untrue things. But I have learned that sometimes you do not need to tell people these things are untrue. Sometimes they want to believe these things, like in church.

Can't it be enough that I wanted something so badly that I was willing to risk my life to make it happen?

I just wanted to climb the Eagle Tree.

I read a story when I was eleven years and four months old about somebody who was in love; they did some crazy things because they were in love. I did not understand why they would do these things when I read the story. But now that I've been through my experience with the Eagle Tree, I feel like maybe I can understand a little bit of how that person felt.

That woman was in love with another person, and that made her just want to be with the person. It did not matter what the person was going through, or how the person felt, or what the person was giving them; they just wanted to be with them. That is how I felt about the Eagle Tree.

It is all right with me that the Eagle Tree fell down. That is a natural part of the tree's life cycle. But I feel good that I was able to be with the tree when it happened. Maybe I am in love with the Eagle Tree, or maybe I was in love, before it fell down and died.

And maybe I understand a little bit more why people do the things that they do.

I didn't climb the Eagle Tree to save a bird, or to make a statement, or because I was angry or suicidal. I climbed the Eagle Tree because that was all that I ever wanted to do.

And I did it.

This is the true story.

ACKNOWLEDGMENTS

I am grateful to Matt Haugh, editor Kyra Freestar, and author Ann Pancake for their early reading and sage advice on this novel. I remain, as always, profoundly thankful for my wife, Jill, and my children, Kate and Nick, for their continuing support and gracious gift of time to write.

I am also grateful to my editor at Little A, Carmen Johnson, for her assistance and advice. I was privileged to work for the second time with the marvelous copy editor Elizabeth Johnson. Thank you both for your insight.

Other early readers whose insight nurtured this book include the wonderful Olympia writer Gabrielle Kirouac Byrne and the writer and critic Alec Clayton, whose perseverance has been an inspiration to me over the years, and whose name I use with his permission here.

I also remember, with fondness, my time teaching at the Pathways School in Montrose, California, alongside Rosemary Healey and Cyndi Bennett Hughes. I remember the students I had there, who showed me the glory and insight that can be found through listening closely to people who live with a variety of neurological differences. I am honored to have had the opportunity to learn from you. I should note that I myself am not on the autistic spectrum; I can be considered "neurotypical," and I therefore may have taken liberties with March's experience. Any errors here must be attributed to me, not to my teaching colleagues and certainly not to the powerful and unique voices of my students, who continue to serve as inspiration to my work.

It is also useful to note that the LBA Woods are a real wooded area in Olympia, and during the time of the writing of this book, the woods were in fact purchased by the city of Olympia as a park, instead of being used for a proposed housing development. Many citizens of Olympia worked tirelessly to make this happen. My main character's passion is inspired by their work.

I appreciate the help of scientist and Olympia-based endangered species expert Emily Teachout for her insight into the life cycle and habitat of the marbled murrelet. I owe a debt of gratitude to Jeanne Ponzetti, past editor of *Douglasia*, the journal of the Washington Native Plant Society, for her active encouragement of *The Eagle Tree*. On the topic of trees and botany, I also appreciate the insight and assistance of Michael Ramsey, my brother-in-law and a lifelong naturalist and employee of the Washington State Department of Natural Resources. I am not a naturalist or botanist myself, and, again, any mistakes of fact or substance must be attributed to me alone, not to my sources or editors.

Finally, I am grateful to you, my reading audience. I have posted by my desk a series of rejection letters from publishers—for my own work and for the work of other writers I admire. One of my favorites is this one:

"These stories have trees in them."

—*Publisher's rejection for* A River Runs Through It,
by Norman Maclean

AUTHOR NOTE

The science and information about trees, wildlife, and human perception in *The Eagle Tree* are based on my research and first-hand experience. If you are interested in reading about topics mentioned in *The Eagle Tree*, here are useful books and online resources:

NEURODIVERSE EXPERIENCES

Asperger/Autism Network (AANE). www.aane.org

Autistic Self Advocacy Network (ASAN). autisticadvocacy.org

Grandin, Temple. *The Autistic Brain*. New York: Mariner Books, 2014.

———. Emergence. New York: Warner Books, 1996.

Higashida, Naoki. *The Reason I Jump: The Inner Voice of a Thirteen-Year-Old Boy with Autism*. New York: Random House, 2013.

Robison, John Elder. *Look Me in the Eye: My Life with Asperger's*. New York: Broadway Books, 2007.

Silberman, Steve, and Oliver Sacks. *Neurotribes: The Legacy of Autism and the Future of Neurodiversity*. New York: Avery, 2015.

TREES AND TREE ECOSYSTEMS

Arno, Stephen, and Ramona P. Hammerly. *Northwest Trees*. Seattle: Mountaineers Books, 1977.

Davis, John. *The Earth First! Reader: Ten Years of Radical Environmentalism*. Layton, UT: Gibbs Smith, 1991.

Flowers, Dick. *Recreational Tree Climbing: A Newcomer's Guide*. Atlanta, GA: Tree Climbers International, 2003.

IPCC, 2014: Climate Change 2014: Synthesis Report. Contribution of Working Groups I, II and III to the Fifth Assessment Report of the Intergovernmental Panel on Climate Change [Core Writing Team, R.K. Pachauri and L.A. Meyer (eds.)]. IPCC, Geneva, Switzerland.

Jepson, Jeff. *The Tree Climber's Companion: A Reference and Training Manual for Professional Tree Climbers*. Longville, MN: Access Publications, 2000.

Mudd-Ruth, Maria. *Rare Bird: Pursuing the Mystery of the Marbled Murrelet*. Seattle: Mountaineers Books, 2013.

Preston, Richard. *The Wild Trees: A Story of Passion and Daring*. New York: Random House, 2007.

OLYMPIA, WASHINGTON

Bulosan, Carlos. *America Is in the Heart: A Personal History*. New York: Harcourt, Brace, and Company, 1946.

Chew, Ron, ed. *Reflections of Seattle's Chinese Americans: The First 100 Years*. Seattle: Wing Luke Asian Museum and University of Washington Press, 1994.

LBA Woods Park Coalition. lbawoodspark.org

Morgan, Murray. *The Last Wilderness*. Washington Papers. Seattle: University of Washington Press, 1976.

Procession of the Species in Celebration. www.procession.org

ABOUT THE AUTHOR

Ned Hayes holds an MFA in creative writing from the Rainier Writing Workshop at Pacific Lutheran University. His historical novel, *Sinful Folk*, was nominated for the Pacific Northwest Booksellers Association Award. *The Eagle Tree* is based on his past experience working with children on the autistic spectrum and on family and friends he knows and loves. He lives with his wife and children in Olympia, Washington. More about Ned Hayes can be found at NedNote.com.